How they run the country

Nineteen Short Stories of Canadian Politics

by
Tex Enemark

◆ FriesenPress

Suite 300 - 990 Fort St
Victoria, BC, Canada, V8V 3K2
www.friesenpress.com

Copyright © 2015 by Tex Enemark
First Edition — 2015

All rights reserved.

No part of this publication may be reproduced in any form, or by any means, electronic or mechanical, including photocopying, recording, or any information browsing, storage, or retrieval system, without permission in writing from the publisher.

ISBN
978-1-4602-7062-2 (Hardcover)
978-1-4602-7063-9 (Paperback)
978-1-4602-7064-6 (eBook)

1. Fiction, Political

Distributed to the trade by The Ingram Book Company

Table of Contents

Introduction	i
Dedication	iii
Copyright Matters	v
Acknowledgments	vii
"I Don't Want to Write a Memoir!"	3
The Campaign: a Short Story in Four Parts	17
1. The Hook 17	
2. Mother's Milk 27	
3. The Grind 34	
4. The Choice 47	
The Buddies	65
Chasing the Fillies	79
An Appointment to Cabinet	89
Doing Business With The Government	107
Clemow Avenue	119
How One Person Makes a Difference	129
The Plan	145
How Ottawa Buys Airplanes	159
Reputations	169
Why Jim Thompson Never Became Prime Minister	185
Some Odd People Get into Politics	201
Thinking in Egypt	209
Sometimes Things Just Turn Out Badly	229
Jake's Appointment	239

Introduction

These stories are works of fiction, although historical names are used in some of them and some of the plot lines may bear some similarity to actual happenings. However, any resemblance to anyone, living or dead is entirely coincidental and not intended.

The purpose of these few stories is to give the reader a look into how government and politics work. That is, how politicians think, what it's like to live with the pressures of decisions and what kinds of issues confront governments, elected politicians, and their staffs. The stories go from the recruitment of a candidate, through an election, to appointment to Cabinet then to decline in political fortune, and defeat. In between are stories about political staff, a lobbyist, an Opposition MP who takes things seriously, a Government MP that does not, political leadership and even how a single person missing from a situation changes the outcome.

Dedication

To

Honourable Ron Basford, PC, (1932-2004)
Minister of Consumer and Corporate Affairs
Minister of National Revenue
and
Minister of Justice
In the Government of Canada 1968-1978

And

Honourable K. Rafe Mair
Minister of Consumer Services
Minister of Consumer and Corporate Affairs
Minister of Environment,
Minister of Health
In the Government of British Columbia 1975-1981

Both of whom demonstrated to me the idealism, drive,
honesty, sacrifice and dedication to the public good
to which all elected officials should aspire,

And to my wife Sandra, who has lived all this with me.

Copyright Matters

Sony/ATV Music Publishing hold the rights to "The Beatles'" song "Nowhere Man" and refused the use of four lines of lyrics mentioned on page 5.

The lyrics for "The Ballad of Weldon Chan" are quoted on page 7. The music and lyrics were written by Arthur W. Hughes in 1960, but he died in that year and no record of copyright could be found.

Acknowledgments

During the over seven year gestation of this collection of short stories I have been very lucky to be able to turn to old friends for help, information, encouragement, and reassurance. While I take full responsibility for these stories, I want to thank those that read drafts of them over the years, sometimes made suggestions for changes, helped refresh my memory of earlier times in Ottawa, and were otherwise encouraging: Gordon Gibson, Harry Swain, Roy Derrick, Cam Avery, Ron Hamel, Mary de Toro, Perry Anglin, Jim Gilmore, and Bob Heath.

I also thank particularly Ron Riter for doing the copy edit of the manuscript. I did not realize what a poor grasp I had of punctuation and grammar until I saw his corrections.

And thanks also to Leslie Kumar-Misir for providing the cover photo.

I'm sure there remain faults with this collection of stories, but the responsibility is mine alone.

Reminiscence

"I Don't Want to Write a Memoir!"

They laughed a little too loudly at the memory Wilson had evoked, and other patrons took notice of two men in their 70s with tears running down their cheeks, accompanied by a man in his 40s laughing along with them, but with a little less enthusiasm. In the atrium at the Ferguson Point Teahouse, as it was no longer called, it was lunchtime.

The three were John Dawson, straight, tall, slim and balding in a dark blue suit. He was a former financier, a political professional of long standing, a collector of fine art, and a recently defeated Member of Parliament, thus reluctantly retired, he said. But nobody believed he was retired.

Wilson Emerson, dressed in a dark brown business suit, was another whose career had ricocheted from law to politics and back, a lifetime friend of Dawson's.

Introducing the third man to Wilson, Dawson said of a short, middle-aged, blond haired man in a brown sports jacket and red tie. "This is Sam Greenfield who represents a Toronto publishing house. You've heard of Toronto, haven't you, Wilson?

It was a long standing joke between them that nobody in Toronto in their Party had the slightest idea that British Columbia existed.

"He's bent on talking me into writing a memoir. I don't think so."

When they had arrived they were waved through and the three found a table in the far corner of the atrium where, up against glass, they would have both some degree of privacy and a panoramic view of English Bay. Wilson watched the Toronto guest take in the view across the water including—Wilson silently counted them—seven moored freighters awaiting cargoes and beyond, to the University out at the end of Point Grey. He said nothing.

The Ferguson Point Teahouse had its beginnings on Vancouver's Stanley Park's heavily forested southern waterfront as part of Second World War defense works. After the war, it did in fact become just a teahouse, frequented during warm summer days by those seeking a light snack during leisurely drives and walks though the Park.

As Vancouver's eateries became more sophisticated in the '70s the owners recognized that they had one of the City's great locations giving them an opportunity to upgrade both food and ambiance. They added a greenhouse-like structure on one side, and then another wing. Yet the place maintained its charm, and its unequalled view. Eventually, it was sold and the new owners changed the menu, unfortunately, and the name. Since they kept the phone number, it was a decade before Wilson realized that the name had changed because he and his friends still called it The Ferguson Point Teahouse. It was a favourite place for John Dawson, and his lifetime political comrade Wilson Emerson to lunch after the view from the Vancouver Club was blocked by a new hotel.

As they sat, a waiter had brought them bread, butter, menus and water They had begun to reminisce during the drive over, trading 'old war stories' about past election campaigns.

"A problem, y'know, John, is where you start with a memoir. There's a million great campaign stories. You'd have to have some of those."

Dawson nodded, uncertainly.

"C'mon, John, you have some great ones. Dawson seemed reticent.

"Do you know," continued Wilson, addressing Greenfield, "that we came close to total disaster in one campaign because the advance guy for the event didn't check the music?"

"The music?"

"Yeah, the locals had a band there to create a mood before Trudeau arrived, and to play music when he walked in. Usually, as you know, it's some campaign theme music, or a march, or 'Happy Days are Here Again' or something. But this was a local rock band pressed into service. Nobody checked their music or told them what to play, or when or what not to play and the advance guy just assumed everything was all right.

"The sons of bitches played 'Nowhere Man' when Trudeau walked in. Could've cost us the whole goddamn election."

Dawson, somehow, had not heard the story and Greenfield could not see how music—or the lack of it—or its quality, destroyed a political campaign.

"Nowhere, man?"

"No, no, 'Nowhere Man,'" said Wilson. "The Beatles tune from the mid-60s. Went like this," he started to half-sing in a low voice and then said, "Dammit, I can't recall the words.

"But it just says he's a nowhere man in a nowhere land making nowhere plans. The words go on to say he doesn't have a point of view and doesn't know where he's going, and that he's blind except he sees only what he wants to see. It repeats that message—better than I can describe it—obviously—a couple more times. But the message is clear. The guy's going nowhere and stands for, believes in, nothing.

Wilson visibly shuddered.

"Can you imagine the fun the reporters and editorial writers could have had with that? Particularly in that campaign where there were no policies and when the national campaign director was deliberately 'low-bridging' Trudeau. Making sure that he said nothing was in fact the strategy. The election Gods were on our side. Nobody in the media caught it. Me, I almost did my pants."

Dawson began to laugh out loud, and was soon joined by Greenfield. Both could imagine the embarrassing headlines.

Wilson paused in his narrative. He was not laughing. He didn't see the humour of it. Wilson realized even after many years that the whole experience still scared him.

"Then there's the time," continued Wilson, "the advance guys working on Trudeau's tour missed grasping that the local group planned a surprise, and produced Trudeau's father's long-lost 90-year-old second cousin, and introduced him on stage at the end of the day's events. The only thing that caused the media to miss the fact that Trudeau was speechless was that the old guy dropped dead right there on the stage. Jesus."

"Yeah, I was there," recalled Dawson. "I can't for the life of me figure out what the locals were trying to prove. I couldn't see a single vote to be gained by the whole thing, even if the old geezer hadn't died."

"Remember the Globe headlines? Something like '426 attended, 425 did not die of boredom?' and the campaign manager jumping up and down in front to the reporters yellin', 'You're just a bunch of ghouls, you're just a bunch of ghouls'. It was awful."

He shook his head, at the horror of it, even decades later.

But when Dawson began to laugh, so did he, and Greenfield.

The waiter returned.

"We'd like a bottle of Burrowing Owl Pinot Gris", said Wilson. He looked at Dawson for approval. Dawson responded, teasingly, "Can you not afford anything better?" but Wilson nodded to the server. Greenfield had no reaction.

There was a long period of silence. Both Wilson and Dawson were looking out the window. Greenfield reached for the bread and butter.

"Local campaign organizers." Dawson picked up the theme.

"There was a manager who had insisted that they could win the riding if only the PM would just stop for five minutes on his way through to the airport. The organizers in Ottawa said no, that the PM only did three events a day, and this would make four and the PM was in a bad mood and all the usual Ottawa office bullshit. The ridiculous thing was that the guy was right. The PM's cavalcade was going right through the guy's riding and a five minute stop was not the end of the world.

"So the local campaign manager said nothing. Stopped arguing. Then when the cavalcade approached, motorcycles and all, he just wandered out into the middle of the street, right in the middle of the traffic and lay down. Everything came to a sudden halt. The candidate was waiting there and jumped into the PM's limo—security was the shits in those days—and before anyone knew what was happening in 30 seconds he persuaded the PM to get out and make an impromptu speech and get some photos taken. He already had a crowd there waving signs, and had tipped-off the media.

"In the meantime, all hell is breaking out in front because the campaign manager is struggling with the motorcycle cops and the RCMP security guys are sorely embarrassed. Finally some campaign aide comes up and reports success, the campaign manager stops struggling, the cops help him dust himself off and the cavalcade proceeds. He was right, too. Won the riding by 200 votes. Who knows, maybe the stunt did it."

The waiter returned with the wine, pulled the cork and after Wilson waved away the opportunity to taste it, he half-filled three glasses.

"Orders?"

After they ordered, Wilson picked up the conversation where Dawson had left off. By this time the restaurant was nearly full, but not noisy.

"You know, some of the things that happen in election campaigns are a complete mystery. In '62—you remember—headquarters in Vancouver sent us—I was working in an up-country riding that time—a box. A small cardboard box. It contained 50 small 33 RPM records, the kind that went into jukeboxes. Yeah, now who the hell these days even knows what a jukebox is, or was, or anything about 33 RPM records, either?

"Anyway, on one side of the disk was 'The Ballad of Weldon Chan'. You remember the story? A Chinese immigrant back in the days when few Chinese were let into the country? The Diefenbaker Tories tried to get rid of him. It became a cause célèbre. In the meantime while he was fighting Immigration I think he opened a small vegetable stand on Hastings Street and then disappeared, leaving his wife to run it and do interviews with the media. There was a great embarrassment about the Mounties not being able to find and deport him."

Dawson grinned as the memory came back. Sotto voce, he sang,

"Oh, Weldon Chan, where are you hiding?

Oh Weldon Chan where are you hiding?

Oh Weldon Chan, where are you hiding?

Don't you know the Mounties they always get their man?"

They both began again to laugh out loud, two elderly men with tears streaming down their cheeks, laughing. Greenfield, too, began to laugh. Other diners looked at them, curious, for the Teahouse was now nearly full.

Wilson regained control first.

"I wonder whatever happened to Weldon Chan. I think he stayed. He's probably a multi-millionaire by now. Made a fortune in the vegetable wholesale business. I should check Wikipedia."

"Well," offered Dawson, if you recall, 'The Jelly Bean Song" was on the other side. Remember the lyrics?"

"No, but it was about the Diefenbaker government having to reduce the value of the dollar by seven and a half cents in the middle of the election campaign."

"Have you any goddamn idea what was behind those records and what we were supposed to do with them?'"

"No. Never."

"You know," said Wilson, "I asked our campaign chairman. I said, 'Y' know, some money we could use. Pamphlets we could use. Signs we could use. A visit by Pearson we'd appreciate. What the hell are we supposed to do with these? How does something like this happen?'

"Now, he'd been around politics since before radio. Before Mackenzie King, in fact, since he started in 1917. He was a smart old guy."

Wilson laughed, reflectively, "About the same age we are now…no, maybe a little older. His name was Sidney Smith, he was a Senator. He had this big head, and a very large, expressive face, and large eyes that swam around in big, brown, horn-rimmed glasses.

"He says to me, his big eyes rotating in these glasses as he stares at the ceiling, then at the floor, and then at us, 'In every campaign, people you've never seen before come in off the street with magic-bullet solutions to winning. If only this, that, or some other thing could be done, the riding's a sure win. It's always nonsense. You win campaigns with hard work, not magic. Some managers throw them out, or argue with them. Me? I always agree, but say rather sadly that it would cost money, and we didn't have any.'"

"He then sort of paused, and shook his head.

"'This time somebody found the money.'"

"I Don't Want to Write a Memoir!"

Again, they both started to laugh and, again, there were some curious stares from others, but fewer this time. Greenfield smiled.

Wilson wiped his eyes with his napkin.

"These are funny stories," said Greenfield, and undoubtedly amusing to some, But I think we have in mind something else."

The waiter arrived with the food and the three ate in silence for about two minutes, two of them thinking old thoughts about campaigns long ago, and Greenfield wondering where all this was going to lead. Wilson spoke first.

"Well, said Wilson, we could start with our days in student politics, if you liked.

"Remember the early student days, the political club at university? Some great stories."

"Don't get me started." Dawson paused. Then he started.

"I remember how we packed that meeting in Montreal and got Simon elected when everybody said he didn't have a hope. Stampeded the meeting." He shook his head. "What a disappointment he was."

"Yes," Wilson said, keeping it moving, "and when we organized that big political meeting in the Common Room at university and invited that up-and-coming Ottawa comedian— who just happened to be in town— Rich Little—along to provide the entertainment? Somebody just knew him and called, and out he came. Put on a great show for a thousand students. No charge. The guys downtown couldn't figure out how we did it when the gambit got front-page coverage in the Vancouver Sun. A coup."

"Yeah," interjected Dawson. "But a very real part of the problem of telling that story and many like it, with all their glory is, 'Who today knows who the hell Rich Little is, or was?' You know, and I know, that he was internationally famous in the '60s and '70s, but does Greenfield, here, know that he was a famous comedian and show business personality for a long while. But the last, oh, 30 years…? Greenfield is our reader demographic, here, Wilson. If folks in their"—he looked a Greenfield, again, trying to decide if he were in his late thirties or early forties—"thirties can't relate, well, what the hell?

9

"Then there is technology. Before email and internet and stuff, there were more face-to face political meetings. People actually met and discussed things. Policy was discussed, if you can imagine that. It was a lot friendlier, more collegial and, frankly, a lot more fun. How do you explain that, before Blackberry, and instant communications, things were a lot different? It's like the difference cars made replacing horses a hundred years ago. Revolutionary. It's just changed political discourse and relationships fundamentally.

"Political parties have been replaced by what are really 'marching and chowder societies'. Members used to get together, sometimes monthly, and discuss policy and issues, and have serious discussions. Now they just gather for fund-raising dinners and gossip about nothing of substance. And you don't even have to be a member of the Party. The sense of common purpose, of collegiality, of purpose has all been lost."

Again, Dawson shook his head.

But Wilson was getting into the spirit of the thing, and kept on.

"Remember the new executive elections at the Ottawa convention, and this girl from the University of Montréal methodically seduced four of the six guys elected in the next two days? The only guys who resisted her were you and a guy from Alberta."

Dawson laughed at the shared memory.

"You, of course, were homely and shy. She probably only half-tried, you were so ugly," said Wilson.

They both laughed at that one.

It was Dawson's turn.

"Remember the party in that motel out on Montreal Road in Ottawa, when the girl had a seizure and fainted inside the locked bathroom and we had to bust the door down? We had a time explaining that to the motel owner. Wonder whatever happened to her?"

Greenfield interjected.

"In this book you're going to write, it would be better and more interesting with Ottawa government and political stories, not the human interest stuff," he said, happy to finally be able to say something. "So far so much of what you guys are talking about is funny to you, and to people that are political nuts maybe, but its all too 'inside' to grab the average reader interested in politics and government."

Dawson smiled.

"That means I should leave out the time, after a particularly heated Cabinet meeting, when two Ministers got into a fist fight, and the House Leader got a black eye trying to break it up? Is that what you mean?"

Wilson only looked at him with a raised eyebrow. Dawson decided it was time for serious talk.

"Wilson, this guy has asked me to write my memoirs. I don't want to write my goddamn memoirs. What do you think?"

Wilson. looked at Greenfield, then at Dawson.

"What are you planning to do with your time if not write your memoirs? You know, you have a lot to say after over 50 years in politics, if you choose to say it. And if you're truly retired," he teased. "You certainly have the time."

"Oh, I'll find something to do. Been asked to go on two boards. A good charity wants me. I had a call from a poly-sci prof wanting to know if I'd like to spend a year teaching politics. Lots of things. But memoirs? What good would that do?"

Dawson had turned to the guy from Toronto, addressing the question to him, and he responded.

"Well, as your friend says, you go back a long way. You've seen a lot of things from the inside over more than 50 years. We Canadians have forgotten huge amounts of our history because so few good memoirs are written, memoirs that tell it like it is—or was. Most are just self-serving puff-pieces retirees write to see if they can improve the reputations they had when they left office. None that I've seen really deal with the big issues, the hard decisions, the personalities as they really were, and the scandals. We want a hard-hitting, honest memoir. Something that maybe adds to the dialogue in this country about its politics, but mainly we want a memoir that will explain to the readers what a person sees and experiences in a lifetime of politics. The risks, the rewards, the diversions, the inside stories about events, some descriptions of personalities....not so much an 'I went there then I did that' kind of memoir that justifies your life, but something readers can learn from."

"Yeah, I know, I know," said Dawson, finally. "But the problem is, if you tell the unvarnished truths, nobody will ever speak to you again. You end up stirring up old animosities. You might face a squall of lawsuits for slander. You offend the Official Secrets Act. Old friends are hurt. On it goes. We Canadians get along because we tolerate each other's frailties so well. An honest memoir messes all that up."

"I'm sure you can still tell the stories and avoid that. You do, in fact, have a reputation for diplomacy, when diplomacy is required," the publisher's representative said.

Dawson looked at him.

"I suppose. But nobody would read it. And how do you tell the stories that are all about the human side of politics? The sad stories, the disappointments, the treacheries, the deals that are made and the deals that are broken. All that stuff. You can't."

Wilson thought for a minute, then spoke.

"Well, John, I think there is so much to tell from 50 years that you really can't tell it all, anyway. Three hundred pages wouldn't cover five percent of it. Surely there are ways you can tell some of the best stories without, well, without messing up a bunch of people's lives?"

There was no response from Dawson as he buttered a bun. Wilson tried again, this time in an effort at humour.

"How about you write it and then these guys publish it after you're dead?"

Dawson looked at him, and stuck out his tongue.

"Explain to me, please, sir, what's the fun in that?"

"Yes, what's the fun in that?" responded Wilson.

Dryly, Greenfield offered that his house would not really be interested in that sort of arrangement, anyway.

Dawson went on:

"Then there's the fact that many—maybe most—of the most interesting stories are complicated. If you want your audience to understand, you lose them in all the background stuff. And what is politics all about, anyway? It's a lot of people talking and thinking. No action. People like action. They like crisis. Good politicians avoid crises. So, I tell a story about how some kind of disaster was avoided by astute action, a lot of palaver, and clever manoeuvring? A big yawn. Politics is all guys like you and me and him having lunch and BS-ing. Boring."

"Oh, come on. You know better and I've heard you yarn for about 40 years. You know how to tell a good story well. Mind you, one of your strengths as a story-teller is that you don't allow yourself to be unduly constrained by the truth."

Dawson ignored the compliment with a grunt, and then continued his previous thought.

"Well, it's one thing to talk and tell tall stories to friends after a long day and a few drinks, and maybe stretch a truth or two to be entertaining or make a point. It's something else to put pen to paper and play with history and with reputations. I just don't have the interest to back up everything I say, and think, with the solid research that would be needed. I'm too old to agree to spend years in the bloody archives. If I were to write a memoir, it'd have to be bulletproof, or it would be my reputation that would be blemished more than the reputations of others. I just can't see it. No." Then he carried on.

"But you know there's a great story about when one Minister found himself sharing a box at Grey Cup in Vancouver with a Cabinet colleague he loathed. The colleague, a gregarious Irishman, pretty well along after a half-dozen drinks, and oblivious to the other Minister's feelings about him, kept getting past the first Minister's accompanying assistant to sit next to him, and bellow drunken observations about the game into his ear. During the half-time break, the Minister motioned to the assistant to follow him to the men's room where, with venomous emphasis, he said to the assistant, 'If that son of a bitch gets next to me for even a second before the end of the effing game, you are fired. Here. Right now. You walk back to Ottawa. Understand?'

"The assistant, who was a big guy, and no wimp, did as he was told, and was in a constant wrestling match with the increasingly drunken

Minister for the rest of the game. I sat behind them. It was hilarious to watch."

Wilson smiled. He'd heard the story before, somewhat embellished.

"Yes, I've always thought the whole idea about 'Cabinet solidarity' was overdone. Well, what about the memoirs?"

Greenfield interrupted. "Look, we are happy to give you a lot of latitude in how you tell the story. As I say, we've seen too much of self-serving—and frankly boring—examples of plainly descriptive memoirs. We want readers to come away from your book saying to themselves, 'Oh, that's how candidates are recruited, or campaigns are run, or how it feels to be a Minister, with all that responsibility. I think Canadians would like to know what motivates people to get into politics. What's the effect of political life on families, on friendships? We want them to understand what goes through a politician's mind when he has to make tough choices, or when he's torn between doing what's right, and what's political. We'd like to give readers a sense of the…oh…grittiness of politics, if that's the right word. What I've heard here over lunch gives me a sense that there is, in fact, a book here. Some kind of book. Somewhere."

Coffee arrived. There was a long silence. Each had a long look out the window, across the grass and the parked cars, over the water to the freighters and the land beyond. The meal check arrived. Greenfield reached out and covered it with his credit card.

Dawson broke the silence.

"Ah, I don't know. First of all, I'm not sure I can write. I'm no Scott Fitzgerald. It'd be a lot of work. But I agree some of the stories deserve to be told. Let me think about it.

A pause.

"What kind of advance're you offering?" he asked with a small smile. I'm a retired guy on a pension now, you know."

ELECTION

The Campaign: a Short Story in Four Parts

1. The Hook

Charlie was late getting out of Court and ran across Georgia Street to the steakhouse where he had agreed to meet Senator George Vail promptly at noon for lunch, knowing how annoyed he was with tardy people. Charlie had no intention of annoying the Senator, and he paused only briefly at the maitre'd's desk before spotting his host and then striding directly to the corner table.

As he regained his breath from his dash across the street he wrestled himself out of his wet raincoat. The Senator watched, saying nothing until Charlie sat down, adjusted his chair and unfolded his napkin, placing it over his lap.

"Well?" said Charlie.

"We haven't had even a few words in about three months and I thought I'd better call you. You don't have a lot of time to make a decision and I wanted to try to remove any inhibitions you might have."

"There are no inhibitions and no lack of a decision. I told you, clearly I thought, that I have absolutely no intention of running in the next election, whenever it is. I told you that and the reasons months ago. Nothing's changed. I don't understand why you're not looking elsewhere. You need a 'star' to win East, if you can win it at all, and I'm not it."

There was a short silence from George, and he began to say something just as the waiter interrupted with a pitcher of water and the delivery of menus.

"Thank you," he said to the waiter, then returned his attention to Charlie, looking him squarely in the eye.

"Charlie, why do you think I'm asking you to run in East?"

"You need a candidate that you think can win. I don't think I can win, but more to the point, I can't afford to win. I've not been a partner in the firm all that long, and am just beginning to make some money and if I were elected, which is admittedly highly, highly doubtful, I'd take a cut in income of about sixty percent. My wife would likely divorce me, my children would be without shoes and a higher education, and my partners would be very, very unhappy."

The Senator thought for a moment. The assessment of the consequences of winning was likely reasonably accurate.

"You're wrong. I'm not looking at you as a candidate that can win because I don't think we can win that riding. But it's important that we run as good a candidate there as we can find. I'm tired of fielding fourth-rate ethnic candidates and immigration lawyers only interested in soliciting business and hoping for a piece of the patronage pie. I want a candidate we can be proud of, who has something to say and will stand up and say what he thinks. You're it. And there's a lot in it for you in exchange for six weeks of your time."

This frankness surprised Charlie. His experience in the outer reaches of politics since he'd been a political activist in university 15 years before was that party fixers—and that's how he thought of the Senator— were always assuring people that they tried to recruit to run that getting elected was a sure thing.

"Spell it out," said Charlie, as the waiter arrived to take their orders and as he buttered a Parkerhouse roll. Charlie ordered a steak sandwich and a Caesar salad. George ordered the lobster bisque and a lobster salad.

"And a carafe of sauvignon blanc," said George.

"A Canadian for me. Draft if you have it," said Charlie. A single beer was acceptable, given that he had a quiet and undemanding afternoon, he thought.

The Senator did not like spelling things out. There was, he thought, a thin line to be negotiated without being accused of something improper.

"There are several benefits. Perhaps most important are personal. You're a rising young figure in this community. The broader community, not just the legal community. You've served in some well-known charities and community organizations, and developed some profile. You've developed a positive relationship with a few members of the media because of your commentaries on a couple of important legal cases and some social issues. These are the sorts of things that move you from being a "grinder" or a "minder" in your firm—and no one disputes your legal talent—to a "finder," where the bigger money and the prestige is, where the corporate directorships are. You get your name on the door. You become the kind of guy that draws new clients to your partners, and this puts you into the upper income levels of the practice of law. You run, and do it well, and you're much closer to that status."

Charlie said nothing.

The Senator went on.

"But, as well, you have things to say. This is an opportunity to establish yourself as someone who is not necessarily marching to anybody else's tune, and certainly not to that of the Prime Minister and the Party establishment. We need people like you. Not only the Party, but our whole community, the country, needs folks like you. You'll get a lot of people's gratitude, mine as well as the Party's. That you take on a riding that everybody says can't be won makes you look, among other things, courageous and idealistic. Stop smiling. There are some substantial brownie points in this for your firm if they keep you on the payroll during your time away from the office, which I'm sure they will. You're 37 years old, Charlie, and this is a really good investment in your future. A solid, realistic investment, and it's only six weeks."

He looked at Charlie for a response.

"You don't think I can win?" said Charlie, somewhat disbelieving the Senator's message.

There was a pause as the wine and beer arrived.

"Not a hope, frankly. Our polls show we can hold what we have in B.C., maybe pick up one or two seats, but East isn't one of them. Not by a long shot. We have traditionally been 20 points down there, and nothing has changed."

Charlie scoffed.

"I think I would look like a fool to run in a riding I couldn't possibly win, and to suffer a humiliating loss would be a personal setback of considerable proportions. I can't follow your logic here at all."

"Well," said the Senator—he frequently began his sentences with 'well', "that just depends on how you—we—spin the story. You know, and everybody knows, that if candidates only ran in sure-thing ridings, most election races would go by acclamation. Of all the seats in the country, only about 50 or 60 out of 256 are really uncertain in most elections. Then about every third or fourth election, there's a sweep. The Tories win big, or we win big. In those elections, all bets are off, and almost everything's in play. Anyway, this is not one of those elections. A relatively small number of seats will change hands. This time the power of incumbency is huge. Of course, in the next election after a sweep, many seats usually return to the parties that previously held them. There is a huge equilibrium in Canadian politics that means a shift of very few votes ordinarily defeats and elects governments. Usually no more than about five percent. The NDP margin in East is more than four times that. An impossible hurdle. Don't worry about it."

Seeing no objection from Charlie, George continued.

"The point here is that you make it clear from day one that while to are working to win, winning is not necessarily your main objective. Rather, you say you are running to say some things that need saying. Then you say them. We'll see you get a good campaign manager, and that you are more than adequately financed. I'll see that you get policy and speechwriting and PR support. You'd be someone who'd would put some excitement in what promises to be a pretty dull campaign."

Still no reaction from Charlie.

"Let me put it another way. In this Province, we need someone articulating some vision more forward looking and regionally sensitive than will come out of the candidates who think they can win and who are intimidated by the thought of making even the smallest mistake, or saying anything that might upset the editorial writers. Or, quite frankly, than will come out of the official campaign platform drafted by the heavy thinkers back east. This could be a dull campaign and you could add some colour to it, if you get into the spirit of the thing."

Charlie began to say something, then paused, then went on.

"You say I can't win. You're sure? Absolutely sure?" Charlie emphasized the 'absolutely', and squinted, looking closely at the Senator's heavily lined face, and into his green eyes as he asked this. He wanted to make sure he was getting an honest answer. He always thought he could tell if someone was lying by looking carefully at that person's face and into his eyes. The Senator, as he answered, passed Charlie's scrutiny.

"Absolutely? Absolutely. Not a chance. It's a riding we've not won in living memory. Despite some electoral boundary and demographic changes, the NDP have it sewn up tight, and this isn't our time. They have a good organization, an incumbent candidate who knows all the tricks, is a household name, and has done some good work, I hate to say. And it must be said that some issues are on their side. That's why it's perfect for you. You can run, say what you like, within reason, of course, and come out of it with a high profile your partners will envy. Go for it."

"This is insanity," said Charlie, shaking his head.

"Why?" responded the Senator.

"Because politics is supposed to be a serious business. You run because you want to win. You work your ass off, you get up at five a.m. to go and stand on a bridge or a street in the driving goddamn cold rain, with signs asking passing motorists—most of whom live nowhere near your riding—to vote for you. You troll up and down the street from dawn until after dusk anxiously trying to shake hands with individual voters most of whom try to avoid you like the plague. Then, at night, you start making the rounds of the bars, or do all-candidate meetings, or attend coffee parties where people who know nothing of politics and ordinarily care less ask questions based on ignorance and to which there usually are no sensible answers. You put up with insults, bad food, the likelihood of pneumonia and the possibility that you might say something stupid that ruins your reputation for life, all in an exercise in democracy. You are not supposed to be running to, well, just for the fun of it or just because you have nothing better to do. I don't know that I could put myself through all that if I were not serious."

This was, the Senator thought, more difficult that he thought it would be. Then lunch arrived, and they discussed generalities while they ate.

Suddenly, Charlie changed the topic.

"I don't have any personal money to put into a campaign."

The Senator suddenly realized that he had Charlie on the hook. Now began the careful task of reeling him in.

"Not a problem. We'll see that the campaign is fully funded. I have a top-notch guy already lined up to head a finance committee."

"I have some of my own ideas. I'm just not going to be prattling the Party line," continued the lawyer.

"Not a problem, unless you start disavowing it. You want to be talking about the future, about the things that are not in anybody's platform. Talk idealism and all that John and Bobby Kennedy stuff. You know, Bobby was always misquoting George Bernard Shaw, 'Some see things as they are and ask why. I dream of things that never were and ask why not.' That kind of thing. Ask why not. That's what we need. Our whole purpose in getting you to run is to show that this Party has bright, attractive, young candidates with guts and ideas. All the better if you say things that demonstrate how you are going to speak up for B.C., within reason of course, when you get to Ottawa."

Charlie grinned. "Not a problem. But what about an organization? East is not the riding in the city with the greatest organizational depth."

While the Senator had been speaking, Charlie had been steadily working his way through his meal. Now finished, he took a good swallow of beer.

The Senator thought for a moment. The wrong answer here could sink the whole pitch. He spoke carefully.

"Look, Charlie, we can't do magic. You know and we know that you are not going to win. We'll see you're properly financed. We'll get some advisers and a good campaign manager. We can get the PM to come into your riding. We can make you look good. But we just can't mobilize the three or four hundred people you will need to go out and knock on every door, or phone every voter, three times, so you could win this riding if the numbers were there. The numbers aren't there and campaign workers are a scarce resource, our scarcest resource, unfortunately. We just can't afford to spend those people-resources on a sure-to-lose riding. I'm sure the riding association can find fifty people, and you have some personal friends that can help, but that's all I can do." He sounded properly apologetic.

Charlie beamed. "That's all I could ask for." Indeed, he had crossed an emotional bridge from doubting skeptic to hesitantly hopeful aspirant. The Senator hid his joy.

"I'm prepared to talk this over with my wife and partners. You say there is no way I can win?" he asked one more time as he rose from the table and picked up his briefcase.

"Do you see us sweeping the country?" responded the Senator?

Charlie looked at him, then rose and put on his wet raincoat.

"I have to get to the office. You'll get the bill? I'll talk to my wife."

The Senator drank the last of his wine thoughtfully. So far, so good, he thought, in advancing the Prime Minister's plan.

That night Charlie broached the subject with Sally. Her initial reaction was stark disbelief, coupled with the look on her face reserved for the taste of something very sour.

"You have to be practical, dear," she said in her patient response. "I wouldn't like to be dipping into capital to do this, and we'll be without an income for the duration of the campaign, will we not?"

"I'll not run unless I have 110 percent support from my partners because, in part, this is an effort to advance the reputation of the firm. And that means I'd continue drawing my salary from the firm," he replied.

"This is good publicity for them, and they'll know it. Besides, we get a certain amount of business from the federal government and if our party wins which is a reasonably good bet that is likely to increase."

He didn't want to sound mercenary so much as practical.

"But what if you win? What's an MP get paid? 15, 20 thousand a year? You would take a…what…sixty, seventy percent drop in income as a backbencher, maybe something like 45 percent if you were in the Cabinet? How would we manage to live, what with the mortgage on this big house, alone, and the kids' education, never mind the extra expense of you living in Ottawa?"

"MPs get paid 12 thousand a year in taxable income, and another 6 thousand in untaxed, unaccountable expenses, so its actually worse than you think. I'd use up most of that six thou with a second place to live in Ottawa.

"But, if there was the slightest likelihood I'd get elected, I wouldn't even be thinking of this. The fact is it is a riding we have only won once since forever, and that was in highly unusual circumstances. On the other hand, it's an opportunity for me to stand up for some things I believe in and say some things that need to be said by someone in our Party. I'm not deluding myself, I have no roots in that riding, and I'm not an ethnic candidate that can look to picking up overwhelming support from any one community. The NDP candidate has worked hard, has a good organization, a good reputation and there's no reason why she shouldn't be re-elected with a clear majority."

Sally was not convinced.

"But what if there were some…catastrophe…and you got elected? What would we do?" The tone of her voice was one of real worry.

"You'd be stuck there at a peon's wage for four years, losing touch with the law and your clients, and seeing the boys and me only on weekends most of the year. I just don't know how we could cope with that.

"I'd rather you didn't, dear," she said gently, with a hurt tone in her voice. He knew then that if he ran he would be doing it without Sally's support.

However, as Charlie had promised the Senator, he met with his partners the next day. They were all more realistic than Sally. Most of them knew something of the political history of East. They knew there was no risk in letting Charlie run that they would lose him to politics. Charlie had put his case, answered a few questions, then he left the room so the partners could talk freely.

Ten minutes later, he was called back to hear the decision.

The senior partner was in an expansive mood in summarizing the discussion.

"Charlie, if you run I'm pleased to say that your partners—even those not of your Party—are unanimous in our support. We'll maintain your monthly draw and, if you are elected"...he paused here to savour a chuckle... "we'll work something out so you can continue to maintain your lifestyle by putting some time in at the office. So in seeking public service you are, hopefully, not at risk of suffering too much financially."

Charlie thanked them. This was more than he had expected. But they too had done the political calculus: his running was a good investment in public, government and client relations for the firm.

He went home at the end of the day much happier than he had left. Sally's discouraging words of the previous evening had left him a little depressed all day, even given the support of his partners. He had called the Senator and brought him up to date. He did not go into detail about the support from the firm, but told the Senator that without wifely support, as he knew, politics was not a happy business. The Senator agreed he knew.

After dinner, over coffee, with the boys dismissed to do their homework, they sat in the den while he described to Sally his meeting with the partners. He emphasized their financial support, post election, if the worst should happen. At this point the phone rang and a few seconds later their oldest boy, Cal, put his head through the door.

"Mom, it's for you. I don't know who. Some man." The head disappeared before she could ask anything else. As Sally rose to go to the phone, Charlie got up and went out to the front yard to turn on the sprinklers. It was spring and Charlie was beginning to take an interest in countering a winter's attack on his lawn. He got into a discussion with his next door neighbour about fertilizers and aeration and it was 15 minutes before he got back to Sally. She was again sitting in the den where he had last seen her. She had a thoughtful look on her face.

"Charlie, if you want to go, you have my support. Unqualified, absolute support. Go do it."

The look on Charlie's face was one of total surprise. He then realized it might have something to do with the phone call.

"Who was on the phone?"

"The Prime Minister. He told me why you must run. That you have a very important role to play in the political life of this country, and if people like you don't run then…the other people… run the country." She shuddered as she said 'the other people.' She disliked the Opposition more than he did. She thought they were nasty, short-sighted, uncaring, narrow-minded and greedy. And those were their least objectionable attributes, in Sally's view.

She went on.

"I guess I was being selfish, but I guess I feared that the voters might see in you what I see in you, and vote for you. Charlie, run, but if you win…." She left the thought unexpressed, but Charlie knew what she meant.

"The Prime Minister?" he asked.

"Yes, it's a conspiracy. But I couldn't say no when he asked. I couldn't say 'no' to any Prime Minister, I guess, but he put it in both personal and patriotic terms."

Charlie wondered about the call. The Prime Minister. He hadn't asked to talk to Charlie, apparently, but then Charlie had had numerous conversations with him over the years, mostly when he was Minister of Justice and Charlie had done some work for the Department. That, and his involvement with the Party, and his work on law reform. The Senator must have called him this afternoon, thought Charlie, and told him that he'd have to close the deal with Sally. Well. They really did want him. And maybe Sally had it right, there was a conspiracy. But how in hell did the

Prime Minister have the time to call a sure-to-lose potential candidate's wife? The political world was full of mysteries.

2. Mother's Milk

The Finance Minister flew in to be the speaker at what turned out to be an uncontested nominating meeting that went very well, with a larger than expected crowd, thanks to some 'whipping-in' by Party organizers. The Party had in the past run ethnic token candidates in East, but the Party's media people had sold the idea to both the local activists and to the media that the Party was really serious about winning East this time and expected Charlie to be the man who could do it. They explained that, in the past, if a Chinese candidate was chosen, other ethnic groups abandoned the Party, and vice versa. Charlie was acceptable to everyone as both an outsider and a non-ethnic. It was political nonsense but had a certain curious appeal, which the media generally accepted.

What in ordinary circumstances would have been a small story on page 9 of the Vancouver Sun, then, was on the front page below the fold. What he had said at the meeting was given prominence over the words of the Finance Minister. It was a good story, and it buoyed him up considerably because it was a good start.

Charlie had spent the past few days cleaning up files in his office. He conceded to his partners that since there were some he just could not pass off and for the six weeks of the campaign he'd put in a few hours a week keeping them going with some help from the juniors. An election call was rumoured to be coming soon, and Charlie wanted to be ready to go full time.

His phone rang. It was Senator Vail.

Charlie had no sooner said "Hello" than the Senator began a monologue. Clearly, he was in full-speed campaign mode.

"Charlie, its George. I've lined up Peter Holt to be your fundraiser. He'll call you within the hour. He has a bunch of guys, and a box full of cards with names of previous contributors and hot prospects. You got to meet today—no later than tomorrow—and get the fundraising going. Look I got other things I got to do to get this Provincial campaign going. I'll talk to you later. Bye."

All Charlie had said was hello. He returned to the papers on his desk. Peter Holt, whom he did not know well, would be fine. He was a finance guy, but one with a reputation for integrity.

A few minutes later the phone rang again. It was Peter Holt. He too began without ceremony.

"Senator Vail asked me to chair your finance committee. Glad to. I've got some guys to help and I'm setting up a meeting for everybody for breakfast tomorrow. You available? 7:30. The Club."

"The Club" of course meant the Vancouver Club, the oldest and most prestigious in a city of three gentleman's clubs and several golf clubs. Charlie understood this, although he was not a member.

Charlie thanked him for taking on the task, and said he'd be there.

"Also, I want Howie Cohen on the committee," he added.

There was a pause at the other end. "Look, I know Howie. He's a good guy, but we've never had any Jews on this committee before. I'd like to keep it that way."

Charlie could feel the hairs on the back of his neck stiffening, but he kept his temper.

"Well, you've put me in an awkward position. I've known Howie for a long time. Since university. He called me yesterday, said he'd like to help fundraise. I don't know what I would say if now I didn't call on him. It would really ruin our friendship."

If Peter was not persuaded, he was at least sympathetic.

"As I say, Howie's fine, but there are others on the Committee… look, why not just leave this to me. I'll call Howie and put him to work separately."

"You mean its fine for him to work, but not to attend breakfast meetings at the Club? Separate but equal? Is that the message here?" Charlie's voice raised a little. He was clearly annoyed. Peter understood that. He was momentarily silent.

"I'm just saying we are not into what I would characterize as the Jewish way of fundraising."

Obviously, there was not going to be any agreement, here.

"Peter, I really appreciate what you and your team are doing. Certainly I'll be at the Club at 7:30. I'll bring Howie, and introduce him around. So we'll see you tomorrow." He hung up before the conversation could be rejoined. With no follow-up call from either the Senator or Peter, Charlie felt he had weathered his first difficulty. He called Howie, who was delighted to come to breakfast. Even in the Vancouver Club, which had not accepted Jews as members until recently.

The two of them arrived a few minutes early and, as the others arrived, Charlie introduced himself to those he did not already know, which was four of eight, and said hello to the others, as they came in. It was, he reflected, something of a WASP establishment group. Nobody who lived in East, that was for sure, he thought wryly, but he recognized that most probably had business interests in the riding.

Peter asked everyone to help themselves to the scrambled eggs and bacon buffet, and Charlie wondered if the bacon was some kind of message from Peter regarding Jews. He dismissed the thought as he saw Howie place six slices of bacon on his plate. When everyone was seated Peter began by saying that everyone knew why they were there, and he introduced Charlie.

Charlie spoke carefully, hoping to set the right tone and get the fundraising effort begun properly.

"Thank you for coming," he began. "Raising money is not one of the great, high-profile jobs in politics and there is not much glory. So let me thank you in advance for volunteering." He smiled a little, suspecting some of them had not exactly volunteered. He suspected also that more than a couple of the attendees were significantly to the political right of where he stood.

"It is an axiom with which you are all familiar, that money is the mother's milk of politics. The best policies can't get articulated, organizers can't get hired, advertising can't be bought, and signs can't be painted without the money we depend upon you fine gentlemen to raise. And so your work is vitally important to me and I thank you.

"It is sometimes said that politicians don't want to know where the money is coming from. Well, I'm different. I don't want the campaign to be accepting money from what I might call questionable sources. I gather from Peter that he expects to have about seven weekly meetings like this and I'll attend each of them, if I can. I really do appreciate the work you're doing. I know it's not easy. Some of your contacts don't like the Prime Minister or our Party or, very likely, me. But I don't want anyone promising or even hinting that a donation gets them anything special. The people you are approaching, these are all people who have done very well in life. They can, each of them, afford a few dollars to help support the democratic process, and that's what they're doing. Any time any of you feel you want to talk to me about any of this, please call me. As I say, I am immensely grateful to each of you. At the end, when it's all over, it might be an idea to have a reception where I could thank each of them personally, if you think that's a good idea. Peter?"

Peter reached into a large leather case, the kind used for carrying legal briefs, and brought out a metal box about a foot long and seven inches wide. He opened it, revealing it to be a card-file box, about three quarters full of five-by-seven-inch cards. This was the list of former contributors and hot prospects. Each card was held to a second card by a paper clip. Each had identical information on it about each individual donor's contribution history, contact information, who had contacted the person last, and with what results. He started through them alphabetically.

"Allison, Harry J.?"

A middle-aged blond fellow at the end of the table immediately said, "I golf with him. I'll take it."

Peter passed one card of the set down the table, and noted the recipient's name on the matching card.

"Anderson, Frank S.?"

A guy Charlie remembered as Bill, said he knew him through his church. He'd make the call.

"Argue, William F.?"

There was no response.

"Nobody knows him?" Apparently, no one did. Charlie knew him a little, and understood he was sometimes unpleasant. Maybe, he thought, they all knew him.

Howie Cohen, after a pause, said, "I'll take him."

And so they went through the box to G. That was about 60 names, and most of the seven people making calls had about seven calls to make. Howie had 12, and had taken every name that no one else knew, or didn't want to take. Peter seemed to not want anyone to have too full a load the first week.

After, Charlie made a point of thanking Peter. He knew that Peter wasn't entirely happy with Howie being there, but he said nothing about it.

The next Monday, Peter Holt called the meeting to order and once again opened the filing-card box. Ham was the meat of choice that morning. Sixty cards in the box had now been re-filed from alphabetical order to the names of the fundraiser that had the card. Peter also produced a lined yellow pad on which to make notes. These would later be transferred to the file cards.

Once again Charlie thanked the members of the group for their hard work and for coming. Then he sat back to listen. If the folks who finance election campaigns did not like him and wouldn't support his candidacy, he wanted to know, and know early.

Peter began the formal part by turning to the fellow to his immediate right, Harry Lee, who Charlie understood was in real estate development, and asked him to report. It quickly became obvious to Charlie that these collectors had done this before.

Harry reached into the left-hand inside pocket of his jacket and pulled out seven blue cards, some with attached pieces of paper, which were cheques.

He began his litany. "Harry Arthurs, $200 last time, I got him up to $250 this time," whereupon he laid the blue card and the cheque on the table.

"Dave Carson, $200 last time, same this time. John Douglas, $100 last time, I tried to get him up this time but no go. Maury Fayer was out of town, and Frank Bateson did not return phone calls. That's as many as I got to this week."

Charlie noted there was no comment about anything related to his candidacy, and watched Peter make notes on his yellow pad as the next fundraiser reported. The note said, '3 of 7 cards/ $1700 last time, $550 so far'.

The next fundraiser had six cards, two cheques, and similar excuses about his failure to reach the other four names. And so it went around the table.

Charlie was not concerned—in was early in the campaign, everything was going well, and he knew that, however you might try, you just couldn't always get someone on the phone immediately. He felt good that no one said anything negative about his candidacy harming fund-raising.

The last to report was Howie Cohen. Charlie had earlier asked him how he had done, and Howie had replied, "Fine," making it clear he didn't want to talk about it. Charlie was concerned that with 12 cards, he'd got bogged down and would look bad to the others. However, when Peter called his name, Howie reached into his inside jacket pocket and pulled out what could only be described as a wad of paper.

He began, as he went through his blue cards: "Fred Axelson, $200 last time, $300 this time, Bill Argue, 200 last time, same this time. Jeff Edson, $300 last time, $350 this time, and another $500 from his company; Mike Ellenberger, $200 last time, $400 this time; Walter Gemmell, $300 last time, and I could only get the same from him this time, which disappoints me, 'cause he's had a good year. Ralph German $100 last time, $300 this time—personally— and, again, $500 from his company; Sam Glass, $300 last time, $400 this time."

And so it went until there were two blue cards left of 12, and no more cheques.

"Walter Crerar is on a cruise, and absolutely unreachable. Tom Cernetig and I discussed a suitable donation. He gave $300 last time and offered the same this time, but I think he's good for 5, if nobody objects."

He then looked over to Peter. Charlie, for his part, was carefully watching the other members. In essence, Howie had raised in a week what he was supposed to in a month.

Clearly, Charlie thought, Peter was searching for something to say, then finally settled on, "Thank you, Howie. That's excellent work."

Charlie stole a glance at Peter's yellow pad, summarizing Howie's collections. It said, "$2400 last time, $4750 this time."

Peter then said, "I'd like to now pass out a few cards to replace the ones you have turned in. Without pushing, Peter managed to pass out enough cards to get from G to K. Again, Howie took twelve cards.

Turning to the group, Peter said, "OK, same time and place next Monday. Has anybody any questions?

Nobody had a question but Howie.

"I have some personal contacts. Would you mind if I canvassed them?"

No one, needless to say, objected.

A week later, early in the morning of the second Monday of the campaign, Charlie went bus-stopping. From 6 a.m. to 7:30 he was driven along two major arterial roads from bus stop to bus stop. He would leap out of the campaign van, introduce himself to the gathered bus riders, jump back in the van and go to the next stop. A half-dozen supporters would pass out pamphlets. By keeping track of what time he was at each stop, and knowing most bus riders were creatures of habit, Charlie's organizers could plan that he efficiently meet every bus rider in the constituency by election day. As well it gave him early morning street visibility and this, in turn, generated chatter among the strap-hangers.

Afterwards, Charlie again attended the fund-raising breakfast. One from the previous week was not there—he was out of town— but a new member had joined the group. As they all milled around having coffee, and then helped themselves to the ubiquitous buffet breakfast, this time with pork sausages, five of the fund raisers asked him how the campaign was going, how he was enjoying it, and otherwise demonstrated an interest in the goings on. There were some comments about how the Prime Minister had launched the campaign but—and Charlie listened very carefully—there were no negative feelings expressed by anyone. This encouraged him.

Again, Howie outdid the others.

The following Monday, Charlie didn't attend the breakfast, but Peter called him afterwards to report that—Charlie said, 'proudly' when he repeated the conversation that night to Sally, "….. Howie brought in $5200 we were not expecting, from his own personal contacts."

Charlie was satisfied there would be no more remarks about Jews and about Howie from Peter.

3. The Grind

Charlie went to the campaign office the first Monday it was opened, after the fundraising breakfast, a few days before the election was called, just as though he were going to the law office. The office manager was the only person there and was busy on the phone. Charlie knew it was ridiculous for him to be at the campaign office that early because nothing much happens in a campaign office early that concerns the candidate and, in this case, the campaign activity had not yet begun. He recalled one old guy telling him years ago that, "Elections are won at night. Any time you see a campaign office closed in the evening, it's a losing campaign."

He went across the street to have a cup of coffee and work on some speech thoughts.

About 9:45, Charlie looked up from his work to see Ted Early go into the campaign office. He gathered his papers and crossed the street. Ted was directing some workers that were moving scrubby furniture in through the back door. He noticed that over the weekend some cubicles had been roughly constructed to cut down on the background noise that would disturb volunteers telephoning voters. There was a largish room with a door in the back corner that had some decent furniture in it and a boardroom table. That was obviously set aside for him, so he went in and dropped his papers on the battered desk.

The Campaign: a Short Story in Four Parts

He joined Ted in the supervision of the workmen.

"This job doesn't need both of us," said Ted, directly, crisply. "Please go back to your office and make lists. Any concerns you have, any questions, any needs, any thoughts. We then want to start planning a campaign. We've got about three days, according to the CBC, before the PM dissolves Parliament, so we have to get going." He was very business-like. Charlie liked that.

"Yes," said Charlie and, like an obedient child, did as he was directed. Ted joined him about 15 minutes later.

"We've got to get everything straight between us right away. You game?" said Ted, with no preliminaries. Ted had been another of the Senator's 'volunteers'. Charlie knew him only by reputation and, looking around, decided they wouldn't be overheard and nodded.

"OK," Ted began, "it's like this. I think I'm pretty good. I told the Senator I'd like to be given a riding that we did not hold but had a chance at winning. I figured that it was worth taking two months off work to do. So what's he give me? The least likely-to-win riding in the Province, maybe the country, and a glamour-boy candidate who, with all due respect, knows nothing about electoral politics. Am I being unfair? No? Nothing personal here, Charlie, but I have to ask, are you going to work your goddam ass off like a real candidate, or just show up once in a while to cheer up the troops?"

Charlie immediately liked Ted.

"Nothing personal here, either, Ted. I really appreciate it that the Senator asked you to come here and I'm grateful that you agreed to do it. I know your reputation. I've the same doubts that you do about winning. But it's the Senator's theory that by my running I can tie up some NDP resources, and I can say some things that candidates in more winnable ridings can't say, but things that deserve to be said in the interests of a...shall we say...regional campaign. My job is to speak up for British Columbia and this might help the others. I plan to work as hard as you make me work. You want me on the street Burma-Shaving at 6 a.m. and I'll be there. Kissing babies, main-streeting, whatever. You tell me, and I'll go. And while I may know little about electoral politics—as you put it—I know enough not to try to be the campaign manager and the candidate both."

He paused, noting the appreciative look from Ted about their respective roles.

"However, I do have to put in an hour or two most days at the office. There are some important things I couldn't pass off entirely. I'll do that first thing in the morning after bus-stopping or whatever else I do, and the fundraising breakfast. Say 9 to 10 or 10:30. The rest of the day and into the night is yours. That okay?"

It was. The election was called the following day, and the first week of the campaign passed more quickly than Charlie thought it would. Although there were times that seemed slow, most of each day presented problems and issues with which he enjoyed dealing. Most of it was, in fact, fun, he admitted to himself. It wasn't all dealing with fools, fanatics, or little Old Ladies in Tennis Shoes, of both sexes, whom he learned were referred to as LOLITAS among the campaign staff. It was certainly different from most days practicing law which someone had once likened to the picking of fly manure out of pepper while wearing boxing gloves. No, each day was different, every day had its challenges, and despite the years he had spent on the fringes of politics, he now realized that nothing compared with being in the ring yourself, and nothing prepared you for the ring. He began to keep careful notes of whom he met, what they said, and how they fitted in to the constituency mosaic.

Volunteers had been slow coming in after the nomination but the pace picked up with the election call and the office opening. He was humbled a little by what new volunteers said to him when he first met them, usually in the office. They thought he was a great candidate. They said they were really happy that he had run. One said something to the effect that it would be a wonderful change to work for somebody whose real objective wasn't a seat on the Immigration Appeal Board. All the upbeat comments made him feel good, too. The volunteers, all thinking he would win, gave an unexpectedly upbeat atmosphere to the office and the campaign.

By the second week a rhythm set in. Mornings invariably began at 6 with meeting his morning campaigners, a dozen or so who accompanied him when he stood on the sidewalk beside the busy commuter routes and waved at passing motorists, or rode his campaign van from bus stop to bus stop, passing out pamphlets. He referred to them, affectionately but discreetly, to Sally, as 'the morning lunatics'.

His campaigners carried signs which were to be held in order for the motorists: INTRODUCING…CHARLIE…WARREN…YOUR… LIBERAL… CANDIDATE.

The others said HONK… IF YOU VOTE… LIBERAL, and VOTE.. LIBERAL.. FOR BC.

As the campaign went along, there would be different messages, and this was known as Burma Shaving, after the shaving cream company ads popular in the United States before the days of fast, four lane highways. The company over about 35 years put up about 300 sets of up to six small signs on fence posts along country roads across the U.S. with a commercial message for passing drivers. Usually, the messages rhymed and were often mildly humourous, like 'In Cupid's little / Bag of trix / Here's the one / That clix / With chix / Burma-Shave'. The political burma shaves are seldom either rhyming or funny, and most of the time the erstwhile candidate is waving at motorists from outside his own constituency, but it had become an expected rite.

Also, early in the campaign, he learned the art of bus-stopping. That is, on days he was not Burma-shaving, he showed up to introduce himself to bus commuters as they waited at their stops. The campaign staff thought this was useful because the people already on the buses would also see the candidate. In modern election campaigns TV is far too expensive for individual candidates, so visibility had to be developed in other, much less expensive, informal, ways.

Just as the campaign began, Sally asked what she could do to help. Charlie said he'd ask Ted.

Ted said, "nothing".

"Nothing?" responded Charlie.

"Yes, nothing. Oh, we'd like to see her in the office making coffee, thanking volunteers, attending all-candidates meetings, but I'm not going to run another campaign just for her."

"I don't get you, Ted."

"Look, there are some wives who try to become the campaign manager or the volunteer coordinator or other things for which they have no qualifications and they make mistakes that campaign workers resent. In other campaigns, the wife does separate events. I've seen coffee parties, fashion shows, media appearances, all kinds of foofarah. Its a nightmare to keep a candidate's spouse organized, it creates all kinds of complications for the campaign organization, it runs the risk of creating an big error that the media notices—like if the spouse says something really, really inappropriate, and it puts extra stress on the candidate who mostly just needs a wife who can see that the kids are looked after and offer him a hot meal and an island of calm in all the chaos. So, nothing. Thank Sally for offering."

Charlie did. The next day Sally came down to the office and had a quiet chat with Ted, just to get everything straight. She spent until 3 o'clock thanking volunteers, making coffee and being cheerful. She then announced she was going home to make the candidate's dinner. She did the same most days, and she showed up at the all-candidates meetings, and politely refused to answer questions from reporters. Ted was happy. His kind of candidate's wife.

As the second week of the campaign closed, Charlie was pleased to note that a press release the campaign public relations staff had issued, reporting on remarks Charlie had made at a seniors' home, had merited eight column inches in the Vancouver Sun. In the second week there were two more stories, both of which put him in a good light, because the newspaper printed what his people had written.

More to the point, there was a mention on Monday, and another on Friday, of the goings-on in his campaign in the most-read gossip column in the Sun which appeared on the lower right corner of the second front page. It was considered a "must read" for the political and chattering classes. Again, he was pleased.

On Sunday, Sally asked him how items like his got in the column, and Charlie had to admit he had no idea. He didn't know the columnist, David Byrd, but understood him to be a long time sports reporter with a drinking problem who had only recently taken over the space from the fellow who had built the column into the "must read" that it was.

It occurred to Charlie that, with about 30 other candidates, Liberal and otherwise, in the Vancouver area, two of whom were Ministers, there had only been two mentions in the past week of all of the other Liberals. There had been one each for the NDP and the Tories. Something seemed to him to be not quite right. He decided to ask Ted Early.

Early, faced with the baldness of the question, "How come three mentions of my candidacy in news stories, and two last week in the Byrd column? I'm an unknown candidate running in an unwinnable riding. What's going on?"

Ted shuffled his feet and looked at the floor.

Charlie suddenly had the feeling this was something he should know about, had to know about.

"Speak!"

The campaign manager looked up at him and sighed. "You don't wanna know."

"Yes, I do wanna know," responded Charlie, imitating Ted's off-hand slang response, and emphasizing 'do'.

Ted looked at Charlie and saw the seriousness of the question. "I got a Sun reporter on the payroll."

Charlie, whose political instincts were growing ever sharper by the day, looked at Ted to see if he meant what he said.

Alarmed, Charlie said, "What? You better tell me!" It came out louder than he intended, and he looked into the campaign office area to see if anyone noticed. No one did.

Resignedly, Early began, "Well, I know what you're thinking, but it didn't start out that way. This guy came to me the day after the election was called. I know him from other movies, and he moonlights. I've hired him to write press releases a couple times. He asked me if we could use some PR help and he told me he wasn't assigned to cover the campaign, so no conflict of interest. At that point, I thought it was a good idea, without thinking about it too much. I know, I know," he responded to Charlie's look of alarm.

"I paid him $200 up front. But then I couldn't get him on the phone over the next few days. When I did, finally, he said that while he wasn't working on campaign coverage, he had to fill in for those who were, and apologized for not being available.

"We then discussed the situation. I wanted my money back. He mentioned he had five kids to feed on a reporter's salary. He volunteered to make sure our press releases got looked at by the guys that decide what goes in the paper, and he said that David Byrd was a friend and he could get items in the column if we wrote them. It wasn't intentional, Charlie, but I can see how it looks."

Early was truly apologetic, Charlie thought, but that didn't deal with the potential problem.

"See how it looks?" Charlie almost wailed as he put his hands up to his ears, covering them. "See how it looks? Jeeez, Ted, if anybody finds out about this…."

There was a momentary silence.

"Well, I'm not going to tell," responded Early, defensively. "You're not going to tell. Sure as hell, he's not going to tell. Nobody else knows. How's anybody going to find out?"

"How did you pay him?

"Out of my own pocket. We didn't have a campaign account set up until the next day."

"Jeeez…" Charlie let the thought go unexpressed.

Charlie's unusually positive coverage in the Vancouver Sun continued. He became a little embarrassed by the questions from other candidates about how he did it. In his own defense, Ted said that Charlie was saying things that were newsworthy, while most other candidates were not.

The third week, Charlie heard about what became known as the "big sign project." Ted Early at least told him about half the story, anyway. Charlie learned the other half later.

By the second week of the campaign, the sign crews were out putting up small lawn signs. Larger signs would come later. Much to the annoyance of the chairman of the sign crew, Willy Briglio, somebody made a point of removing nearly a hundred of Charlie's signs within days.

"It's the NDP. They always do this."

Charlie asked him how he knew this. Willy's explanation was that the Tories didn't have the manpower, the motive or the interest. "It's the NDP, believe me."

Over the next few days it was decided to do something different with the sign campaign. While most signs were small two-foot square plastic bags stretched over a wire frame pressed into the ground and others were three feet by four or four by eight, made out of cardboard or plywood, the idea of "something different" was to build a really big sign. A Really Big Sign, as Ted put it.

The design was to be six separate signs, each containing one letter of Charlie's surname, and each made of three pieces of plywood mounted on two 16-foot long, two by six boards. That made each sign 16 feet high with each letter being eight feet by 12. There were two more signs of equal size, one of which said only "Vote" and the other "Liberal."

The strategy was to line the signs up, one on each of eight front lawns, so the sign was spread out to cover half a block, and could be seen a long way away. Like, from Alaska.

"Sort of a giant, 24-hour-long burma shave effort," said Ted.

They had found a busy street with almost a block-long stretch of Liberal homeowners anxious to take a single big sign, Early told Charlie. Three were visibly delighted when the candidate showed up to help put up the signs

Willy, the sign-crew chief, had arranged for a large crew to be there to erect the signs, which was remarkably easy. It took about six helpers to raise each sign, and each sign was held firmly vertical by six simple guy-wires staked to the ground. Electric extension cords from each house wound across the grass and up to lights mounted on the top of each sign, so they could be brightly lit at night. Ted, it turned out later, had another reason for lighting the signs.

The media arrived in force. Three TV stations wanted to get numerous shots of Charlie helping to put up signs. One TV outlet had pictures taken from a helicopter. The newspapers had photographers and were busy interviewing everyone and they too wanted Charlie posed as helping with the signs. That night it was the lead item on all the TV stations, and the next morning front page in the papers. CTV and the Globe had featured it nationally as "Canada's Biggest Campaign Sign." The ecstasy around the campaign office was palpable. Momentum, as they call it in politics, is when you do something unexpected and everybody says, "Great!" and more volunteers show up.

Following Monday's meeting of the collectors Charlie heard from Peter that three attendees reported that people who knew they were collecting for Charlie, but who were not on any list of prospects, had called to donate money having seen the sign publicity.

The central campaign committee downtown was both delighted and annoyed, Charlie heard, because it hadn't been told of the media coup in advance, couldn't take any credit for it with the national campaign and it was a stunt that should have been done, the Senator's people said, in a riding where it could do some good. Charlie, perversely, was pleased by the negative feedback from "downtown". Ted was overjoyed.

One candidate called to ask if Charlie had any objection to his campaign doing the same thing. Charlie didn't, but it was a media bust.

Now, while Charlie was very happy with all the attention, and Ted was delighted, Charlie then learned that Ted had not told him the whole strategy of the big signs.

Four days after the signs went up, Ted caught up to Charlie at 7:30 a.m. as he was waving madly and mindlessly to an endless stream of passing automobile drivers, some of whom honked their horns in response the to the burma shave message, "HONK…IF…YOU… VOTE… LIBERAL… CHARLIE…WARREN.

"What are you doing here?" said a startled Charlie, who knew Ted usually slept late.

The Campaign: a Short Story in Four Parts

"We caught the sons-of-bitches," was the excited response. "You have to get briefed and we have to discuss what you're going to say at the press conference at 10."

"Caught which sons-of-bitches? What press conference? What the hell is going on?" Ted had an unwilling Charlie by the shoulder padding of his jacket, dragging him along.

"Let's get in the car," rasped Ted with real urgency. "I'll explain it as we drive."

The two got into the back seat of the Chev that served as the car for transporting the candidate joining Charlie's aide and driver for the campaign. He was a university student, good company, discreet, and a very good and careful driver.

"OK, give."

"You know the big signs?"

"Yeah."

"Well, I didn't tell you the whole story. We didn't think the NDP could resist sabotaging them, so we've had them staked out for the last three nights, 24 hours a day. Last night they showed up and cut the wires. The signs are all down. A real mess. We got it all with TV cameras, we got still photos of faces, we got license numbers. The NDP don't know they were observed."

Ted had a huge, effervescent grin on his face. He kept giggling.

Why this did not surprise him, Charlie later thought, he didn't know. By now, he had learned just to accept what was happening.

"So, what's the plan?"

"I figure it this way. By 10 we will have done searches of the license plates and know who owns the cars. I think that we call a press conference and accuse the NDP of the vandalism, without any proof or releasing the photos or car license numbers. They will, of course, deny, deny, deny. That's what they always do. Then tomorrow we release the videos and the photos, and the names of who owns the cars."

"Where is the press conference?"

"We haven't set it up yet. But why not hold it at the site of the damage? It's best for the TV stations and everybody else as well. We'll have to make sure the homeowners who participated in the surveillance say nothing, of course, but most are off at work, anyway."

"Let me think about that for a minute," said Charlie. After about 10 seconds, he went on, "OK, let's do it. What then?"

Between 10 today and 3 gives enough time for the NDP to deny, deny, deny. We'll have had noon hour and afternoon coverage, and evening coverage, with the pictures of the signs down and everybody asking, "Who did it?" This gives us lead item on the news tonight, and maybe national stuff. You can take the afternoon off."

This was obviously a joke, and Charlie ignored it.

"Then tomorrow we do another 10 a.m. press conference and release the pictures. By then we can dupe the TV tapes we have and distribute them to the stations by then. We'll do big, big blow-ups of the pictures of the faces and car license plates, and give them out. By then we'll have been able to identify the connections between the vandals and Herself's campaign."

"You actually think there are identifiable NDP workers?" Charlie said, with some doubt. "I don't want to make charges we can't back up."

Ted laughed. "I've seen the photos. I recognize two of the guys myself. Slam-dunk. But I have a friend, who's formerly NDP, and he knows a lot of their guys, and he's going to look at the photos, too."

Then, more seriously, he went on.

"I want you to think about our asking the police to lay charges for vandalism, and we should complain to the Returning Officer for the riding as well as Canada's Chief Electoral Officer. We raise hell—or rather you do—in your press conference. You're a lawyer; you know how to sound totally goddamned outraged.

"Then we let things settle for a couple days," continued Ted, "and we call another press conference and re-erect the signs, and talk about democracy and the sanctity of the election process and all that stuff." Again, he giggled. "We get a third night of good TV, and everybody in the riding, by now, knows who the hell you are and is reminded what kind of people they are. And it's only Day 24."

Ted was, once again, obviously very pleased with himself.

Charlie thought he better ask a question that he thought might be asked of him.

"Why didn't you tell me the whole plan?"

"Oh, you might have objected, or might have got all principled on me, or doubted it would work, or worried about it. You didn't need to know."

Charlie reflected on this, then spoke carefully.

"Reporters on the payroll I didn't need to know about? An entrapment scheme of the NDP I didn't need to know about? What else is there, Ted that I don't need to know about?"

"You don't have to know about any of it." This was said very soberly.

"Well, said Charlie, shaking his head "I hope to hell we all get through this thing without anybody going to jail."

There was no response from Ted. Just as well, Charlie thought.

The press conference, the NDP denials, the release of the photos and names all went as Ted had thought they would. The police had not laid charges but Charlie thought they well might. The Chief Electoral Officer a few days later issued a very strong warning letter to every candidate in the country. More publicity for Charlie.

The media coverage of both the event and the re-raising of the signs was, as Ted kept saying, "Blockbuster, just blockbuster." He was very, very happy at the way the campaign was going, thought Charlie, and Sally agreed.

The public relations volunteers continued to crank out press releases praising Charlie, and dreaming up items for the Byrd column. They, too, were happy because they had more material to work with, given Charlie's willingness to court controversy. An embarrassingly large percentage of what they sent to the Sun got published, and even the Province newspaper began print material from Charlie's campaign.

Willy the sign chair kept saying to Charlie, "See, I told you it was them guys in the NDP." By now he had almost all his signs up, and very few were coming down. There was a debate going on in the campaign about buying more signs because the canvass crews were coming back with requests from residents for signs for their lawns. All in all, everyone was happy with what was turning out to be a flawless and fun-filled campaign.

By this point in the campaign about two dozen of Charlie's lawyer-friends were out door-knocking, another couple dozen personal friends had shown up, and Charlie's mother, previously totally apolitical, was in the office phoning. His Dad was working with the sign crew.

In the middle of the campaign, Ted organized a party for all the campaign workers. Charlie spoke briefly, thanked them all, and asked each of them to recruit a friend to help. The following week another seventy five workers showed up to phone and door-to-door-canvass.

By the fourth week of the campaign, Charlie paused to consider how much he was enjoying it all.

He found getting to know the volunteers was, in itself, a rewarding experience. He was impressed by the many and varied reasons they had for working for the Party or for the PM or for Charlie. The hours put in by some, particularly women, were huge. Charlie thought, towards the end that win or lose it was an enthralling and humbling experience.

Despite being new to the campaign trail and political debate, he was finding he could pretty well match Herself in all-candidate meetings. He went prepared, knowing that the NDP would have the meeting hall packed. Ted, who felt such meetings were useless, and a diversion of campaign volunteers from more useful work, begrudgingly allocated enough Liberal workers to protect Charlie from being totally shouted down, but that was all.

For every appearance, on the basis of his communications advisers, he made a point of saying one particular thing, or emphasizing one issue. Press releases, quoting what he said, were printed ahead of time to make the reporters' jobs easier. Before the meetings, Ted had Charlie record five, one-minute or thirty-second radio clips, each putting his message a little differently. Tape recordings of the five clips were given to the radio reporters. They were usually assigned to cover two or three or more similar meetings each night, so being able to use Charlie's canned comments was appreciated. The journalist community was noticing that

Charlie was gaining confidence and his campaign was offering a professionalism lacking in most of the other campaigns.

Among themselves some reporters began to wonder if, against the huge odds of the traditional NDP vote margin, could Charlie possibly win? The NDP had recovered following the sign-event disaster. Often, NDP campaigns in East would be looted of talent to support other candidates. But this time Herself put her foot down, insisting her troops stay put. She was, Ted commented several times, a formidable campaigner and the NDP organization was superb. It was a kind of grudging admiration from one professional toward another.

For Charlie, who was working hard, the campaign was a grind of early mornings, late evenings, and constant tension from worrying that he might say something wrong. But he was getting used to the grind, and found he liked it.

4. The Choice

The big surprise came on day 38. The Senator caught up to Charlie by phone at his law office at 9:30 in the morning, and suggested they have lunch at the Club. As it happened, it was a slow day on the campaign trail for Charlie. He reflected that at this point in the campaign the pressure was largely off the Senator. Candidates were nominated, campaigns were all underway and as far as Charlie knew everything was under control.

But Charlie wondered for a minute about the luncheon invitation. The Senator, he thought, should have time only for winning campaigns, ridings he had reason to hope he might win, and ridings or candidates that were creating, or likely to create, some kind of problem. Charlie thought his campaign in East did not fit any of those categories. A short congratulatory phone call from the Senator during the sign affair had been their only contact in weeks.

As usual, the Senator was at the Club first, holding court in the foyer with other arrivals who wanted to know about the campaign.

They went up the wide staircase to the dining room, with the Senator commenting in passing on the campaign as a whole. It was nothing that was news to Charlie.

The Senator asked Louis, the maitre'd, for a quiet table against a window. Charlie sensed a serious conversation that the Senator did not want shared with others.

They sat down and spoke to the server simultaneously about drinks. Then the Senator glanced at the menu and wrote down his choices for lunch on the order form. Charlie watched him, and when the Senator looked up, Charlie promptly ordered.

"What's up?" enquired Charlie. He wanted his curiosity satisfied before the Senator gave a tour d' horizon of the whole campaign. As far as Charlie was concerned, they could have the wider discussion later.

"My, you're impatient, aren't you?"

"Well, we wouldn't be here if it were not important, and I only hear from you when there is something I might view as trouble, so, yeah, I'm impatient."

The Senator had broken an oat cake and covered half of it with butter. Now it was Charlie's turn to do the same as the Senator bit into the oat cake, chewed a minute and swallowed.

"Something not unexpected is about to come up, and I wanted to prepare you."

Charlie had a premonition that this was real trouble for him, and his stomach muscles tightened.

"What?"

"Your NDP opponent might be in trouble. Its been bubbling for weeks. Legal trouble. I didn't really think it would jell during the campaign, but it'll become public next week, and you gotta know about it."

"Legal trouble? Legal trouble? Herself's in legal trouble?"

"Yes. Story is that she took a two-month holiday in Australia last summer—winter there, you know, but pleasant. She stayed with friends, former Canadians. As it happens, some of her friends were…how shall I say this…allegedly not quite honest, so the story goes. They got into some legal trouble and dragged Herself in with them. Fraud. It's not clear what all she knew and when, or that she is in fact culpable, but there's been a police investigation going on in Sydney for several months. Charges are going to be laid next week, and I am told the Aussies will be seeking her extradition from Canada to stand trial."

In a campaign of surprises, this was for Charlie beyond his imagination.

"You're telling me that a week or so before Election Day the Australian government is going to be seeking extradition of a candidate standing for election to Parliament and charging her with fraud or something?"

"That's what I understand."

"How do you know this? No, you won't tell me that. How sure of your facts are you?"

The Senator shrugged as Charlie asked the first question, then looked for several seconds at his soup which had just arrived before he picked up his spoon. Waving the spoon a little he responded, "I know. You needn't think I am trafficking in gossip. Just let's leave it there. I know."

Charlie turned to a second line of enquiry.

"OK, what do we do? What do I do? How do we handle this?"

Charlie was sitting with a sandwich in front of him. While the Senator finished his soup, Charlie took a bite out of the sandwich and he began to think not of how such an event was going to be handled but of its effect on the campaign. His campaign. His electoral chances. The light slowly dawned.

"Oh, Jesus Christ," he breathed, only loud enough for the Senator to hear him.

"Yes," responded the Senator. "You've been running a good campaign. The media have been paying an extraordinary amount of attention to you, why and how I don't know, and I'm not asking. I'm not sure I want to know. I wonder if Ted has pictures of a Sun editor doing something unnatural with a goat, or something, but I don't want to know. But there's no rational explanation.

"Anyway, the signs thing did serious harm to the NDP campaign, not just in East, but elsewhere. Your own on-the-ground campaign is going well, I hear. You've got adequate—more than adequate—money I also hear. I guess I wanted to give you this heads-up because it now moves your riding from the 'just might win if he gets all the breaks and there's a national sweep' to the just might win column. You better think about this."

Thoughts were going quickly through Charlie's mind, more quickly than he could sort them out.

"What do I do?"

The Senator, not seeing a tantrum in Charlie, leapt.

"You get ready to host an event in your riding for the Prime Minister. He'll be there a week Friday, as part of his last-week-of-the-campaign national tour. I don't yet know what we will do with him, or what time of day, but he's agreed to come to East."

"He knows about…the Australian…thing?" A glimmer of light revealed itself to Charlie.

"Yes."

"How long have you known this might happen?"

"Ummm, about, oh, uh, three months." The Senator looked a bit embarrassed.

"So all this has not come as a complete surprise to you," Charlie said, matter of factly.

"So now the extraordinary effort to get me to run, and to get me all the financial and organizational help I needed, that all now makes sense. I wondered, you know."

"Yes."

"You are a son-of-a-bitch, aren't you?" Charlie offered, without any malice.

"Yes, but that's been said before. Please understand, Charlie, my job is to win seats for the Party and the Prime Minister. It's not easy to recruit really good people. They want promises, assurances, Cabinet seats, Senatorships…all sorts of things, if they run and lose, or even if they run and win. Some baldly ask for money. And of course, in B.C., almost all lose. Always have. So we get too many second-and third-raters because most first raters can't be bought—that's not the right word, but you get my drift—can't be recruited no matter what the inducement. The sacrifice of privacy, of personal opportunity, of income, and the demands of public office, they are all just too much for most first-class people. And who in hell in B.C. who has ever visited Ottawa wants to live there? So I guess I sometimes have to stroke and cajole and plead and wheedle and whine, and sometimes I cry, and maybe cheat a little, if I have to, to get as many good people as I can. I hope that I can elect enough Cabinet-material-MPs so the PM can appoint enough good people from BC that can do a good enough job for this province that maybe next time its all a little easier. One reason we don't win as many seats here as the polls say we should is because we don't run candidates that are as good as we should be running, and poor candidates lead to substandard campaigns. You're the quality of candidate we should be running in every riding."

Charlie said nothing.

"And," continued the Senator, "every so often along comes opportunity. "No," he put up his two hands and crooked the first two fingers of each hand to signal quotation marks, "Capital O Opportunity, to recruit a first-class talent, a first-class mind, the kind of guy that really should be in public life, someone with principles and commitment to ideas and…" his voice faltered.

"Charlie, forgive me. But I saw a, maybe, 10 per cent chance of sending you to Ottawa. And I grabbed it. I hope you understand."

"But you knew that Herself was in trouble?" Charlie persisted.

"Yes, but I learned it entirely by happenstance, and I was never sure it would really go anywhere all that soon. You want to know?"

Charlie nodded. He needed to know for his own satisfaction, but also he wanted to know that nothing…unprincipled…had happened.

"As you may suspect, I practice a little law from time to time. We had a young associate who decided he wanted to work in Australia for a while, to become completely familiar with the mining industry there and in the South Pacific generally. We have connections to a large law firm in Sydney, and arranged for him to spend a couple years there. He had no sooner arrived when the events in question took place. It was not clear in the beginning that the 'Canadian tourist' mentioned in the media there—small story, buried deep in the paper—had anything to do with the fraud, and nobody paid any attention to her. She has a common name but our sharp young lawyer realized who she was, and tipped me off. The case has had little public attention down there and the media have still not recognized Herself and that she was a Canadian Member of Parliament. However, our young lawyer has been watching closely and Bar gossip being what it is, he has been able to track events quite closely. That's how I know the Australian government is preparing extradition papers. At a point," he paused and looked Charlie in the eye, "somebody will have to call the Globe and help them connect the dots. You don't have to worry about that."

"No, I don't have to worry about that."

"The point is," concluded the Senator, "that if she's re-elected she likely can't be extradited, irrespective of her guilt or otherwise. That point won't be lost on the media, or the voter, and the question posed will be, 'Should you, the voter, help someone avoid a trial for fraud by sending them to Parliament?' The next few days will be fascinating.

"But for you, there's another big problem. What you really have to do is decide."

"Decide what?"

"Decide if you want to be an MP," responded the Senator, almost as though he were instructing a child. "You'll go from about a 20 per cent chance of winning to about 50 percent once this story breaks. You're not unlikely to win. I know your hesitancy about public life, and about the money side. Well, you can probably do something stupid in the next few days to screw up your chances of winning. That's why I wanted to have lunch and tell you about…this. You still have a choice. I do want to say that, in shanghaiing you to run, it was not my intention to trick you. I hoped that you would just get hooked, and decide on your own to run-to-win next time, perhaps in a more promising riding."

"No, I like East, I relate to it." Charlie said reflexively, without thought. He then realized it was true. He digested what the Senator had told him about having a choice. "I understand what you're saying and I appreciate it. I have to talk to Sally. She has to be a part of anything."

"Understood."

The Campaign: a Short Story in Four Parts

The Senator rose from the table, saying, "I'm sorry, but I just must get back to the campaign. I have the PM coming in a few days and everything must go absolutely without a hitch."

"Yes, me too. They will be sending out a search party for me if I don't get back. Thanks for lunch, and for the information and advice."

They made small talk as they went out the big doors of the dining room, and down the wide, carpeted stairs. Charlie reflected for a minute on the silence of the place, given that it was quite full at lunch. "No music," he thought, "that's the difference."

On his way back to his campaign headquarters Charlie's mind was a mist of confusion. Ordinarily his thoughts were clear, analytical and lawyerly. Not so now. As he arrived at his headquarters, he consciously put it all aside until he could talk to Sally.

It was a quiet and undemanding afternoon. There was another story in the Vancouver Sun about the previous night's all-candidates meeting, and he was quoted favourably. Yesterday there had been another mention in the Byrd column. That made 10. He could afford a slow afternoon, and was thus able to go home early for dinner, saying he'd be back to the campaign office at 7:30 to help work the phones. He thought it important that he do his share of that sort of grunt work in the campaign.

The kids were somewhere else when he arrived home, and his wife seemed to have dinner preparation well under control. He hugged her from behind, then poured himself a glass of ice water.

"Have you got a few minutes for a serious chat?" he said to her, rather formally. She responded with a quizzical look, dried her hands on a dish towel, and followed him into the den.

They sat down and he began, "You remember the terms under which I undertook to run? No chance of winning, good experience, good for my reputation, and for the firm, etcetera, etcetera?"

"Yes." What was he getting at?

"Well, so far, so good. No mistakes, good media, good, solid campaign, etcetera, etcetera.

"However, everything is going to change. I just might win. We have to decide now if we want to win."

He related the Senator's news over lunch, and added what Ted had told him about the campaign. They were getting very good results from both the door-to-door canvassing and the telephones. More volunteers were coming in the door each day. In the beginning, he had been told that, in that riding, if they could get 50 workers, they'd be lucky. The campaign manager had given him the latest numbers that afternoon: over 400. There would be 100 per cent single-canvass coverage of the Riding, well over 70 per cent of a second canvass and maybe the best 30 per cent would get a third canvass.

"It's becoming a problem to keep everybody busy," Ted had said. "I know this sounds funny, given the riding and the strong campaign Herself is running, but it almost smells like a win." He'd shaken his head in disbelief.

Sally seemed to have no response, then shook her head.

"What do you want to do?

He looked at her with that look that people who have been married a while give their spouses when they don't know what to say, and he shrugged.

"No, I didn't put that right. What do you want to do?" she repeated, emphasizing 'want'.

"I honestly don't know. I went into this as a bit of a lark. A mid-life break from the ho-hum and the humdrum. The campaign has engaged me. I've enjoyed it. I've enjoyed the challenge of something…new, something…that has meaning. It's going to be difficult—and I didn't see this before—going back to the law after this."

Ruefully, he admitted, "I guess I'm hooked."

He shook his head while Sally sat silently and listened to him work through his thinking.

"You know, for the first time in my life, I think I'm doing something… important." He had emphasized 'important'.

"But," he continued, "this doesn't take away from the realities of life. We both know what the implications of my winning are, financially, in terms of our life as a family, in terms of our…security…privacy.…"

The Campaign: a Short Story in Four Parts

Indeed she did. Just then she realized that she, too, had been getting positive vibrations from the campaign. "I guess we better discuss this," she said.

"Well, I have to be frank with you and tell you I'm confused," he responded.

"One part of me shrieks, 'NO' and wants to run back to the law office. Another says, 'You were put on this earth to do more that sift through paper, and make arguments in court that you don't yourself believe. Life is more than earning a good living.'"

"I'd like to win, I guess, I'd like to get into the hurly-burly of public life and see if I can do some good, but I shrink from the thought of all the time we'd be separated, about the loss of privacy." He hesitated. "And about the loss of the money, too, I guess."

"How could you really have a choice, as the Senator says?" Sally asked.

Charlie thought a bit.

"Oh, I could say the following." He then laid out a statement that would sink him, a "mistake", made just a day or two before the election. She nodded.

"You wouldn't do yourself a lot of good with that kind of comment. You'd look really stupid. You'd undo a lot of what you have achieved in the campaign."

"That's right, but I could then resume a sort of fetal position and return safely to my law office and get on with life. Everybody'd forget in a week. Every candidate, every politician, mis-speaks from time to time. So, its not really a huge problem."

"Charlie, only you can make this decision. But let me make four points. First, you have never, ever been a quitter and your persistence is one of the reasons I married you. Second, you have a wonderful sense of public policy and public good. Third, we'll figure out a way of living on whatever you get paid. We've lived on spaghetti before and we can do it again. Fourth, if you lose is one thing, but if you throw this one, if you give up and run back to the office, you'll regret it. Every day, as you make your way to the office to sift through the flyshit in the pepper, you'll hate it. And after a while you'll start to not like yourself very much, either, Charlie. No, you make the decision, because you have to live with it. But, I guess I agree with what the Prime Minister told me that night," she paused, "if good people don't do it then the bad people will. You're good, Charlie."

Charlie thought about Sally's long summary.

"You know, my Dad has often said that at the end of a man's life his measure is in what he did to make the world a better place. I guess this is one of those forks in the road."

Charlie reached over to the phone, picked up the handset, and dialed from memory.

"Senator, I'm in. Damned if I know how we'll make the mortgage payments if I win, but it's go for broke." He was not conscious of the pun.

"That's good, Charlie, because when the PM is in town we're doing a big evening rally—the biggest one we'll have in B.C.—in your riding."

"Oh, Jesus," said Charlie. "My campaign manager thinks things like PM's visits detract from the serious business of running a proper campaign."

The Senator laughed. "Well, he's not alone in his thinking, but he'll love this one. Look, I gotta go. Thanks for that, Charlie, you've restored my faith in humanity."

The next day Charlie took his four notebooks, by now full of names, into his office for his secretary to transcribe and organize. He thought that after the campaign there were a lot of people he had met who he would want to keep in touch with, and that would begin with many thank-you letters. He wanted to be ready. And he knew he had a large number of personal thank you letters to write by hand, too.

The PM's visit was a triumph. The national media interpreted it as the beginning of an electoral sweep of the country. Earlier in the week, the news of the criminal charges in Australia against Herself broke, along with the Aussie government's application for extradition. The national media pounced on it, and the pundits commented how the scandal was harming not just Herself, but the national NDP campaign.

Charlie absolutely refused to comment on the whole matter, either privately or publicly. He didn't need to. The Tories, the NDP themselves, and the media saw to it that everything that could be said, was said. It was a huge boost to Charlie's campaign in the final week. Another hundred volunteers showed up. The smell of victory, the very smallest of hints, has that effect.

On the Saturday before the vote, the Vancouver Sun editorialized that the Liberal government deserved to be re-elected, but endorsed one Conservative and one New Democrat for, it said, their personal qualities.

The editorial ended, however, with an endorsement of Charlie that he found, frankly, embarrassing in its effusiveness, remarking particularly on his policy views as "refreshing."

"I'd best enjoy it", he said to Ted and Sally over a drink. "If I get elected, it'll be the last good press I get, I expect. It's all downhill from here."

Charlie went to the final meeting of the fundraisers, just before the polls opened on election day. It was just a review of the fund-raising effort. There was a spirit of bonhomie in the room. The invisible barrier between Peter Holt and Howie Cohen was long gone. The committee had gone over its fundraising target by 54 per cent, and Howie's efforts, they all realized, were a significant reason.

They asked Charlie about the campaign, and about the PM's triumphant appearance in the riding the previous week. He was able to pass on some inside stories the PM had told him. They were fascinated.

As the breakfast of crabmeat omelets ended, he thanked them very much for their efforts, and said that in a few weeks he'd be organizing a cocktail party to which they should bring their spouses and to which they would also invite the contributors.

As he left the Club, Charlie realized that, win or lose, he was becoming a politician. These men who had raised money for him he now had to forge into a loyal group of permanent financial campaigners. He realized that, if elected, he'd have to go to them from time to time and ask their advice. If defeated, well, he'd start to plan for the next time. He'd have to organize intimate dinners for them with Cabinet Ministers and otherwise feed their egos. That it was all a subtle part of building a political base, as well as a political organization. He knew he needed a base in the business community as well as in the riding, and this was where he would begin.

Mentally he listed all the community leaders he had met in the riding. Most were not supporters of his Party but getting them on side to some degree would be absolutely necessary if he were to become an effective, riding-oriented MP.

There's not much a candidate can useful do on Election Day until about two in the afternoon. Charlie and Sally had voted early. Since Ted had taken his driver/aide away from him for the day to work on getting voters to the polls Charlie had to drive himself. He visited a dozen polling stations, thanking his scrutineers. Mid-afternoon, he went back to his headquarters and, just like any other election-day campaign worker, busied himself with phoning identified-Liberal voters and urging them to get out and vote.

One lady, who sounded to Charlie like she was elderly, responded, "Oh, Mr. Warren, you bet I'll vote. I haven't voted in years you know, no Liberals worth voting for and I always used to vote Liberal, but I'm voting this time. I like what you say. You stand for something."

The day's activities reached their crescendo about 7:30, when almost suddenly a great silence settled over the campaign headquarters. The phoning was over, and almost everyone had left to go out to scrutineer the counting of the 300 or so ballot boxes.

Ted Early came into Charlie's office and shut the door.

"I've no idea if we're going to win tonight, but I'm optimistic. But I'd like to say something now, win, lose or draw. I was really pissed when the Senator asked me to 'volunteer' to be your campaign manager. I thought you'd be nothing more than a sunny day candidate who'd show up twice a week to cheer up the troops."

He paused.

"Yeah, really pissed."

Charlie smiled. "Disappointed you, did I?"

"That's what I wanted to say, and apologize. You've been a great candidate. Let me do my job. Did as you were asked. Always in good humour.

No big ego shit. I want to say, when you run again, and whatever happens tonight you will run again, I'd like to do it again."

His voice was soft. He was asking.

Charley smiled.

"You did a helluva job, Ted, and I'm grateful. I really am. Let's see what happens tonight, and have lunch tomorrow noon at The Teahouse, and unwind, talk about things. I really can't focus just now."

Ted smiled and opened the door and went out into the near silent office.

Sally had come to the headquarters about three and pitched in with the phoning. She came to Charlie as the silence descended.

"Now is the hard part," Charlie said to her, "the long wait. Polls close at 8. I've been figuring that there might be a trend early on to give me solace, win or lose."

Her response was a laugh.

"There's nothing for you or me to do for the next while," said Charlie. "Let's go for dinner. Someplace good. I'll buy Champagne and we can toast a great adventure. Win or lose, it has been great."

An early trend in the riding, unlike the country, was not to be. The depth and commitment of the NDP organization and its voters held, almost, and it was not until after 11 that Charlie was declared a winner, by a razor-thin 225 votes, based largely on a much larger Liberal voter turnout. There'd be a recount, for sure, Charlie said to everyone who asked. But 225 votes would be tough to overcome, Ted had said.

Herself came over to his campaign office a few minutes later to concede, in a very gracious speech that Charlie's workers listened to politely, and politely applauded. She offered to sit down with him in a day or two and brief him on constituency issues. Charlie was touched by her gracious manner in losing.

"I hope I can lose with similar grace when the time comes," he whispered to Sally.

The victory party was one not to be forgotten in size, enthusiasm, and noise. Just after 11:30, Ted caught up to Charlie in the swirling mass of overjoyed humanity.

"Phone call. You gotta take it. In your office."

"Who?"

"The PM."

He got to the phone and closed the door in a vain search for some quiet.

"Hello?"

"Charlie? Congratulations. A well fought campaign. There were lots of solid wins tonight but I'm particularly pleased about yours." It was a booming, expansive, happy voice.

"Thank you, sir. It's been a long one, and hard-fought."

"Yes. Look, Charlie, I appreciate that you ran when you really didn't want to, and you didn't bail when you could. But I meant what I said to your good wife. The country needs people like you, and if good people aren't prepared to serve, and if people like me don't keep trying to bring good people into politics, then bad people will get the job, and the whole counry suffers."

"Yes sir." Charlie wondered what else to say. "I appreciate you calling, Prime Minister. It's late there so I'll let you go."

"Not yet. Charlie, I know the financial sacrifice here is substantial. So I want to tell you something, but I want your undertaking that you'll tell no one."

Charlie thought it odd that the PM used that particularly lawyerly word "undertaking", the commitment lawyers give to one another, often orally, that is a promise above promises, that it will not be broken.

"You have my undertaking," responded Charlie.

"OK. Look, Charlie, I really am delighted you are joining us in Ottawa. The news of the makeup of the new Cabinet is at least a week away. But I want to tell you, now, that you'll be in it. Usually, I think a new MP should learn the ropes for a year or so…but…this is different. It'll not be a senior position, Charlie, but a place from which you'll be able to understudy some good people and move up. I put my money where my mouth is, Charlie. Remember that. Should help with the finances, hey?"

Charlie truly didn't know quite what to say. It was, with the better expenses arrangement that Ministers had, effectively double the pay of a back-bencher, but still about a 30 per-cent cut in income.

"Thank you, Prime Minister," was all he could muster. Then, "Can I tell my wife?"

The PM chuckled through the phone. "No, but you can at least tell your wife that all MPs will be getting a raise next year."

"Thank you, Prime Minister. I'd better let you go now." The din from the victory party made it difficult for Charlie to hear.

"No, one more thing. I've gone to great efforts to recruit you, and get you elected, Charlie, and I want to say some things now, because there may never be another opportunity."

Charlie fleetingly wondered if, somehow, perhaps if the PM had pulled strings with the Australian government, but the Prime Minister continued.

"You've made a mark in this campaign for progressive and imaginative thinking, Charlie, but you'll now be a member of the Government and you'll have to develop a habit of verbal caution, outside Cabinet. You said some things about enlarging the role of BC on the national scene, and about Western alienation. Good themes, but very dangerous if pursued too far, too fast. Be careful, Charlie."

"Yes, sir."

"Years ago we had another very bright young Minister from B.C. who was a progressive and who accomplished great things. His name was Ron Basford and he was fond of reminding the rest of us that everyone in public life is only just one poorly thought out sentence from political oblivion. One disastrous headline has destroyed the careers of too many otherwise sound politicians. Remember that, too, please, Charlie.

"Well, enough of that. Thus endeth the lesson." There was a weariness, at last, in his voice.

"Sorry. It's been a long day, a very good day, and I'm just a little philosophical about things. Good night, Charlie."

"Good night, Prime Minister. And thank you for everything."

The line went dead. The campaign was over for the Prime Minister, for the Senator and for Charlie. Now, thought Charlie, we have to begin planning for the next one. He sat in the near darkness, ignoring the clamour of celebration for a few minutes.

"I wonder what I have really learned over the last two months," he thought. Then he answered himself.

"In politics I guess what is to be expected is the unexpected." He said it out loud. Twice.

Later, in bed with the lights out, he recounted most of his conversation with the Prime Minister to Sally. Not all of it. He was conscious of keeping some things from her, something very unusual in their marriage. And he was suddenly aware that this was only the first. As a member of the Cabinet, there would be a great deal he could not share.

Sally listened quietly, asking few questions. As the evening's excitement passed, and the weariness of a long campaign asserted itself, they both drifted off to sleep.

Backbenchers

The Buddies

Some thought the two MPs were unlikely buddies. Paul was from the rural west. Bill from urban Toronto.

Paul was from his Party's populist wing. He fought strongly for the people of his riding and the interests of his province. He was outspoken, blunt and often profane. He had hard prejudices and was not given to much introspection. He could be mean.

Bill was a policy wonk, business-oriented, quiet and restrained, a man of carefully measured words and cautious judgments. He didn't care much for the hurly-burly of retail politics, but reveled in the exploration of ideas, of public debate and private discussions of big issues.

Paul was tall, robust but not fat, and wore a suit like it was pyjamas. Bill was of average height and slim. He dressed like an English country gentleman and carried himself with an air of urbane serenity.

Paul's humour was earthy, Bill's was of the drawing room. One would not have thought that these two would become the close buddies they were. But when Bill was elected to Parliament about nine years after Paul, the mutual attraction was immediate and Paul took it upon himself to be Bill's mentor on all matters political.

This was perhaps natural. Paul was born to hold elective office. His father and his grandfather had been Members of Parliament. His grandfather had been a provincial member as well, while his father had been a distinguished Federal Minister.

Bill, on the other hand, had wandered into politics rather obliquely as a career diversion for a middle-aged, recently divorced man. In fact, elective politics had not been his idea at all. He was a professor in a Graduate School of Business in a Quebec university. He wrote some very provocative articles in the popular media about economic policy which had caught the attention of the Party's leader.

The Party was, at the time, in desperate need of new ideas, new faces, and new directions. Bill found himself rather suddenly and before he had given any thought to elective office described as a "rising star" in Canadian politics. He was unaware of the Leader's interest and the Party managers' attempts both to recruit him and to find a smooth way for Bill to get a seat in Parliament.

For Paul, who had had to scramble his way into politics the hard way—even if he did come from a distinguished political family—this was a bit unseemly. People should want public office, he thought. They should seek it. They should work for it. They should train for it. Politics was, for Paul, not a game in which amateurs were welcome. When he first read about Bill and learned of the extraordinary attempts being made by the Leader and the Party wise heads to woo him into public life, Paul was more than a little offended.

But by the time Bill arrived on The Hill, Paul had seen enough of him in the media to think that this was one time the Leader was right in his judgment and he, Paul, was wrong. Paul was determined to seek out Bill, to befriend him and to teach him the finer points of the art of politics. And so the friendship began. Soon it ripened. They became almost inseparable.

Most mornings they met for breakfast in the cafeteria in the West Block of the Parliament Buildings. Their offices were separated by four others on the second floor of the same wing of the Confederation Building, 200 meters to the east. They usually walked to caucus meetings and to the House of Commons Chamber for Question Period together. They would share a drink at the end of most days as Paul taught Bill politics and the ways of the House of Commons and Bill schooled Paul on other-than-parish-pump politics and policy.

You see, it was clear to everybody that their Party was almost sure to win the next election and that Bill was a shoo-in for a senior Cabinet seat. There was no doubt in anyone's mind—although the details were both secret and denied by everyone—that Bill had been promised an appointment with destiny as a key figure in the Government after the next election as the price of his entering politics in the first place.

Paul, on the other hand, had aspirations but he had carefully calculated that he was unlikely to be included in the Cabinet and he resented it. There were many from his Party elected in his province, so numbers were against him. He was aware that others had skills he didn't have, and his manner sometimes was a shade too blunt, his language a little too colourful, his policy thoughts somewhat shallow and unvarnished. Some said he lacked the finesse a Minister needed. Thus, either consciously or unconsciously, Paul's reaching out to Bill was a search for someone to mentor him in becoming a Minister.

One of Bill's interests was transportation. He got himself assigned to the House of Commons Transportation Committee. Paul then asked to be transferred from the Fisheries Committee to Transportation, making the case that transportation matters were a lot more important to his constituents out west than were fish.

The Transportation Committee is one that does a lot of traveling, inspecting ports and railways and airports, holding hearings in the nooks and crannies of a large country for which transportation services, infrastructure and operations were the nation's life blood.

And thus as the Committee travelled the country, Paul and Bill spent many evenings together, working away on bottles of scotch, and sifting through the public issues of the day.

For Bill, the experience was like one long tutoring session with a single graduate student. For Paul, it was an opportunity to fill in many of the dark crannies of policy ignorance that had plagued him. He developed an appreciation of some of the relevant concepts of economics, public finance, and policy development. Not suddenly but noticeably after about two years, Paul was able to deliver more sophisticated and nuanced speeches both in the House and on the stump. He became better dressed and sported better manners. He was less inclined to bursts of outrage or anger. Bill's lessons about the bigger picture issues had found a home.

Paul, for his part, was a virtual travelling political encyclopedia that he opened for his buddy Bill. Outside of Quebec, there was hardly a town in which he did not know someone—that is, someone active in the Party. Often the Party organizers would arrange some kind of intimate political event for that Party's MPs on the Committee to meet with the local Party activists. Paul, who had his own 'trap-line' in the Party would see to it that his local contacts were not overlooked for invitations. But even in the many towns the Transportation Committee over-nighted that were too small or too politically inconsequential or where the Party apparatus was inactive, Paul nearly always knew someone to call and somehow some sort of meeting or party or coffeeklatch was organized. Paul introduced Bill to everyone, never forgetting a name, much to Bill's constant amazement. Bill's academic knowledge of public policy was thereby leavened by contact with the often ignored Common Man in Canadian politics, the local community activist.

Slowly, Bill's appreciation of politics matured. He learned what "consent of the governed" meant on Main Street. He learned that there was often a great deal more common sense away from St. James Street or Bay Street than in downtown Montreal or Toronto.

Thus, like ying and yang, the two complemented one another's political shortcomings. They learned from one another, and each came to deeply appreciate the strengths of the other.

Bill, not long after he arrived in Ottawa, bought a condominium with a lovely view next to the Rideau Canal where he lived alone, having been divorced the year before he was elected. He seemed to have no regular or intimate lady friends. Thus his life changed from one of being a married academic in a large cosmopolitan city, wherein he had lots of time for a variety of activities, to one of a single and almost single-minded politician, busy most evenings that he was in Ottawa with constituency mail, speech-writing, and policy discussions, sometimes with other caucus policy wonks.

Not having come into politics through the expenditure of blood, sweat, toil and tears, Bill had little appreciation of the hard work and sense of fulfillment of constituency work. He begrudged the weekends spent in his constituency and the drudgery and dullness of attending to the minutiae of concerns that are the lifeblood of being 'a good constituency politician.' He eschewed the habit of attending every wedding, funeral, and birthday party, a habit that gave joy to those of his colleagues with lesser ambitions and, he thought, lower intelligence. He'd rather spend off-hours in Ottawa reading, researching, sometimes cross-country skiing in winter or sailing in the summer. Sometimes he co-hosted small and genteel dinner parties with Ethel Barrie, an older MP who lived in the same building, where policy discussions lubricated with fine wine often went far into the night.

Paul, on the other hand, was religious about regular visits to his constituency. It was large and rural. Even if he went there every second weekend, which he tried to do, it might well take him two months to get around it, by which time people would sometimes say, "Haven't seen ya in 'bout six months, Paul. You gettin' too used to the soft life and easy livin' in Ottawa? You likin' those subsidized meals in the Parliamentary Restaurant too much to be payin' 'tention to your folks and our problems?" These were usually said in jest, because everyone knew how dedicated Paul was to his riding and its issues.

Paul, however, always thought he was playing catch-up in his constituency work, and it worried him. In a lifetime of political experience, he had seen dozens of good, dedicated, bright, and worthy MPs defeated because they had not done their constituency work as well as they might have. He had seen these able people then, in the shadow of defeat, find they were unemployable, having little but a meager Parliamentary pension to live on, or maybe no pension at all. Yes, after a lot of years, a long-term Parliamentarian's pension was handsome indeed, but before six year's service and two elections it was nothing and even after 10 years it wasn't much. He was determined to spend his life in Parliament and had no interest in post-political-life employment. Thus, his dedication to seeing his constituents almost every second weekend, without fail.

As the relationship of the buddies matured, Paul often brought Bill home for dinner. He had bought the modest house in the Alta Vista area of Ottawa because its location was practical from Paul's perspective: it was about midway between The Hill and the Airport. Paul's wife, Barbara, was an excellent cook, a good conversationalist, and almost as knowledgeable about politics as Paul. She was unfailingly optimistic when the two politicians would become depressed about the recent polls, some new piece of government policy—for they were in Opposition—or their Party's poor showing in the House.

Barbara, for her part, played the role of cheerleader and wise counsel well. She was, at 45, still a woman who could turn heads at cocktail parties. There were some who thought she had married beneath herself with Paul who was, when young, too political, too bellicose, too, well, shallow.

But Barbara would hear of no criticism of Paul and they appeared, after 22 years, to be happily married, with much in common. Their life together was, as she put it once, "comfortable". With their two children now off at university, Barbara busied herself with Parliamentary Wives' business and occasionally went with Paul to the riding to help with constituency work. Home life away from The Hill was quiet, with only a little entertaining.

Thus it was one Thursday in January two years after Bill first arrived on the Hill that he was at dinner at Paul and Barbara's. As with many other alternate Thursdays over the past year, on his way home he drove Paul to the airport so Paul could catch an evening flight back to his constituency for a weekend of riding business. Paul grabbed his suitcase out of the back seat of Bill's red Mercedes, bid him goodbye, and went through the revolving doors of the Ottawa Airport. He checked his bag and boarding pass in hand walked down the hall to the Air Canada First Class Lounge—a "perk" for Parliamentarians—there to pass an hour and have a drink.

Sometimes there were other MPs heading home to talk to, sometimes senior public servants, and sometimes prominent business people. He rarely found an hour in the Lounge a waste of time, even if he only used it to catch up on phone calls.

That night, however, at about the time the flight should have been called for boarding, there was an announcement that he should identify himself to desk staff. He was then told that Winnipeg was weathered in and his flight would not be taking off and that the airline was retrieving his bag from the plane. They offered alternative arrangements the next day, but that was of no use to him and he spent 15 minutes calling his constituency assistant to ask her to wind things down. While he was making his phone call one of the other MPs, similarly indisposed, offered him a ride home.

He got out of his colleague's car, fished his suitcase out of the trunk, bid farewell, and began his walk up the driveway. It was only then that he noticed the unmistakable red Mercedes parked in the driveway. It was, by now, 9:30. The house was unlit. Paul stopped in his tracks, and dropped both his suitcase and his briefcase to the ground.

With a suddenness that startled him he concluded that it was very unlikely that Bill and Barbara were sitting in the darkened living room watching television. His old anger welled up in his gut and he was ready to run into the house and kill somebody. But just as quickly, the new restraints that Bill had drilled into him asserted themselves. The flush in his face receded. His hands unclenched. He breathed again. He picked up the bags and walked closer to the house and put them down. Leaning against Bill's car, oblivious to the winter dirt on it's door rubbing on to his overcoat, he lit a cigarette and drew on it slowly. He considered the alternatives. He had, he had thought, a solid marriage. Should he just ignore what he pretty much knew was happening and walk down the street and flag a cab that would take him to a pay phone somewhere? There he could call Barbara and tell her of the flight changes, giving Bill a good 10 minutes to get out.

He thought about that option for most of the cigarette. This was the peaceful, un-confrontational, civilized way to deal with it. He could then deal with his knowledge of Barbara's marital transgression in a cool and rational way, quietly raising with her that, "maybe something is wrong with our marriage" and see what happens. He could slowly withdraw from his relationship with Bill. Create some space but maintain a professional relationship.

He was tempted. Very tempted. But he realized such an approach was just not in him. Paul was angry and hurt. His trust in his wife was utterly shattered. He could not spend another hour in her presence with this knowledge or suspicion weighing in his heart. He knew it was beyond his ability to hide his emotions.

He considered other alternatives, like making a lot of noise entering the house, so that Bill and Barbara could somehow put the best face on the obvious. No, he couldn't do that, either. He had to know, absolutely, what was going on. Catch them in the act if necessary.

What should he say to Barbara? He had no answer. Bill? His mind hardened on Bill. He felt a betrayal, a bitterness and an unprecedented savage anger. As he thought about Bill, he considered some of the very basic conversations they had shared over the previous two years while on the road. They had talked about public duty and private honour. They had talked about friendship, and personal values and loyalty. Paul realized that a large part of his admiration for Bill lay in what he, Paul, had gained from those conversations.

"He's a phony," Paul said to himself as a plan began toform.

He dropped the second cigarette and ground it out with his heel. Ignoring the suitcase and briefcase standing in the snow-covered driveway, he approached the side door to the house, the one by which he ordinarily entered. He knew the route to the bedroom from that entrance and that he could navigate it silently in the dark. He quietly inserted his key and turned both the lock and the door-handle. The door noiselessly gave way and then swung open. He stepped inside, and closed it. He removed his overshoes and then his shoes in total silence, hung up his overcoat, then began his slow walk down a short hall through the kitchen and into a longer hall in the bungalow.

The master bedroom was at the end. From the hall nightlight, he could see that the door was slightly ajar. He could hear voices talking, almost inaudibly.

Paul stood outside the door for about a minute, trying to listen to the conversation, but also slowly putting his hand through the doorway, searching for the light switch. The light was not a bright one, but he saw in an instant that the couple were in bed. Bill was on his back, talking. Barbara was over on her right side, leaning on an elbow, listening.

"Thank God," thought Paul, "I didn't catch them in the act."

Barbara uttered a yelp of surprise at the light and then, seeing Paul, a scream of horror. She sat upright, trying at the same time to cover herself. Bill, equally startled, but more restrained sat up and said very calmly, "Paul? What are you doing here? You're supposed to be on a plane."

Paul overcame a renewed urge to throttle him.

"The plane to Winnipeg got weathered in," he said levelly. "I think we better talk. I'll be waiting in the living room."

He left the room, noting that Barbara was scrambling to get into a bathrobe, while Bill, less hurriedly, swung out of bed and leaned over, presumably to find his socks and underwear. Paul's last glimpse of the room was of Bill's trousers folded carefully over a chair seat and his suit-jacket hung neatly over the chair back. It was not a scene reflecting spontaneous passion.

Going into the living room, Paul glanced at the furniture, took off his jacket, and threw it carelessly over the back of the chesterfield. He chose to seat himself in the overstuffed chair that faced both the chesterfield and an upholstered upright chair. He wanted to see how the lovers would seat themselves, and he wanted to be in a position, physically, to direct the conversation.

While he waited, he thought about Barbara, and his own transgressions. There had been a short affair with a Committee staffer years ago, when the Committee travelled. It was just sex, for both of them, he thought. They liked one another, she was unmarried, and there was little to do at night in most of the small towns the Committee visited.

He didn't think much of it at the time, or even now, because there was nothing emotional in the relationship.

Then there was the longer relationship with his constituency assistant in the riding. In fact, she was the one that had started it one night after a lot of drinking. One thing led to another, and before long sex was a regular but discreet part of his constituency trips. But, again, it wasn't any kind of emotional connection and she was single.

Then, after a year, she announced her engagement and quit Paul's staff. She ended the relationship just as she had started it. It didn't bother Paul. He considered it just one more way of keeping warm during a cold prairie night. He had known that he deeply loved Barbara, and nothing was going to destroy that.

But now, as he awaited the arrival of Barbara and Bill, he wondered if, in fact, he had the right to be too sanctimonious. He decided he did, because the relationships were all different.

But why had Barbara done this? Was there something lacking in him, he asked himself? Was it that his near-total dedication to politics left little time and emotional room for her? Was it menopause? The options sped through his head. He reached no conclusion.

Barbara came into the room hurriedly about two minutes behind Paul. She had taken the trouble to run a brush through her tousled hair, but that was her only concession to enhancing her femininity.

"Paul…?" she began. Whatever she planned to say froze in her throat as Paul looked at her with a coldness she had never before seen. She sat down silently in the upholstered chair and examined the backs of her hands.

"Ah," thought Paul. "She's not going to sit on the chesterfield, making room for Bill."

Bill came into the room a minute after Barbara, his jacket on, his tie spilling out of his left jacket pocket. His shoes were neatly tied and except for the lack of a necktie he appeared not a bit perturbed. He looked at Barbara a little uncertainly, then at the chesterfield, and sat down. He looked expectantly at Paul.

"Bill, you are a despicable piece of dogshit. A disloyal, lying bastard, a betrayer of friendships and a phony son-of-a-bitch," Paul began. "But first things first."

He turned to Barbara. "You stayin' or you goin'?"

Quickly, Barbara understood she was maybe being given a second chance, and she responded firmly, clearly. "I'm hoping…I'm planning… to stay." She seemed to Paul to be a little less tense and one or two of the lines in her face loosened.

"Then you and I can talk later. Now, I want to talk to Bill."

Bill decided to try to get a word in. "Paul, this is all my fault. I'm the guilty one here. Don't blame Barbara…."

Before he could say more, Paul waved his arm, dismissing the entreaty.

"Look, it's one thing to fall off the wagon once or twice," he said, implicitly excusing his own past behaviour, "but it's quite clear that this has been going on for some time. You two are playing house. I should have noticed the increasing quality of the food served…on alternate Thursday nights as…as…Barbara, um, showed you her, ah, various talents."

He glanced at Barbara, whose faced was flushed with embarrassment, then back to Bill.

"You should know that my first inclination tonight when I stood in the snow outside and realized what was going on was just to come in here and choke you to death." He paused. Bill gave no sign of reaction. "I still might."

"Now, look," started Bill, impatiently, and not prepared to suffer a lecture, "I'm everything you say, and I am dreadfully sorry. I don't know what to do or say to…try to seek forgiveness, but…."

Again, Paul interrupted him. He knew if Bill started to talk, that even in these circumstances, he could manipulate Paul around to thinking how very inconsiderate it had been of Paul to come home unexpectedly. He wasn't going to give him that opportunity.

"Look, shithead, there is no forgiveness," Paul said harshly. I will not share my Party, or my caucus, or the House of Commons, or even this goddamned city with you. What we are doing here, right now, is trying to figure out how you get out of Ottawa, how you get out of politics, how you go back to whatever miserable little life you had before...."

Disbelief crossed Bill's face. "You're babbling. You're talking nonsense. This..." he waved toward Barbara, "has nothing to do with politics. It's between you and me and Barbara." His voice had raised some above its normal calm, low tones.

Paul was about to yell another string of expletives, but restrained himself. This was going to be argued on his terms.

"No, Bill, you don't understand," he went on, quietly. "Things in politics are done in certain ways. You have proven yourself unfit, by any measure, to be respected by your colleagues in the Party and the House. You will either agree to get out of politics or I will take this whole thing to the Leader. I'll take it to the caucus, if necessary. I'll publicly destroy you. You'll never get into Cabinet if you stay, and if you can't get into Cabinet, you have no reason to stay. So...go!"

Suddenly, Barbara's face flushed again, and once again showed tension. The thought of her affair becoming public, of being the subject of common gossip and press attention....

"That's silly," responded Bill, a little louder this time. "You'd not do any such thing. You'd make yourself the laughing stock of the city—a cuckold—you'd destroy any promise or possibility of a reconciliation with Barbara," he waved toward her, "which I think you can see she wants and I think you want. You wouldn't dare take this public. You'd never be in Cabinet yourself. Your constituents would laugh. Don't try to con me, Paul."

Still calm, Paul said, "Bill, you don't want to tempt me. But you and I have spent a lot of time drinking scotch over the past two years. You know me pretty well. You know I have hates. Single-minded, blind, unreasoning hates. I sometimes deal with them poorly, irrespective of consequences, and you have counseled me on the consuming and dangerous nature of hates.

"Well, right now I hate you, I hate you more than you can ever know, or even imagine because where you come from you people think it's sport to sleep with one another's wives, close friend's wives. Well, where I come from it's a capital offence. We shoot people for messing with our wives, and nobody goes to jail for it. Now, I'd like to kill you, I truly would, but that would be too kind. No, you have now been here long enough to want to play a big role in government after the next election. I hate you so much that irrespective of consequences—to me, to Barbara, to… anything—I will destroy any chance of you realizing that ambition.

Bill's response was wide-eyed, disbelieving silence.

"Now, tomorrow morning, I'll make an appointment to see the Leader—he's in town, I know—and you and I are going to go see him, or I'll see him alone. If I go alone, I'll tell him about tonight, and dump further action on his lap. If you come, you will tell him that, after two years, you have decided that political life is not for you and that you'll be resigning from Parliament as soon as is convenient. Do you understand?"

Bill, finally grasping the enormity of what he was hearing whispered, "You're crazy. You won't do it. You can't do it. The Leader won't do it."

"Bill, there are political facts. One of them is that I might be more influential with the caucus than with the Leader, and he needs me. He doesn't need you. I'm the key to his credibility with much of the western caucus. If I decide to make trouble, the Party will divide and will lose the next election, and he'll never be Prime Minister. You, on the other hand, have no political base, either in the Party or outside. You think you're important because you're a policy whiz. But you do nothing to sell the things you believe in to the rank and file, or to the public for that matter. Even after all I have tried to teach you about politics, you're still a hothouse flower. You still need somebody to look after you.

"No, Bill, You're just a sort of public intellectual, and they're a dime a dozen. The Party can rent somebody else just as easily and cheaply as it rented you. So recognize you are expendable and just go," he said contemptuously.

Bill flustered, and then spoke up, having regained his calm manner.

"Paul, I don't think you have it quite right. I'm the bridge for the Leader and the Party into more seats in both metro Toronto and Montreal, and maybe some other areas. I'm the future, and you're the past. I don't think the Leader will even see you—I'm certainly not going to play my assigned role in this charade—if or when you call him in the morning."

Paul got up and took seven steps over to the telephone on a side table next to Barbara and dialed a number.

"I'm sorry to call so late, but it's Paul Carson and something very important has come up that I simply must see you about first thing in the morning. I need 15 minutes."

There was a pause. "No, it won't wait." Another pause. "I know. My schedule is usually the shits, too, but I couldn't get west tonight because of snow in Winnipeg so my tomorrow is clear. Yes, 10 a.m. will be fine. Thank you." He hung up.

"See how simple it is? You and I are on, one way or another, for 10. You don't have to tell me if you will show up or not. I know you're a dirty little coward, and you'll be there. Now, get the hell out of my house." He waved his right arm, dismissively, towards the door.

Bill stood up, a little uncertainly. He started to move to his right.

"The door's that way."

Bill pointed the other way, "I have to get my coat."

He returned with it. Paul had gone over to the front door, and unlocked it. He then opened it and went out into the cold to retrieve his bags. Bill passed him, stopped as if to say something, but there were no words. He got into the car, started it and backed out of the driveway as Paul watched, suitcase in one hand, his briefcase in the other. Then he turned and went back into the house, locking the door.

"You wouldn't do what you say, really, would you?" she said softly. "You are not that kind of person. You couldn't do it." Barbara's voice was begging, uncertain even after 22 years of marriage; she could not read her husband on this one.

"You just bet I could, and would, and will, if necessary. I'm going to sleep downstairs tonight. You figure out what you want to do. I got some thinkin' comin' about all this. Maybe we can talk on Saturday or Sunday."

He disappeared down the hall. Barbara, tears running down her face, stared after him.

Chasing the Fillies

The election was one of those odd ones that produced a large number of MPs who weren't serious politicians. Federal politics is a hard life. It means a lot of time away from home, mostly spent in Ottawa, a city of limited charm with very cold winters and oppressively hot summers. It means a lot of travel to make political appearances before unappreciative audiences in uninteresting parts of the nation. It means long hours, a great deal of stress on family relationships and the risking of personal reputation. It means, for those who were earning higher incomes, or benefiting from generous expense accounts before, a drop—sometimes a big drop—in income. For those with promising expectations in the private sector who had convinced themselves that they would of course be in the Cabinet, where the money was better, the perks greater, and there existed an opportunity to make a mark on history, but who didn't make the cut, a disappointing term in Parliament was—in those days—four years of low pay, frustration, underachievement, unrequited sacrifice and very likely an unhappy spouse.

Some backbench MPs, most in fact, decide to do their best and find other Parliamentary challenges. They take an interest in the organization of Caucus business and the operation of Parliamentary affairs, or become active in Parliamentary Committees, working to become a Committee chairman, or carving out a reputation in one or two particular areas of policy interest or they do Party work. These might be termed serious politicians.

Some—the small minority—just decide there is nothing of interest for them but, since they are there for a four-year hitch, to simply enjoy the experience. They aren't serious about the work. They line up for the overseas travel. They follow along in events, party too much, organize late-night poker parties in their offices, miss a lot of Parliamentary sitting days or spend most of their time in their constituencies, purportedly on riding business but really for all practical purposes returning to their pre-electoral life, running their businesses or practising law.

A few spend much of their time, as one put it, "chasing the fillies". You see, for many women, middle-aged men who have been elected to Parliament are sexually irresistible.

And available women, to some men, are not to be resisted. In those years—but things are a little different now—Parliament Hill was a place where the irresistible and the available found common solace.

There was a story, carefully repeated to all new MPs by their Whips, of an accidental defeat of the minority Government in a Parliamentary vote on a Budget bill. In Parliamentary tradition, such a defeat would be considered a loss of confidence in the Government, leading to its resignation and a general election. It didn't happen that time because the Government managed to manoeuvre itself out of the crisis, and the media were so mesmerized by the enormity of the stakes in play that few asked themselves why the government lost the vote.

But one journalist decided to track down every MP's whereabouts at the time of the vote. A hundred and two MPs had to be accounted for, and it was easy to account for ninety-one of them. They were on legitimate business. Another nine eventually came up with acceptable excuses. But the last two—who said they had been in their ridings during the vote, and had told that to their Whips—were in fact at their respective secretaries' apartments for three days, oblivious to events, this of course in the days before mobile phones and Blackberries and email. Neither was re-nominated for the next election. Their Party saw to that.

The message from the Whips to the new boys was—again in the days before mobile phones, mind you—"We don't care where you are or what you are doing, or who you're doing it with, we just want to know how to reach you any hour of the day or night."

There were lots of stories, some of them even true, and many of the MPs from that election didn't come back after the next election, even though they ran again. Even their constituents knew they were not serious, and most voters want serious people representing them in Ottawa.

Jerry was one of the MPs who wasn't serious. He'd made some money while he was young, but he sought the kind of status in the community that a little money couldn't buy, and big money was beyond him. So he ran for Parliament in an election where, as it turned out, it was easy for the lazy to get elected, if nominated by the winning Party.

The riding wasn't one that the Federal Campaign Committee in that province thought was winnable, so they paid little attention to who was chosen as candidate until it was too late. When Jerry arrived in Ottawa, he was considered sufficiently inconsequential that nobody took an interest in showing him the ropes. Because he was away from home so much, his pretty blonde wife thought she should travel as well—but not to Ottawa. Thus, with little of interest in Ottawa, and no reason to go home all that often, Jerry began to show an interest in the fillies.

In that era, unlike now, the House of Commons sat three evenings a week, until 10:30. This led to a unique style of life different from later years. MPs often had to hang around The Hill in the evenings, should their presence be needed for a vote. Some busied themselves in their offices with work while some spent their time importuning Ministers for favours. Some just gossiped and read magazines in the lobbies. For most it was a careless mixture of these.

But there was in those days a liquor store in the basement of the West Block—now long gone—and a staff member could be dispatched to buy something. As well, there was a huge ice-making machine beneath the Centre Block in the days before office refrigerators.

Thus, two of the three necessary ingredients for a spontaneous party were close at hand. The third—congenial company—was not far away.

Some parties were quiet and serious—with serious drinking and serious conversation. Some were more festive. And some more intimate.

That was the rhythm of Parliament before Mulroney. He had given up drinking, himself, and seemed to think everyone else should do the same. Evening sittings were done away with. Ottawa, always a dull place became a duller place.

Wednesday evenings, however, were different too, during that era. Most MPs were in town mid-week, and the House closed down at six. So that was cocktail-party night. The embassies, the lobbyists, the visiting firemen all scheduled Wednesday nights for receptions, and Jerry tried to make at least an appearance at most of them—sometimes four or five in an evening, since he was serious about his partying.

Jerry had a routine to his attendance at any reception. He tried to guess who of interest might be there. He would enter, make a quick tour of the room to reconnoitre, and then decide which five or six people or groups he wanted to spend a few minutes with. He then made his tour, drinking no more than a single glass of white wine in the process, and then exited. In this way, he was able to meet a large number of fillies.

When he met one he liked, he might stay for the evening if prospects were good, or he might just note a name for later follow-up. In this way he had a string of half dozen fillies going at any one time and a reasonable success rate.

He was enjoying his time as an MP.

In his second year, he met Jennifer. He went to an embassy party in late September, just as the fall session of Parliament was beginning. It was love at first sight. She was quintessentially beautiful. Tall and slim, with notable breasts, an oval face with fine features, a perfect nose and hair that was gold, not quite blonde. He saw her when he first entered the room, but did not approach her. She was, he sensed, something special. He studied her from various directions for about a half hour, as he feigned interest in a score of other people and conversations. He wasn't a man who lacked courage when introducing himself to a new woman, but he felt once again like he was 17, with a lightness in his belly. With this one he thought he needed a strategy.

He introduced himself. She told him, barely, who she was as she surveyed him. He was tall, almost angular and he often gave the impression that he was awkward, which he wasn't. His face was narrow and slightly irregular, and he had an off-centre smile. The overall impression was far from handsome, but he had a boyish charm that some women—enough women—seemed to like.

Usually, even before politics, he found it easy to make conversation with just about anyone, and with women he had a gift of knowing what they wanted to talk about within 20 seconds of beginning a conversation. But with Jennifer, he found conversation difficult. Part of it was, well, she seemed to have little interest in him, the fact that he was an MP, what he was doing or what he was saying, or even that he was obviously interested in her. She was unresponsive to his efforts to learn more about her and she was a master of the one-word dismissive answer. He found it entirely charming. For about three minutes. She then spotted someone she just had to see, and left him standing there, talking to himself, as she made the briefest of excuses.

He went back to furtively watching her for the rest of the evening. He noticed who she talked to, who she seemed animated with, and who she sought out. He slyly followed after her, talking to the same people. He found out her last name, that she was a junior executive in a large trade association, that she was divorced, 32 and shared a large apartment in a new upscale high-rise near Centre Town with a woman in similar circumstances. Both liked to throw large dinner parties, neither wanted to cook for one, each wanted to live in a better, bigger apartment than she could afford on her own, so they shared. In other receptions later, he learned that both were very discreet, that they shared one car, and that Jennifer was considered very bright.

When she left, he went directly home, forgoing the other receptions that night. He thought about her, and then dreamed of her. This was, he realized, unprecedented. He couldn't wait until the next Wednesday.

He saw her at the third reception, dressed in the day's business attire. She appeared to be there on business which, when he realized the identity of the host, was obviously the case. Again, he studied her. After a long while, he approached her and again introduced himself. She made no reference to their having met before, nor did he. He thought that since the earlier meeting hadn't gone well, he was better off starting again afresh. Nonetheless, the second encounter went no better than the first. Again, she tarried no longer than it took to recognize someone she just had to see. He was puzzled and hurt. For the first time in two decades he began to have doubts about his attractiveness to women. He went home before she left. He wanted to think.

Over the fall and winter he saw her again at perhaps another 15 receptions. He had no trouble, most of the time, knowing which one she would attend, because almost all were business-related. She wore her day clothes to those. The few she went to that were not business she wore dresses that showed her to her best advantage. They did not reveal more than was prudent in a town where appearance is important, but she showed enough well enough to captivate most of the men in the room. Jerry realized he was not the only man who admired her, and he wasn't the only man she was studiously avoiding. At each reception, however, he made a point of trying to talk to her, with little progress being made. He gave no thought to giving up because he was by nature an optimistic and persevering man, but there were nights when he believed that there was no progress to be made.

Occasionally, Jerry would take another woman to these receptions. It was part of being an MP to not appear to be alone or lonely. At the same time, the women he took were women that showed well. That too was part of being an MP out on the town.

One night in May he took a date to an embassy reception, one at which he had no expectation of meeting Jennifer. Yet there she was, and in a spectacular, dark blue, low cut thing. His date was talking to someone so he broke away to have a word with Jennifer. Once again, he approached her, quietly and deferentially. He expected the usual brush off. Instead, he was met with a response that bordered on effusive. She was warm and outgoing. She was animated, interested in what he was doing and forthcoming. She was truly captivating. He immediately sensed the possibilities of the evening and excused himself.

Jerry went back to his date, interrupted her conversation and abruptly suggested they leave. She sought an explanation. He said he had a splitting headache. He took her home—she was a bit grumpy over that—said goodnight unromantically and returned to the reception, all within twenty minutes. Jennifer was still there.

They began to talk. Her company was exciting. She showed an inner beauty that he hadn't been allowed to see before. Other people came over to where they were talking and tried to participate. She ignored them, focusing, Jerry realized, only on him.

Eventually, the party began to wind down. Over the course of the evening he had learned that her roommate had taken the car to Toronto for the week. He offered her a ride home. The offer was accepted and they left, her arm possessively in his. He sensed a willing warmth in the short ride to her apartment. He parked the car and turned to kiss her. She responded. They sat there and kissed for a while, saying little, and then she suggested they go upstairs for a nightcap. Jerry didn't want to scare her away by being too aggressive but resisting temptation was not one of Jerry's weaknesses.

They went into her apartment which he could see, even in the gloom, was obviously large and well appointed. She turned on the light in the kitchen creating enough light in the living room to which she waved him while she opened a bottle of white wine. She had noted, somewhere, somehow, not only that he drank white wine but preferred a Pinot Grigio.

They sat on the sofa, talking, then kissing, then becoming, slowly and carefully, more intimate. Jerry was in love and was being tender and careful. Light from the street enhanced the mood. Finally, taking courage in hand, he asked, "Should we go to the bedroom?" She nodded. She was tall, but not heavy, and he was strong. He picked her up and carried her towards where he knew the bedrooms were. She motioned to a door, and he pushed it in with his foot. "Don't put on a light," she whispered. There was enough light from the street that he could see where he was going and, later, what he was doing.

It was, he remembered, a marvellous experience. Later, he never went into details when he told the story, which he did with great skill. He never told "Jennifer's" real name, but he thought it had lasted for about two hours. They went to sleep, a sound sleep fuelled by alcohol and extraordinary sexual release.

He never told the next part of the story, or knew of the last.

He woke up suddenly. Bright spring morning light flooded into the lightly-curtained room. He was disoriented briefly then the events of the previous evening flooded back. He began to smile with the memory. Jennifer was still soundly asleep, her long hair tousled gold across the pillow.

He looked around the room, which was painted a pale, pretty green. The furniture was tasteful modern teak. Danish. The diaphanous drapes were a complementary green. The wall was decorated with framed pictures. He stopped the survey. The photographs were pictures of him, Jerry. There were four of them. Each different. Each about two feet square, in frames

Confusion flooded his mind. Then he thought he understood. She had been playing him for how long? Six months. Like a fish. He felt stupid. Made a fool of. He couldn't think of what he'd say to Jennifer when she awoke. Jerry carefully got out of bed and dressed. Quietly, he left the apartment, his face still burning with embarrassment. He made a point of never speaking to Jennifer again. But she always smiled at him when they met.

Jennifer, for her part, awoke a half-hour later, equally confused to find that Jerry had left. She called his office later in the day. Her call went unreturned. She called again. No response. He avoided her as best he could when he ran into her at parties. She was disappointed. That evening, still confused, she had confided to her room-mate some of the details.

"Y' know, I fell for that guy months ago. I guess I should have melted then, but his sheer persistence caused me to wonder how long he would hang in. When finally I decided to surprise him with a spectacular night, and the photos, to demonstrate how I felt about him I guess he didn't understand. The pictures were a compliment, not an insult. I'd fallen in love with the guy."

It is said of dogs chasing cars that they would not know what to do if they caught one. Some men are the same about some women.

An Appointment to Cabinet

Louis Henderson had sought public office for three reasons, a combination of boredom with the practice of law, ambition and a desire for public service. He knew these were the reasons, but never answered in his own mind what the relative proportions were. Thus, he had served a term on the local school board and two terms as a municipal councilor and then, somewhat prematurely, the opportunity came for a nomination to run for a seat in Parliament for a Party that was almost certain to form the next government. He thought he could win and went about assembling a nomination team that, would see him through to victory on election night.

The decision to run had not been all that easy to make, however. He had to negotiate with his partners in the law firm. They were reluctantly supportive. Reluctant because he would be a loss to the personnel and talent mix that makes for a successful and balanced legal business, but supportive because they admired him and believed he had a contribution to make to public life. But even if he lost, which some thought likely, his higher profile in the community would be good for the firm.

At the age of 45, he was as they say financially comfortable and his wife, Irene, had a career of her own, while their two children were just launched at university. Prudent financial planning had meant university costs could be met without strain, even on a backbencher's indemnity.

Since before Confederation until recently, being elected to the House of Commons or to a Provincial Legislature was nothing like a full-time job. It was not long before that the House in Ottawa sat for only three or four months a year, Parliamentarians travelled by train, and the farmer-Members could be home for spring planting. MPs did not have constituency offices, and for most of the year lived lives little different from their neighbours. The pay of parliamentarians reflected the very part-time nature of their jobs.

By the early 1960s, the workload of Parliament became greater, the sessions longer, the travel more demanding, the separations from families greater, and the role of MP became pretty much full time, if one were a serious MP. Parliamentary salaries and pension arrangements lagged behind the new reality for some time. Louis came along in the middle of the transition.

And so Louis went to Ottawa to learn to be a parliamentarian. He wasn't included in the Cabinet and hadn't expected to be. He threw himself into his new work with all the drive and concentration of a trial lawyer—which he was—preparing for a big case. He quickly tallied who was who in the Party's and the Government's power structure, and adjusted his approaches to his tasks with these in mind. Asked by the Whip or the Caucus Chair to do something, he did it uncomplainingly. Asked by a parliamentary colleague to come to his riding for a speech or fundraiser, he agreed with alacrity. He enjoyed the debates in the House, the camaraderie of politics, the learning about policies and regions of the country with which he was unfamiliar as the Committees he was on travelled. He made a positive contribution just about everywhere.

Like most new arrivals to the House, he was generally unknown to the media, his colleagues, and his Party but, over the next two years as he gained political experience and visibility it became a consensus that he was 'a comer', someone who was serious about politics and government, who was thoughtful about his choices, had something positive to say when he spoke, and was destined for a place at the Cabinet table within his first term.

Louis, however, refused to play political games to advance his cause. He didn't backbite his colleagues. If he had a criticism, he said it quietly and directly to its subject. He made a point of getting to know a number of the press gallery members because he wanted some media attention for what he did and said and he wanted to understand how media people worked and thought but he stayed away from the shameless self-promotion common among politicians. He also knew that to rise in politics better communications skills were vital.

After two years, Louis considered his apprenticeship complete and began to consider his future. After several months thought he decided that, however much he enjoyed what he was doing, he would not seek re-election if he were not in the Cabinet. It wasn't that he was bored after two years but rather that he knew that he would be bored not long after four, and the backbench offered inadequate opportunities to contribute. If he could not make Cabinet, he decided, he would turn his attentions elsewhere. Maybe run for Mayor.

In his view, there would be two opportunities for promotion. The first should come, he calculated, in the coming few months—just past halfway through the Government's mandate, as the Prime Minister sought to address the weak spots in the Government and its policies. Several of these were clear, some of near-term importance caused by poor performances in the House, and other fundamental, longer-term issues that underperforming Ministers were not addressing. He figured that six—maybe eight— members of Cabinet were for the high jump if the PM were doing his job. However, it would not just be six or eight new appointees to Cabinet but rather some would be kept and moved to other portfolios—promoted or demoted—in the parlance of politics as an attempt by the PM to better match the problems he perceived with the talent he had available. This was a cold calculation on Louis' part but that was what trial lawyers do every day. He concluded, quite dispassionately, that given any sort of fair consideration, he would be offered a Department.

There was also the great likelihood that just before the next election the Prime Minister would want to make some further appointments to ease out those who were not seeking re-election and to put a fresh face on a government seeking a new mandate. Louis decided to try for the early opportunity.

Again, he did so directly. One day he found himself in a private conversation with the Prime Minister who had sought his advice on some small matter. At the end of the conversation he said, "I'd like to say something further."

"Yes?" responded the PM.

"I assume you will be addressing some changes in the Cabinet in the next few months. At least, the rumours are starting. I'd like to be considered, but I'm not going to mount a campaign or anything. I think you're aware of who I am and what I've done here the last two years. I've been loyal, constructive, discreet, and hard working. I have ability and ideas. My area of the country is not over-represented in Cabinet, and I believe I've something to contribute. That's all I have to say."

The PM looked at him without response for a half minute, then said, very carefully, "Louis, you're correct to say I've noticed you and, further let me say I've appreciated your quiet support. This is more appreciated than you likely know because every Prime Minister puts up with an enormous amount of jostling among a large number of self-important prima donnas both in and out of Cabinet. I can't promise anything other than a fair consideration, whenever. Is that okay?"

"It's all I could ask for, Prime Minister. I just ask that my name be on the list for consideration."

The spring term of Parliament recessed in mid-June without Cabinet changes and Louis returned to his constituency for an almost three-month break. He hadn't spent as much time with Irene as he have liked over the previous year and thus his suggestion of a holiday in Europe was greeted with enthusiasm. They would go after he'd done three week's work in the constituency, rebuilding relationships. He had an efficient and politically astute staff, in any event, and everything was well under control.

He called the Prime Minister's Principal Secretary two weeks later.

"I know you can't tell me what you can't tell me, but my wife and I are going to be driving around Europe for three weeks from the last week in

An Appointment to Cabinet

July and will likely be out of touch for much of the time. Is that going to cause any problems with the PM's plans for the summer?"

Such an enquiry put in that way was perfectly clear to the Chief of Staff. He responded in a similar fashion.

"No, I don't think so, although you know how this business is. But if you're planning a return to Canada about mid-August, you should check with me about passing through Ottawa."

That understanding in hand, Louis and Irene went off to London for a week. Then Paris for a week. Then they drove east across France to Luxembourg and from there to Trier, the ancient Roman city on the western edge of Germany, at the head of the Mosel Valley. Louis and Irene loved the Mosel, its particular German wines, the food and the scenery. They ended up in Frankfurt to catch the flight home.

A week before, Louis had called the Principal Secretary. The response had been guarded.

"There are no guarantees in this business, Louis, and even the timing of things gets screwed up, but in my judgment you'd be well served to drop by Ottawa. Let me know your plans."

That was enough for Louis.

The holiday, although well enjoyed, had been largely taken up by discussions between the couple about Cabinet. They discussed how an appointment would further restrict his time at home. Should Irene take a leave of absence from her job? Or quit entirely? Should she move to Ottawa? Was he going to have to re-arrange their investments to avoid conflicts of interest? What were the implications for the kids? There was a run of other questions, some relevant, others not.

Then there was speculation about which portfolio he would get. He went over the list in his mind, rejecting some, conditionally accepting others as possibilities. Agriculture? No. Not from a farming area, no interest. Fisheries? Not from a fishing area. No interest. National Defense? Not much interest. Foreign Affairs? Finance? Too senior for a new boy. Justice? Yes, that interested him, as did Industry, Trade, and several other mid-range portfolios. He and Irene discussed his thoughts about a half dozen possible portfolios and what he would do—or like to do—in each of them. But they realized that whatever portfolio, it was all in the PM's hands and speculation was of no consequence. He'd take what he was given, and be thankful.

"The point is, Irene, across the government there is a crying need for some vision and more active, visible, intellectual leadership in a bunch of Ministries. We should be looking at long term issues, the challenges of the next 20 or more years, They are coming at us quickly. But I've seen that most Ministers are in their respective ministerial swamps, too busy fighting the daily alligators of politics and not focusing on the future of the swamp. I'd like to do things differently."

He didn't realize how common that same thought was to other aspiring Cabinet Ministers, and how soon the demands of the swamp overwhelm good intentions.

Irene mostly listened, nodded her head, shook her head, or commented briefly and often pithily in response to what were often lengthy monologues by Louis. But despite the preoccupation with Cabinet possibilities, they visited museums, sat drinking coffee or wine in sidewalk cafes, and chatted about the things that married people do.

Irene flew home. Louis went to Ottawa, got in late, and slept the clock around in the modest apartment he kept eight blocks from the Hill. He rose before noon and went out on to the balcony and looked across the Ottawa skyline, unconsciously counting the Canadian flags. Ordinarily he could see 16. There were 16 today. He called the Principal Secretary.

"Your timing is pretty good. Can you hang around for couple of days? I'll try to work you in, maybe tomorrow afternoon. We'd appreciate it if you would say nothing to anyone about anything and avoid talking to anyone in the media. There are about a hundred rumours out there and, with it being mid-summer and nothing much of substance to report, the columnists are sitting around speculating and making things up."

The Principal Secretary laughed at Louis' response.

"You are talking to a mute, invisible man."

Louis walked down O'Connor Street to a bookstore on Bank Street, and bought four large books that he'd been wanting to read. He bought some groceries, then returned to the apartment. He didn't call his office staff in Ottawa or in the constituency. Irene, if she were asked, was to respond that Louis had gone fishing. A little joke. Louis had never fished in his life, but now he was fishing for an appointment to Cabinet.

The next day, just after lunch, the Prime Minister's private secretary called. Could Louis show up quietly at the PM's Centre Block office about 3:30? Louis could. He arrived without being observed by any reporter by walking in the door the tourists used, rather than the Members' entrance.

The PM greeted him with some warmth. Having not been close to the PM personally, this was something new to him. He responded carefully and correctly.

"Good afternoon, Prime Minister."

"Sit down, Louis."

Louis moved to an upright upholstered chair to which the PM had motioned.

"How has the summer been?"

Louis briefly reviewed the trip to Europe, "I wanted to get a good vacation this year because likely next summer will be taken up with getting ready for an election the following year if I decide to run again," said Louis, matter of factly.

The Prime Minister straightened in his chair. "Are you considering not running?"

Louis realized he'd perhaps said the wrong thing.

"No, not really, but I consider my period of apprenticeship over. I came here in the hope that I could actually contribute, actually do something. I guess I think that I'll be bored as a backbencher two years from now, and will have trouble getting up the necessary enthusiasm for an election campaign, frankly.

"Politicians lacking enthusiasm for the job aren't what you want, I would guess."

He tried to make it sound as just a normal consideration of the future, but realized half-way through that the issue would likely be settled then and there, with the offer of a portfolio or with a pleasant conversation as to why there was no offer, but encouragement for the future.

The PM relaxed.

"Well, maybe we can address your future right now. As you may have guessed, I'm working on some changes in the Cabinet. You're the last interview, and I hope you'll be pleased." The PM saw Louis visibly brighten.

"Louis, I'm offering you the Department of National Revenue. Its not the most senior portfolio, but it's a great place in which to learn."

The PMs words trickled off as he saw Louis' face change from ruddy and relaxed to pale and taut. Louis, for his part, felt his stomach tense and his cheeks tighten. He stumbled for words. It was the one Department that he and Irene had not discussed

"Please don't think me ungrateful, Prime Minister, but I can't accept that portfolio."

This was not what the Prime Minister expected. He covered his confusion.

"Why?"

Louis had recovered himself from the shock somewhat.

"Well, this will likely sound strange, but I know too much about those…awful bunch of people from my time in practice. It's a Department of, how can I put it, sadists. Mean, nasty, untrustworthy, double-dealing, harsh…I run out of adjectives. It's a Department that, in trying to collect taxes, makes the lives of too many Canadians just awful. They decide you've been evading, and that's that. They don't listen to explanations. They give no quarter. And taxpayers are stuck defending themselves from bankruptcy, from the loss of their businesses and reputations and it's just an awful experience. No, 'sadists' isn't too strong a word.

"As Minister, these people would be acting in my name. I'd be in effect sanctioning their behaviour. Prime Minister, I just couldn't do it. I couldn't."

The PM had taken this in with detachment, once he was over the initial shock.

"But as Minister, you could fix what you think is wrong," he said, reassuringly, soothingly.

Louis thought briefly. "That's a good theory, and a very worthwhile objective, but National Revenue is the ultimate 'Yes, Minister' portfolio.

So much is delegated, and has to be delegated, that Ministers have little real influence or flexibility. The harm, the evil, takes place at the lowest level of the bureaucracy, not at the civilized upper levels where Ministers operate. It's a matter of initial recruitment, of training, of first line supervision. The whole…how can I say it…'working ethic' of the Department would have to change. It's beyond the time and energy of any one Minister to reform it."

He paused, reflected, then went on.

"I'd be in a constant rage about what was being done in my name. No, thank you Prime Minister, but I just couldn't do it. I've seen in Court, in case after case, up close, how those guys do things. I couldn't live with myself."

The PM grunted.

"Look, Louis, you're a solid and rising talent, I'm sympathetic to your…ethical problem…but I just don't have any other place else to put you. I'm truly sorry. That's just reality."

"I accept that, Prime Minister, and I'm not taking this position because I'm trying to negotiate something…more senior. I mean no disrespect and will happily take on any other task you ask of me, in or out of Cabinet. Any other task. But not this one."

The PM looked out the window to the U.S. Embassy, across Wellington Street, appearing thoughtful for at least a minute, Louis thought later, likely assembling his words.

The PM sighed and said, "OK, Louis, but I did my best as I said I would when we chatted a few months ago. I guess had I known your views on Revenue, I maybe could have done something, but everything else is sewn up now, and the announcement's tomorrow, so I just don't have any manoeuvring room. I'm sorry."

Louis rose, silently shook the PM's hand, and left the room. He found his way to the elevator and, still unobserved, made his was down Metcalfe Street towards his apartment. He stopped at a liquor store, bought a bottle of scotch and picked up soda at a corner store. Upon reaching the apartment, he closed the drapes to darken the room, took off his shoes, mixed a weak drink, turned the air conditioning to a lower temperature, sat down and put his feet up.

He considered the meeting with the Prime Minister. He wondered if, just if, he could have handled it otherwise, and decided he couldn't. He called Irene and told her of the meeting. Since she knew of his feelings towards the tax collectors, he need make no long explanation.

"What are you going to do now?" asked Irene.

"Oh, I'll go into the office here for a couple days, be home for the weekend. I guess I'll work the constituency next week then maybe you and I ought to go on another vacation. You got any time off due?"

"Only a few days, but let me see what I can arrange."

With that, the phone call ended.

Louis was still suffering from jet lag. He undressed and went back to bed for an hour's nap. He didn't sleep. His mind kept turning the meeting with the PM over in his mind. He then had the mad thought of phoning and telling the PM it'd all been a bad mistake. But he couldn't do that, either.

At five o'clock, he rose, dressed casually, and went down the street to the grocery store to buy a steak for dinner. Standing in front of the meat counter, he felt a heavy hand on his shoulder. He looked around, then smiled in surprise.

"Well, Don Polika, as I live and breathe. How are you?" Polika was a fellow government MP who had an apartment in the same building as Louis.

"What're you doing in town?" responded Polika, ignoring Louis' question.

"Oh, on my way home after three weeks in Europe. Going to spend a couple days in the Hill office catching up. You?"

"Same, minus Europe. I got a tighter race to face in two years than you do."

Each knew the other was lying. Each thought the other was in town to be close should the PM call. Neither voiced his thoughts.

"What are you up to tonight? I'm going to cook myself a steak with lots of onions and mushrooms. Want to join me? Then we can swap lies for a couple hours, but I'm still a little jet lagged, so go home early."

"Great idea. I'll buy my own steak. You got potato puffs, frozen peas and the other accoutrements of a deluxe bachelor dinner?"

"Yup, but all I have to drink is scotch and soda."

"I'll buy a couple bottles of wine. And salad makings."

The deal done, the two went back to Louis' apartment, and together began to prepare the meal.

"I hear the PM's announcing a new Cabinet tomorrow morning," announced Don, casually.

"Oh, I hadn't heard that. Not much penetrates Europe about such things and I got in late yesterday and spent most of the time in the bag catching up on my sleep."

"Are you in the new Cabinet?" Don couldn't resist asking the question, straight out.

"No."

"Would you tell me if you were?"

"No. But I'm not."

"You were expected by...jeez...just about everybody to be offered something. A guy loses faith if you're not in. I mean, I don't have anything like what you have going for you, and I was hoping, but if you're not in... well...jeez...." he trailed off.

"Well, I don't want to talk about it. What happened while I was away?"

Thus, they got away from the topic of Cabinet appointments. They told one another funny stories and not long after nine, Louis started to sag. He yawned.

"Look, I'm fading, Can we call it a night? I don't think I'm getting old, but I'm tired."

"Sure, sure. Hey, the Cabinet swearing-in is at 9:30. Why not come down for breakfast at, say, 8:30, and we can watch it on TV? See who the ins and outs are?"

Louis nodded agreement as they both rose. They shook hands as Don reached for the door knob.

"Sorry you're not in. You shoulda been."

"Thanks, See you at 8:30."

He thought for a few minutes before he went off to sleep. The die is cast. It's two more years, here. Then off to something else. Louis slept soundly.

Don made a cheese and mushroom omelet, and had gone down the street to buy fresh-baked croissants before Louis arrived.

"Just as good as Paris," pronounced Louis.

With coffee cups charged they turned the television on to catch the commentary of the announcers before the formal proceedings got underway at Government House. Don switched back and forth between channels, but the commentary was desultory.

Promptly at 9:30 the new Ministers and Ministers that were being reassigned filed in and took their seats in the large room in Government House. At that point the announcers knew who would be sworn in as what in the new Government. Louis noted that Ralph Richardson, one of the senior Ministers who everyone had expected to retire was the new Revenue Minister. He said nothing to Don as they kibitzed back and forth discussing the strengths and weaknesses of every new appointment as each was sworn in.

It was all over in a few minutes, then the milling around began.

Don made like he was going to shut off the television, but Louis said, "No, not yet. The PM is going outside to meet the media. Lets see what everyone has to say."

The scene shifted from the interior of Government House to the portico outside, where microphones had been set up. The PM strode up to the dias with a smile that exuded both confidence and mischief, Louis thought later.

The PM looked out into the crowd of reporters, pointed to one and said, "Yes, Will?"

A simple question was asked and answered and the PM moved easily through the remainder for about 15 minutes until, it seemed, there would be no more.

Then the Prime Minister seemed to draw himself up and smiled again. "I want to add one more thing that doesn't appear in the briefing material you have. It relates to the Department of National Revenue."

Louis stiffened perceptively.

"It's been my view and that of others, for some time now, that the Department requires a thorough overhaul. I hear too many stories about the Department behaving in a—let us say—high-handed way towards taxpayers, towards citizens.

"I've been told by people whose judgment I trust that some people— by no means all—in the Department, and I quote from one person I respect,

'...treat taxpayers harshly. That, in trying to collect taxes, the Department makes the lives of too many Canadians just awful. They decide you have been evading, and that's that. They don't listen to explanations. They give no quarter. And taxpayers are stuck defending themselves from bankruptcy, from the loss of their businesses and reputations and it's just an awful experience.' Unquote.

"In my view we have to try to strike a better balance. Taxes have to be collected of course, and sometimes that's not a pleasant job. But it is, in my view, worthwhile trying to reform things. And that's why I have asked Ralph Richardson, who likely knows more about how government departments are run than anybody else, to take this on. Louis watched, transfixed.

"But National Revenue is an unusual Ministry. So much is delegated and has to be delegated, that Ministers often have little real influence or flexibility. And the harm takes place at the lowest level of the bureaucracy, not at the upper levels where Ministers operate. So I think it's a matter of initial recruitment, of training, of first-line supervision. The whole 'working ethic' of the Ministry will have to change. It's not going to be easy."

Louis had sat upright as the PM began to describe this new initiative. Here were his own words being spat back at him. He was without speech.

Don noticed that he had sat up straight.

The Prime Minister went on.

"Now, this is not going to be an easy task," he repeated. It is, quite frankly, beyond the time and energy of any one Minister to address."

Louis heard more of his own words.

"Thus I will be appointing, as Minister Without Portfolio for National Revenue Reform, Louis Henderson, to help the Minister. He's been out of touch in Europe, which is why he's not here at the swearing-in this morning. I understand he gets in to Ottawa later today."

"You lying son-of-a-bitch," blurted Don, toward Louis.

"The son of a bitch," said Louis to the television set simultaneously, almost yelling.

Don, not as surprised as Louis at the PM's words, but quite confused by Louis' reaction, could only get out, "What? What?"

The Prime Minster continued.

"Mr. Henderson is a rising and able parliamentarian with a lawyer's keen mind and a strong sense of justice. He has had personal front-line experience dealing with National Revenue as a lawyer, and he's just the guy to take this on."

"Now, I have to admit…" at this point the PM gave a nervous chuckle…"that I've not had a chance to discuss this new task with Mr. Henderson, but he has told me that he'll take on any task I ask of him. I think he'll take all this in stride."

This was said, Louis realized, by the Prime Minister knowing that he, Louis, was watching, and it was directed at him, personally.

"The son of a bitch," repeated Louis, lower this time, softer, admiringly.

"I've no idea what you're talking about," interjected Don, obviously confused. "But you told me you weren't in. Now you are. Why is the PM a son of a bitch?"

Louis answered, vaguely, "I understood I wasn't to be appointed. It's as much a surprise to me as to you."

There were a couple more reporters' questions, but that was the end of the press conference, and Don turned off the television.

"Well, goddamn it. Congratulations. You made it. Isn't that great? Don was excited for Louis. "Can't you tell me what's going on?"

Louis didn't know what more to say. He was more than a little confused by the sudden turn around. He shook his head and went towards the door.

"Thanks. I guess I better phone the PMO and tell them that there was a change in my schedule, and I got in yesterday. Oh, well."

"You knew nothing about this? Nothing?" asked Don in disbelief.

"Not a goddam thing. Would I lie to you?"

He shut the door walking quickly, his mind racing ahead.

"Not only a Cabinet appointment, but a job, a mission, something really worth doing," he said to himself. "An opportunity to drain a swamp." He began to run to the elevator.

Staff

Doing Business With The Government

I was just taking the first sip of my martini when my luncheon companion arrived, sliding into the booth in the Canadian Grill of the Chateau Laurier. I had chosen a dark corner where we could make sure we were not overheard. Gordon—my luncheon guest—had said he had to talk to me urgently when he had called an hour earlier so I had assumed a degree of privacy was needed.

In was the spring of 1971. The government had weathered the FLQ/War Measures Act terrorism crisis of the previous fall, things had settled down and we had regained some momentum. I had not seen Gordon, an assistant to Public Works Minister Jack Oaks, for several months and I looked forward to a chat.

"What's up?" I greeted him cheerily. Why not? Everything was going very well in my world that day.

His glance alone caused me a start. His had the look of someone who had just seen something he had preferred not to have seen. He said nothing for about half a minute and I let him settle and order a glass of wine. He didn't bother with pleasantries.

"What do you know about the new buildings the government is building and leasing?"

"What are you referring to? Place du Portage? The Bell Building?"

"Exactly."

"Nothing." But my curiosity kicked in. After a decade of an expanding Liberal government renting cheap, privately-owned, substandard, ugly buildings that were a blight on Ottawa's downtown, a disgrace to the government and an insult to the nation's capital, something had happened and the Government had bought the half-completed Place du Portage project in Hull with the promise to use it to revive that slummy town, and was going to lease space in the Bell Centre, a decent-looking and reputedly a higher-class building. Certainly it looked better than the wartime "temporary buildings" down the street, still in use 25 years after the war.

"Why do you ask?" I enquired.

"I've just strung a bunch of twos together. If they add up as I think they do, we have a major scandal ticking away. You've got to do something." It was a plea.

As an assistant to the Prime Minister, I was used to people assuming I had a great deal more power than I did. The fact was I didn't think I had any power at all, other than the power that comes from being physically and emotionally close to someone who does have power. The Prime Minister, with whom I met daily, often twice or three times, had power. I was only a hanger-on, but one the PM considered useful.

"Tell me what you know, or think you know." I racked my mind to think of any rumour I might have heard about either building. Nothing.

"Do you know how modern buildings are built? Inside I mean?"

"I don't even understand your question."

"Come on, you've been in the new office buildings in Toronto."

He was speaking impatiently, as though I were a rather slow learner. "No walls between offices. Open floor plans, that sort of thing."

He was waving his arms.

"You know, built with the idea that the constant re-organizations that require constant redesigns of floor plans and the moving of walls is both disruptive and expensive. So now space planners—that's a new concept too, I'm told—want to separate people with low portable walls and filing cabinets. Supposedly it makes the air conditioning work better, people communicate better, and a dozen other benefits. The new jargon is 'work stations'; they're no longer offices, and it's a better use of expensive space."

"Well, yes," I said, "But I understand the whole idea has not gone far in Ottawa because of the need to have closed offices for privacy and security, some place where you can lock the doors and leave confidential stuff laying around and not worry about it,"

Where was this going?

"It's going to happen in those two new buildings."

"So far I'm totally unable to see a problem. You're going to have to explain it to me."

My turn to be impatient.

The server came and took our orders. Both of us had long since memorized the Canadian Grill menu and ordered automatically. Then his glass of wine arrived.

He sipped while he considered how to say what he had to say.

"I want to deal in design detail for a minute. Have you noticed that in all the existing government office buildings there are no plants?"

"Plants? As in potted?"

"Yeah. Other than the little ones secretaries have on the corners of their desks."

"I hadn't given it any thought, but yes there are no plants."

"When you think of those new offices you have seen in Toronto, in this context, what comes to mind, then?"

"The offices I've seen use large plants as dividers, to give privacy, to provide…texture, I suppose the architects might say. Yeah, it's a sort of a design feature in all these new buildings. Okay. Now what?"

"Somebody has to provide the plants. Somebody has to look after them."

"What? Why? Does somebody just not go to the wholesale plant supplier, buy a bunch, put them wherever, and let the secretaries water them?" I was growing annoyed with the conversation, downed my martini, and waved to the waiter to order another.

"That's what you might think, and what you might want, but in fact these plants are worth hundreds of thousands of dollars—millions of dollars—all the plants needed for a large building—and when you have plants that are supposed to look good, somebody professional has to look after them, go around every few days, water them, fertilize, remove dead leaves, dust them, keep them happy."

"Keep them happy? I follow you so far. But, again, where's all this agricultural education taking me?"

"Just be patient. Did you know that there's no such business in Ottawa providing such a service? That is the case, in fact. Or was the case until a few days ago."

"So?"

"So a few days ago a business license was issued to Skylark Services Inc. a federally incorporated company. It's president is John Dalton."

"So? again."

"Dalton is son-in-law to William—Bill—Jorgenson, the wealthy entrepreneur, developer, and generous political contributor who, as it happens, is a silent partner in a real estate venture with Senator James out in south Ottawa. Residential subdivision stuff.

"Dalton—as I piece it together— apparently saw the business opportunity and spoke to his father-in-law. They did some numbers, also apparently. It's a potentially good business and very remunerative. Non-union. You hire hippie kids who love plants, university students wanting part time work with no heavy lifting and indoors where it's warm in the winter, air-conditioned in the summer.

"Right now, there's nobody offering the service, and with Skylark getting into it, there's no competition. But it's an easy business to get into, although it requires a bucket of money to buy the plants in the first place. Anyway, once you get a contract with the government, if the plants like you, you are there forever. But first you have to get the contract."

For me the light began to dawn.

"What exactly are you telling me?"

"I am telling you that Senator James went to see my Minister, and I think made a corrupt offer, and it was accepted."

There. It had been said.

"Tell me the details."

"Okay, but for God's sake, you have to keep me away from whatever happens. Everybody involved will have my balls. But I just can't stand by and watch this." His anxiety was increasingly acute and genuine.

I nodded agreement, looked into my new martini, took another sip, and waited for him to go on. Just then lunch came.

He drew a long breath. "My Minister has debts from the leadership campaign. They are substantial. They are in other people's names. People you might call friends, if anybody in politics has any friends. The guy in question who holds most of it has been patient, and quiet fundraising has been going on to get the debt down. As I say, it's still substantial, even though it's about half paid off. The other week the guy—the holder of the biggest chunk of the campaign debt— is in town. He invites me to lunch. He tells me at length a story I happen to know is fiction about how he's under financial pressure and how he really needs to get that debt off his back and would I please speak to Jack about it.

He went on.

"I spoke to the Minister who showed a wrinkled brow in response, then shrugged. Now, I had carried the message. That was all. But a few days later he tells me to talk to Senator James about it. I do. James is, as you know, a great fundraiser. The Senator says he will pass the hat. But he wanted to talk to my Minister. So they have a private meeting.

"Now, I've worked for Jack for—what—two years. He's Public Works Minister, and has a great deal of discretion in the spending of substantial sums of money. To avoid any suspicion of anything going sideways, he never, ever has private meetings with anybody. Not ever. Period. But he spends an hour in his office with Senator James, with whom he has little in common other than that James can help get the financial monkey off his back, sipping Irish whiskey.

"A few days later I was sitting in a meeting with the Minister, the Deputy and some other officials and the topic of the new buildings comes up. Jack asks for a detailed presentation, so he can be informed about what he described as a major departmental initiative. That took place last week. I then get a call from someone in the department—an old friend who buried himself in the bureaucracy and who is a useful back-channel that keeps me up on departmental gossip—who tells me that—and he didn't know how it happened—the department planned to sole-source the contract for supplying and servicing plants for the two new buildings to some new company with no current operations called Skylark.

"As you know, sole-sourcing instead of competitive bidding particularly for large contracts is unusual and rightly avoided. The excuse seems to be there is nobody else in Ottawa. That it would be going to a non-operating company that exists only on paper is suspicious. The fact is that if it had gone to competitive bid the Toronto and Montreal companies would have responded.

"In short, he was curious. He had looked up the ownership of Skylark, had heard of the relationship between Dalton—Skylark's president—and Bill Jorgensen, and learned of the connection between Jorgensen and the Senator. He smelled a rat. He wondered if maybe the Senator had put in a good word on this.

"I told him to please keep his suspicions to himself. I called you. You don't want a scandal. This will most certainly become public at some point—the Auditor General will likely look into it, in any event, because of the single-sourcing, and there'll be a mess. If it doesn't get addressed, I'm gone. I have a reputation to nourish and protect and I want to be a long way from Minister Jack when the mess comes to light.

"I still don't know how all the i's got dotted, but I'm convinced that the leadership campaign debt, the Senator, and the plan to sole-source the office plant supply contract are connected. I'm absolutely sure of this."

The mention of the Auditor General was troubling enough; to most public servants it's akin to displaying a cross to a vampire. Nobody wants to find themselves or anything they are working on subject to the AG's attentions.

But I was more concerned about a scandal that linked political fundraising corruption, a Senator and failure to follow contracting rules, to Ministerial misbehavior. And now that it had been brought to my attention I had to deal with it. If there were a scandal, and if my friend Gordon told investigators, "Well, I did my best; I reported my concerns to a senior adviser to the Prime Minister, and I guess he never did anything," my own goose was cooked. So now I had to do something. But what?

We finished lunch dealing with generalities. Then he interrupted, "What are you going to do?"

"I don't know, yet. I understand that whatever I do, I have to keep you out of it."

The look of relief on his face was plain.

I paid the bill and we walked back down Wellington Street. We parted at the statue of Sir Galahad, a memorial to MacKenzie King's friend Henry Albert Harper. I looked at the statue and the inscription for a minute and reflected on its meaning, then crossed the street to the Langevin Block while Gordon headed up to the Centre Block of the House of Commons.

Back in my office, I told my secretary to give me 15 minutes. The problem was a difficult one. How does one unravel something like this without the media finding out? How do you do it so that, preferably, not only does no one know, but no one notices.

I stood and looked out my window for several minutes, considering the alternatives. Face down the Minister by myself? No, that would only cause him to wonder how the PMO found out. My friend Gordon would be exposed. Call the RCMP? Hah! I might as well post a notice in the editorial room of the Ottawa Citizen. One by one, I considered and dismissed about eight options. At the end of 15 minutes, I knew how to deal with it. I called the office of the Secretary to the Cabinet, and asked to see him. He got back to me five minutes later with the message that if mine were a 10 minute problem, he had 10 minutes. It was the right answer.

Now, Secretaries to Cabinet come in a variety of shapes, sizes, methods, personalities, competencies and motivations. I couldn't have been luckier than at this point to have to place my problem in the hands of Gerry Rollins. He was a long-time public servant of the old school. Self-effacing, generally invisible outside government, discreet, effective and—most important—he knew the location and kept track of the buried bodies.

He met me with a smile. Well dressed in a dark blue suit and a starched white shirt, tall, handsome, hair greying, he exuded not only confidence, but competence. I thought of him at that minute as a doctor I was consulting over a serious illness. I knew he could cure the problem.

"I won't take but a few minutes. I know you're busy," I began.

"I have whatever time you need," he responded, expansively. "I know you're not here on short notice to discuss fly-fishing at the Five Lakes fishing camp." Not only was he wise, I thought, but very perceptive. He knew my ways of operating.

"Well, I don't want to make too much of it, but I heard a rumour that Public Works was going to sole-source a major contract to supply and maintain a large number of office plants needed for the decoration of the open-space-concept office buildings the government is moving into. Now, I know that Public Works is used to sole-sourcing things like architectural work and so on, but I think there might be some danger in this all getting out of hand."

I was being very general and very casual. His eyes told me he knew that I knew there was much more to it. It was well known in some circles that one of my roles in the PMO was political-problem-solver. By his next words, he made it clear that I need say no more.

"I gather your concern is general rather than specific?"

"Yes. This example came to my attention in a cocktail party conversation about how too much government business was going to favoured contractors, and the government may be open to criticism about unfairness," I lied. "I thought I should bring it to your attention. It's a problem even if it's not a real problem yet — it's just not an accusation the PM needs because I think it's groundless."

His response was a questioning look.

I carried on.

"I thought it might be appropriate for you to call the DM of Public Works about it. I know he's busy, and there has to be a thousand contracts a day going out of his shop but he might think it wise, if you were to call, to just do a review of their sole-sourcing policies."

Gerry nodded. "Sounds sensible." He wrote a short note on his desk pad, then turned to me. "Other than that, everything is fine?"

"Just fine."

He indicated by his body language that he had a few more minutes.

"I'm going to have a coffee. Want to join me?" I nodded. "Milk, only." He pressed his intercom button and spoke to his secretary.

"How's the government doing, do you think?" he asked.

A strange question that called for a general answer.

"Not badly. We're recovering well from last fall's events. But then I ascribe to Mackenzie King's dictum that its not the great things a government accomplishes that are important, but the great mistakes it avoids making. We may not be making as much progress on some things as many would like, but we aren't making mistakes, either, although I'm really worried about the draft Competition Act, which might come out in June. That would be a serious mistake. With an election probably next spring, caution is a sound strategy. But I'd hope that, 18 months from now, we're a more…vigorous…government."

He nodded. I think he was agreeing. He had worked for Mackenzie King.

I wanted to change the subject.

"Did you ever give any thought yourself about going into politics? I mean, beside your public reticence—which I think with you is a learned trait and not a natural one—you have all the attributes of a very effective Parliamentarian and would make a great Minister."

He smiled again, considering whether, given his reputation for reticence and discretion, he should even answer the question.

"Yes, I did, although it wasn't my idea. I was approached by a political party and asked if I would be interested in running in the constituency in which I lived. It was a sure thing—or at least as sure as these things are. Implicit was a cabinet post."

He didn't mention the Party, but I knew where he lived. He was telling me it was my Party.

"And?"

"I told them that I'd have to discuss it with my wife. We'd been married for 15 years and, I said, I couldn't even think about such a change in my life without first talking to her."

"And?"

"Her response was that she didn't think a divorced man could get elected in the riding."

We both laughed out loud. He loved the story, I gathered, but likely shared it with few people. I had been let into the inner sanctum of his mind a little bit. I felt honoured. The coffee arrived and we passed another 10 minutes in general conversation.

I left, apologizing for taking more time than I'd asked for.

I heard nothing more about the issue. I was a very busy guy with a dozen problems a day requiring a solution.

About three weeks later, my friend Gordon called. "I just wanted to tell you I've submitted my resignation. I've done my time here and to stay on even another few weeks would really mean I'd have to commit to another 18 months, until after the election."

I congratulated him. "I suppose it's big bucks in the big city," by which I meant Toronto.

"Yes, venture capital banking. A company called Steele Capital. Fits well with my MBA."

"Well, let's keep in touch. I tried to do something about the other, by the way. I've not heard back."

"Yes. It got caught up in a general review of sole-sourcing," he responded, almost with surprise. "A very timely review. It's going to competitive bid." There was a satisfaction in his voice.

"OK, but keep in touch."

"I will. I will," he said, but his contacts over the next two years were infrequent and casual. It was rumoured he was doing very well.

The next time—I suppose the last time I heard mention of office plants—was two years later. The Citizen was running a series about middle level public servants who had opted out in mid-career for the adventures of the marketplace. The first of the series was about Len Lee, who had been Chief of Leisure Products in the Industry Ministry, then he quit, using his pension refund to start a specialty tool supply company called Lee Valley and was becoming a rich man. His success was legendary.

The second article in the series was about another mid-level guy who retired from the Public Works department to get into the business of providing and servicing plants and foliage for the growing number of office buildings in the Capital Region that had an open-floor design.

It was a double-page article. The president of this company was clearly loquacious. He talked about seeing the opportunity and getting out of government in time to get started. Then a big contract for Place du Portage came up and he won the competition. He did it on price, he said.

"You know, the other guys were all from Toronto and Montreal and couldn't operate as efficiently as we could. Besides, we've built a model around hiring university students"—this I knew to be code for "non-union"—"and working around their study schedules. If they only want to work 10 hours a week, fine. We accommodate them. They only want to work Thursday and Friday afternoons? Fine, we work it out. We specialize in hiring science students, and we offer bursary help and so on. They all want part-time work with no heavy lifting and indoors where it's warm in the winter and air-conditioned in the summer. We like to hire people who love plants, people the plants will love back. We think it's the only model for this kind of business."

The words sounded strangely familiar. I recalled they were exactly the words used by my friend Gordon.

Then the interviewer asked how he financed a start-up of something that obviously needed quite a lot of capital.

"Oh, that wasn't difficult. I found a venture capital company in Toronto called Steele Capital, and one of their guys saw to it that the money came. In fact the Steele guy is personally the second largest shareholder...."

I read the last line twice, unbelievingly. Son of a bitch. I'd been had. My friend Gordon, out to stop a scandal, was he? I just bet. He used me to sideline the other guys while he lined up his own position. And I bet that the President, here, was Gordon's backchannel source and the originator of the whole idea.

I thought about it off and on for a few days, and almost gave up. What could I do? I could never prove anything. I would only embarrass everyone if I did anything at all. So much for scandals. The guy running the company had it right when he concluded, "Once you get a government contract, if you handle it right, it's yours forever."

Gordon had made the same point.

Then I thought, maybe that was the real scandal and I turned my thoughts to how I might get the contract cancelled, reviewed, and retendered, maybe getting the government a better contract. Without getting my own fingerprints on it, you understand. Actually, it wasn't that difficult.

Clemow Avenue

Ottawa is a city of many distinct neighbourhoods. Mention where you live, and people will automatically place not only the neighbourhood and its ambience, but your status in Ottawa, a very status-conscious town. Thus, to say you live in Rockcliffe—or more properly Rockcliffe Park Village, because before 2001 it was not then formally part of Ottawa, is to say you are a person of wealth, someone who views status as important, and who likely lives in a large, older house. That is, unless you are a diplomat who has had no choice as to where he lives. There are many embassies and diplomatic residences there, and no poor people. To say you live in Alta Vista is to say that you prefer to live in a newer, smaller house in an inner suburb—that is, one built in the '50s or '60s, perhaps a house with some individuality, one that is halfway between the downtown and the airport—an important consideration if you live on airplanes, maybe. Sandy Hill says old brick houses on narrow lots with small yards and little parking, close to downtown, as does most of the Glebe. Neighbourhoods with "character". To say that you are near Island Park drive says you like large older houses with big yards, and can do without the cachet of Rockcliffe, and so on. Of course, if you don't care where you live, you reside in one of the outlying suburbs.

Then there is Clemow Avenue.

It is an obscure street that runs between O'Connor Street and Bronson, two of the main north-south arteries downtown, and just south of the cross-Ottawa freeway called the Queensway, built on a one-time railway right-of-way.

It's a street of early 20th century houses, mostly built of red brick that is a bit remindful of Rockcliffe but on less spacious lots, with much lower prices. Like Glebe Street to the south, and Powell to the north, the street is shrouded in magnificent old trees but, because the houses are on larger lots with greater set-backs, it has a more genteel air about it. Some of the houses are the embassies or residences of second-and third-tier countries. To live there says you like ambience and older houses, but eschew the snootiness of Rockcliffe because, well, you are enough of an individual that you don't need the location of a home to set your status in life or in Ottawa.

Now, one of the odd things about Clemow Avenue is that people who like the street will wait for years for a house to come up for sale there, then snap it up as quickly as they can whip out their cheque books. The attentions of building inspectors come later.

Thus it was that Cary Harkness lusted after a house on Clemow Avenue. He had accidentally fallen in love with the street when he came to Ottawa on business, years before he found himself living in a tract house in Alta Vista and working in the Prime Minister's Office.

He lived there for four years while wistfully driving down Clemow from time to time, often on summer evenings after the heat of the day had softened a little. He would drive slowly along. He knew—for his realtor had done the research—who the owners were of most of the houses, and he also knew that few would come up for sale in his term in Ottawa, expected to be no more than a few more years.

Then during one of his summer evening drives, he was struck by an inspiration.

Cary Harkness was one of numerous assistants who worked in the Prime Minister's office. There was an Executive Assistant; there was an Appointments Assistant, who looked after the PM's schedule. There was a Correspondence Assistant who supervised a large staff of researchers, writers and secretaries that tended to the hundreds of letters the PM received each day. There were Regional Assistants who, notionally at least, were in charge of liaison between the PMO and the Regional Caucuses of elected MPs. There was an assistant who was in charge of seeing to it that people who turned 85 or older, or who were celebrating their 60th Wedding Anniversaries, received a congratulatory greeting from the Prime Minister. There were assistants in charge of travel planning and execution, since the PM's every move was recorded, photographed, and commented upon, and must be done flawlessly. There were assistants who worked on policy, and assistants that wrote speeches.

Most of the people who seek to work in Minister's offices or the PMO in most governments are of high principle. They are there out of dedication to Party and/or Country. They are there out of idealism, not there for the money, or even the power. They are honourable people.

Cary was not one of them. Let me tell you what kind of person he was.

I first met him during the first week of my first year at university. The university was small then, and while those who came from the city in which it was located brought their high school cliques and connections with them, those of us from small towns in the hinterland used the experience of being in a new place to meet a large number of new people. Cary went out of his way to meet as many people as he possibly could. He came from modest beginnings that he never discussed and a little industrial town he never mentioned. It was almost as though he used the transition to university to reinvent himself, which is about what he did. What I know about his background I learned from his cousin who shared the same name. The voluble cousin thought Cary was a jerk, and was prepared to tell anyone who asked exactly why he thought that.

Suitably warned, I watched Cary as he made his way through university. I noticed that he only dated girls whose families had money and/or position, although the girls were unevenly attractive. For awhile, I thought that his intention was to marry a potential heiress, but from the cousin I learned that, no, that was not the case. He was using his considerable charm to cultivate the fathers of these girls. He was recruiting mentors, men who he could call on for help or advice in the years after he graduated.

He joined the right fraternity.

He joined the political club of the then-dominant political party in the country.

He dressed well enough to give people the impression that he was a gentleman; he polished his manners and prepared himself for a successful life among the wealthy.

Thus it was that upon graduation from law school he was able to arrange to article with the oldest and likely the most prestigious law firm in the city. He didn't find his way there on the basis of his rather mediocre marks. No, he had carefully dated for some months the not-entirely-beautiful-and-less than-charming daughter of the managing partner, leaving the impression that he had what were called, at the time, honourable intentions. Once ensconced in his 13th floor office, however, the romance dwindled.

There were three other students articling with the firm that year, hard workers with marks in the top 10 percent of the graduating class. Cary was apart from them. He had not had their dedication to scholarship at law school, and the menial tasks assigned to articling students did not appeal to him much, either. To the extent he could, he manoeuvred to have the others do the work he disdained.

This he got away with for most of the year, but ended in spectacular fashion.

You see, in this large law firm few of the working lawyers even knew the names of the students. Contact was infrequent and superficial. Thus, when a lawyer wanted some student to do something, direction was given by memo. Strangely, however, the original of the memo was kept in the lawyer's file, and a photocopy went to the student. It was easy for Cary, if he didn't like the assignment, to "white out" his name, substitute that of one of the other students, and proceed to do only work he liked, or work that would bring him praise and attention. Thus, by doing half as much as he was assigned, he had the time to produce praiseworthy work.

Toward the end of the year of articles, the other students, each overworked, realized what was going on. Revenge burned in their hearts.

But what kind of revenge would be truly fitting? They hit upon the perfect ploy.

Learning that the most senior partner in the firm was to be away for a week, they forged a memo from him—none of these memos were signed, of course—that set out a very large and complicated legal problem supposedly facing one of the firm's largest clients. Being very bright students, they drafted a truly difficult legal problem.

So that Cary could not pass off the task to another, the "senior partner's memo" specifically noted the he wanted Cary to do the work because of the fine things Cary's principal — the lawyer who would sponsor Cary's admission to the Bar—had said about him. The memo was given to Cary on a Friday afternoon, just after the senior partner's departure.

It gave him nine days to do what in effect was a month's work. There was no out.

He was in the office about 18 hours a day during the time he had to complete the work of research and writing. He finished it at two in the morning of the Monday it was due. It was, for a legal mind of mediocre ability, a magnificent piece of work of over 300 pages and 400 legal references. Had he done it in law school, he'd have earned the Gold Medal.

But, of course, it was all bogus.

He marched proudly into the senior partner's office at nine in the morning to submit his magnum opus. The senior lawyer was confused. He had asked for no such work. Cary produced the memo. The senior lawyer said he'd never seen the thing, and certainly had not drafted it.

There was, as you would expect, an investigation. It was not complex or drawn out. The three pranksters were more than happy to admit their complicity and, of course, their reasons for the prank.

There was a full review of the files to substantiate the students' allegations while the hapless Cary stood red-faced, caught in a deceitful web of his own making. Two dozen original memos to him were easily found to have been misdirected to others.

The partners of the firm met to consider the situation. They had in their midst, a forger, a phony, a lazy person with a lazy, second- or third-class mind, and no principles at all. Simply choosing him to article in the firm was an embarrassment to them all. That he would forever trade on their high reputation by saying, "Oh, yes, I articled at the law firm of so-and-so," was more than they could take.

Cary's principal met with him to say that, in the circumstances he could not sponsor Cary for admission to the Bar. Cary was staring total catastrophe in the face. It would be the loss of a year, of course, but such an action without explanation would lead to legal community rumours likely to destroy his carefully constructed reputation and severely harm his prospects. But Cary understood that, if the law firm was putting him in a difficult position, Cary had the firm in an awkward position as well, since the scandal would reflect badly on the reputation the firm had crafted over 75 years. Thus he made them an offer, as is said, they couldn't refuse.

Cary said that if he were sponsored for admission to the Bar in the province, he promised to immediately leave the province and never, ever return to practice law there. He knew this would appeal to the firm's partners and, indeed, he had his way. He left town, his reputation intact except for a very small group in the firm who, over the years, gossiped and shook their heads in disbelief as they watched his rise in the world, but who rarely shared their dishonourable secret with others.

Once free of the threat of loss of reputation, Cary made his way to Toronto where he honed his previously described skills of charm and manipulation in a business where knowledge of the law was useful, but membership in the Ontario Bar unnecessary, although his business card said that he had been admitted to the Bar of his home province.

In the meantime, the political winds had changed and he had tacked accordingly. Thus, he found his way to Ottawa shortly after making himself useful to the organization that supported the man who became the new Prime Minister. Not shy, he asked for a job in a Minister's office. This was granted. The Minister was not consulted, nor was he pleased.

Now this Minister was never considered any sort of genius, but he was widely believed to be a solid political talent with a good future ahead of him. He had worked hard for his successes in life, was careful with his money, considerate, and honest. And he saw through Cary right away. A bit of a perfectionist, he used Cary's first mistake as an excuse to fire him. Cary went whining to his friends in the Prime Minister's Office. They tried to place him elsewhere. Since the story of his firing was well known, and the reasons for it, there were no takers. So they found him a menial job in the Prime Minister's office.

Cary didn't actually become an Assistant to the Prime Minister. Rather he became an assistant to one of the Assistants.

He complained not at all. In a world of Insiders and Outsiders, he had made it Inside, if only barely. He set about reinventing himself once again. For instance, since his government-supplied business card accurately described his title, Cary instead had cards of his own printed that said, with magnificent simplicity and vagueness, "Special Assistant to The Prime Minister". This was noticed, but nobody was concerned about it.

His was not a demanding job and as with his time in the law firm Cary was free to wander about doing things other than those assigned to him. Over a period of months he was able to be useful to several genuine Special Assistants, such that they would ask him to undertake certain tasks. If interested, Cary leapt. If not, he begged off.

But one expenditure of time he found useful was to attend meetings. Cabinet Committee meetings, interdepartmental meetings, strategy meetings were all available to him. Because he was on the PMO staff, he was trusted, and because he was so under-occupied with his real job, he could become nearly ubiquitous—attending many, many meetings, involving matters across the whole of the Government. No one was ever very sure why he was there, or who might have sent him, such is the general confusion of most PMO organizations. And he said little, mostly occupying himself with note-taking. He took detailed, complete notes. For what purpose, no one knew.

The notes complemented the photocopies of the Cabinet documents and other briefing and research material that came into his possession; almost everything going on in the government flows through the PMO. During his four years there, he accumulated 63 filing boxes of documents, all neatly catalogued and cross-referenced.

Thus, he developed a knowledge and understanding of the whole government—its policies and ways and its senior personnel—likely unequalled by anyone outside the lifers in the Privy Council Office. And because he was "calling from the PMO" every Deputy Minister and senior official would take his call, answer his questions, or accept his invitation to lunch or dinner. He and his attractive and charming wife became known for their well attended and sparkling dinner parties. And his calls to senior businessmen, "calls from the PMO," also expanded his contact list as well as his knowledge of who was who and how things worked.

In due course, Cary found himself able to take on an interesting task.

An election was coming in 18 months or so. The Party was particularly vulnerable to the loss of seats in one area of the country and a strategy was required. Cary volunteered to prepare a strategy.

Now, it would take someone of Cary's uniquely greasy personality to come up with the strategy he did. It was a masterful document from someone with very little electoral experience. What was required, said the memo in essence, was the appointment of someone senior enough in the political structure to command the resources necessary to turn around the government's political fortunes. He recommended the Minister who had fired him. The Prime Minister's advisers all agreed this was a solid idea of great promise, and the PM invited the designated Minister in for a chat. Since Ministers rarely say "No" to the PM, the deed was done.

But, protested the Minister, while he could act as the facilitator, chairman, and boss of this effort, he needed someone with real political talent to assemble a staff and run the operation.

Cary's memo had anticipated such a demand and suggested as the perfect candidate a senior assistant to the PM. He could not refuse the honour either and he left the PMO, putting Cary in a position to spin an even wider web. Over the next year, as the Minister and the former assistant carried on with their vain task—and it was a vain task—and as things did not go well, Cary was always there to pointedly and sympathetically offer excuses as to why the strategy was not working. By election night, the loss in the area in question was huge and while, in reality, it was a loss for which the whole government bore responsibility, it was the Minister and his carefully picked campaign staff that bore the blame.

The Minister himself was re-elected.

The Prime Minister took a two-week holiday to consider his various options. He had to find a new direction for his government and as part of doing that, restructure his Cabinet. That meant retiring the tired, the old, the unpopular and the unproductive in favour of ambitious minds and new faces.

The staff of the PMO assembled papers on the subject for the PM's consideration, Cary volunteered for the job of clerking the process and was thereby able to put his thumb on the scale of judgments here and there. The PM then called in Ministers, reassigning some, thanking a few, retiring several. Cary's former Minister was retired. No reason was given by the PM, who actually liked the fellow as a person, but since he had been so publicly identified with such a serious political failure, it was necessary that he go. Accountability it is called.

The afternoon of the Cabinet changes, Cary called his real estate agent and told him to expect to see a new listing of a house for sale on Clemow Avenue. The real estate agent was directed to make the offer for whatever was the asking price, with no conditions, in the name of someone the realtor had never heard of before, but he of course agreed. The name was Cary's wife's maiden name. She came from a wealthy family. Cary and his wife had no reason to tour the house because they had been guests in it at social functions many times.

Cary got the house and for a very good price. The owner had just lost his job as a Cabinet Minister, he had told the realtor, and could not afford to carry the mortgage. He would, in any event, be returning to the part-time practice of law in his constituency. He was delighted to have such an expensive house sold so quickly. He told the realtor that he hoped the new owners would enjoy it, that it was a great house for entertaining.

Within weeks Cary left the PMO. Without any evidence to support it other than four years of self-promotion over PMO-paid-for lunches, during which he leaked tantalizing pieces of insider gossip, he had developed a reputation such that several large, well-paying organizations were prepared to have him in their employ at an extravagant retainer. He chose well, rose high, became rich, and nobody chose to remember his faults.

That he had stolen 63 filing boxes of photocopied Cabinet documents was not something he ever mentioned. But the information contained in them gave him authoritative background any time he had to brief a CEO, or advise a client.

His cousin had said about him, though, that Cary had learned early in life that he could slide further on shit than sandpaper. After a few years on Clemow, however, he had made too much money, and had become so socially prominent, that Clemow Avenue no longer suited. He moved to Rockcliffe.

How One Person Makes a Difference

Brent rushed up the stairs to the Vancouver Club and through the doors at 12:15, annoyed that he had been kept in court an extra half hour because the other law firm had sent an ill prepared junior to Chambers, wasting everyone's time. In the gloom of the lobby, the Senator was not in evidence. Brent strode to the reading room at the rear, in the belief that Senator George Vail would be catching up on the foreign news.

George was not there, either. Brent turned to go back to the lobby as the Senator emerged from the men's room.

"Aha!"

"You're late," accused George, a stickler for other people's promptness, although less strict about his own.

"Ah, geez, I had to break in a junior that Dumoulin's sent to Chambers. Sorry."

"Where to? The main dining room?" He answered his own question as Brent nodded.

They went back down the wide hall and through the lobby to the bottom of the staircase to the second floor, each nodding or saying some pleasantry to others who were loitering there, awaiting the arrival of their luncheon companions. Between the two of them, these twin political operators knew half the business people in town, and nearly all the members of Vancouver's most prestigious club. As they climbed the stairs, George said, out of no-where, "Do you think we could fight an election in B.C. with any hope of improving things if one were to be called in the next while?"

Brent reflected. So that was the purpose of the urgent call to lunch. He was a reflective sort of guy in such circumstances. It was his many years as a lawyer. He'd learned that clients tended to be willing to pay more if they thought time had been spent on his answers. And they were more likely to take his advice.

As they entered the main dining room, the maitre d' greeted them by name.

"A quiet table by the window, please, Louis." Louis smiled at the Senator and led the two of them over to a back corner table. The dining room was not full, and the Senator judged they could have a private discussion. As he sat down, he looked out the window to the magnificent harbour view. "I love that view", he said, to no one in particular.

They picked their napkins out of the water glasses as a waiter quietly approached and filled them. Ice tinkled over the edge of the pitcher.

The waiter, surmising that the Senator was host, even though both were members, placed an order chit and stubby pencil in front of him, then wordlessly walked away.

"Not really. That is, not in the sense we could pick up seats. We haven't expected an election and there has been no organized search for good candidates so, no," was Brent's long-delayed response.

George had not expected any other answer.

"What about Centre, though? Might Robbie go again? Could we take that one back from the NDP at least?

Again, Brent thought carefully before answering carefully. "I don't think Centre is winnable for some time because of that goddamn Harbourview Development project and that bloody ugly All-Seasons hotel perched right on the edge of Stanley Park. That park is hallowed ground in this town, as you know, and that we seemed to have either negligently or purposefully stood by and let it happen curses us in that riding for at least one, maybe two more elections. And Robbie is the perceived author of the mess. I doubt whether his own constituency organization would even nominate him again, despite his record, his talents, his energy and his dedication. Everybody thinks he screwed up. And that's that. Finis."

It was a bitter judgment, but George didn't disagree.

"I just can't understand exactly how that happened, for the life of me," said Brent. "It's the ugliest, most offensive piece of development in Vancouver's history. And that's saying something. The architects here in Vancouver seemed to have mostly studied their craft in East Berlin. Or Moscow. It's awful. It's worse than that goddam white shoebox of a department store that Eaton's built at Georgia and Granville. Vancouver will never forgive the Eaton family for that one. And Robbie knew how to stop that mess down the street. How was it allowed to happen?"

He was referring to 14 acres of waterfront land along Georgia Street between the entrance to Stanley Park and Denman Street. For the first half of the 20th century, this land and Coal Harbour— the adjacent water— was an industrial area serving the marine trades. There were boat builders and boat repair works, floating offices, moored tugs and fishboats, and any number of marine service companies. After the Second World War, the area went into a steep decline and was, by the late '50s, an ugly industrial slum. Into this strode a New York entrepreneur heading a land development company which bought up the privately held pieces to assemble five acres of land along Georgia Street, Vancouver's major east-west thoroughfare that led from downtown to Stanley Park—Vancouver's jewel—and beyond that to the Lions Gate Bridge across Burrard Inlet to the North Shore. Since forever, people walking or driving down Georgia could look across the low-rise buildings of the slum and see boats in Coal Harbour, the south shore of the park, Deadman's Island, Burrard Inlet and the North Shore mountains beyond.

When the New Yorker put his holdings up for sale, some local business men formed Harbourview Developments Inc. and picked up both the freehold lands and some leases on water-lots—owned by the Federal government—he had assembled. They then spent several years accumulating the remaining water-lot lease assignments in front of the freehold until they had 14 acres.

The water-lots were nine acres of federal government-owned land administered by the National Harbours Board. Originally true 'water'-lots, that is they were immersed at low tide, they had mostly been filled by a multitude of tenants over the previous 70 years to expand the land area. There were about two dozen individual parcels, many quite small, many no longer occupied, but about half were still being used by operating businesses. In negotiations, businesses occupying the water-lots had to find other sites to move to, and Harbourview Developments had both to pay for all this, and to be patient. It had taken five years. Another year was spent negotiating with the NHB to have all the lot leases consolidated into one lease with a common expiry date many years hence.

Harbourview Developments then took the land package to an eastern Canadian company that operated the All-Seasons Hotel chain, and sold them on the idea of building a hotel on the site. Since the Bayshore Hotel already existed two blocks away, built on the waterfront a dozen years earlier without any expression of civic concern, the deal was swiftly put together. But the new development company was not satisfied with just a 13-storey, 650 room hotel. They went to City Hall with a proposal to build three, 13-storey condominium buildings right on the water and three 33-storey towers along Georgia Street. These were twice the height of any other building in the area. There was to be underground parking for 2000 cars. City Hall approved the plan without a murmur or public hearings, almost in secret.

The buildings were without architectural merit. They were ugly, blocky, grey, Stalinist monstrosities. No consideration was given to neighbours, or sight-lines, or anybody's view from Georgia Street or elsewhere in the mid-rise apartments behind it. There had been, after the fact, a huge public uproar but City Hall had already provided permits. Nothing, the civic politicians said, could be done.

It being that most of the land was owned by the federal government through the National Harbours Board, however, and the constituency was represented in Parliament by one Robbie Burden, a senior Minister, an appeal was made to Ottawa to stop this horror. It was to no avail. The monstrosity had been built, and the development had become the major issue in the subsequent election campaign. Burden had been defeated. Badly.

"How did it happen?" asked George, rhetorically. "They figured out how to get rid of the abominable no-man."

"What?" said Brent. "What's that?"

"Oh," smiled George, satisfied with his cleverness. "It's a reference to a short story by J. Northcott Parkinson—you know, Parkinson's Law—in which he made the point that in trying to get something approved in a multi-layered bureaucracy you had to figure out how to avoid anyone that might say 'no'—that is, the 'abominable no-man.'"

"So, how's that relevant?"

"Well, it's a longish story about how somebody figured out who the abominable no-man was, then figured out how to make him disappear. Poof."

"Do tell. No, just a second. Let's order," interjected Brent.

"Buffet," said George, decisively.

"Me too," said Brent, and George wrote '2 buffets' on the chit. "Wine? Beer?"

Brent nodded. "A small carafe of the House Red. Its an easy afternoon."

George put the chit to the side and looked at Brent.

"Have you not found it curious that a smallish ad agency in Vancouver picked up the All-Seasons Hotel ad account worldwide?"

"Yes. And I was surprised when Terry Everest left Robbie's staff so suddenly."

"It's not surprising when you look at the job he landed," responded the Senator. He went from about $18,000 a year, no perks, no thanks and no future, slaving 18 hours a day, six and a half days a week for Robbie, to about six times that salary as a VP of Abbott Broadcasting. He's making almost as much as you." This latter was a standing joke. Brent was a senior lawyer in a large firm—much larger than the Senator's, and he fought big cases for serious money. Politics for him was an avocation. For the Senator it was life itself.

"I've also been curious as to what it was in Terry's resume that got him a job paying that kind of money," Brent went on.

"Well, I don't wonder, because I happen to know that the radio and TV broadcasting community were very pleased with the work Terry did in getting some legislation through Parliament the previous year. I watched him gently but persuasively push it through the Senate and the House both. It was well done. I happen to know several of the big broadcasters were also very impressed and one even asked me what he could do to recruit Terry. He'd talked to Terry himself, and been turned down. You know how devoted Terry was to Robbie," said George.

The waiter brought the carafes of wine, interrupting them.

"Then the answer maybe lies in the fact—I guess—that Robbie was not equally loyal to Terry." Brent thought this was not exactly true, but voiced the thought anyway.

George knew exactly to what Brent was referring. They all thought Robbie had made a big mistake at the time.

"Well," responded George, "I think Terry thought that."

"OK, so Terry didn't become Executive Assistant when Gillie left, but what does that have to do with Harbourview Developments.?" asked Brent.

"You know, you're an experienced lawyer and politician," George said. "And you know that not much happens by accident. And you know that the best lobby—the best kind of getting a government to do something—or to not do something—is when nobody's fingerprints are on it," George spelled out. "And still none of this you find curious? It was the best, cleverest coup pulled off in a generation, even though I hate the results."

"Okay," responded Brent, "But all I know of some of the background to Terry's concern about Harbourview Developments is that when that bunch of influential people from Vancouver showed up in Ottawa, protesting the federal leases to Harbourview Developments and very angry, it caught both Robbie and Terry by surprise. But after the meeting Terry supposedly said to Robbie that this was serious and he was going to look into it.

"I know also that he called the Transport Minister's Special Assistant in charge of NHB stuff and asked to be provided with a copy of every single piece of paper on the Harbourview Developments file and on that land since—and here I am quoting him, 'since 1896'. Two days later he took all three filing boxes home and spent the weekend poring over them. By Sunday, he was in an outrage over what he found. After that, it became something of a fixation for him and he never took the boxes back to the office. But that's about all I know."

Brent obviously knew quite a lot, George thought to himself.

"Let's get to the buffet while there's still a choice," interjected Brent. The Senator led the way amongst the tables to the heaping buffet table near the entrance door, nodding and shaking hands as he went past friends and supplicants.

They returned to their table, smoothed their napkins on their laps, and each took a mouthful. Before his second, Brent said, "Go on."

"Go on?" responded the Senator, seeming mildly confused.

"And," enquired Brent, patiently, slowly, "what happened next?"

George caught his train of thought.

"Oh, well, Terry showed up in the office early on Monday and tracked Robbie down in the West Block cafeteria, having coffee. He told Robbie that he had spent the weekend on the documents and a memo was being typed and it would be on Robbie's desk by noon, but if Robbie wanted, he could provide a six-word summary. I know this from what Robbie told me. Robbie asked for the six-word summary. Terry said, 'It looks like somebody was bribed.'

"Robbie told me that he asked Terry how he had come to that conclusion. Terry said that, of the total of 14 acres, just over nine were NHB—or about two-thirds. Harbourview Developments had negotiated a deal to get the nine acres from the NHB under three successive 22-year leases for $59,000 a year with no review of the appropriateness of the rent, no inflation adjustment factor, no anything for the whole 66 years.

"However, Harbourview Development was sub-leasing the whole 14 acre package to All-Seasons for $469,000 a year, indexed to inflation and re-opening the lease to adjust the rent every 22 years. Inflation now is running at about 10 per cent a year. So Harbourview Developments gets an increase—an increase mind you— just this year, equal almost to what they are paying the NHB in total. Everything else is pure, incredible, profit. Terry found it outrageous. The NHB over 66 years would get less than $4 million in total. The Harbourview Developments guys would get about a billion, depending on compounding inflation rates. Terry could not conceive of anybody—even the NHB lease negotiators—being that stupid, although I disagree with him. So if it was not stupidity, he reasoned it had to be bribery and he thought all these documents he had would inevitably and eventually become public and create a huge scandal and that Robbie would wear it. That's what Robbie told me Terry said. However, he also thought even without the financial side becoming public that it was a development that was too dense, in the wrong place and if anybody could make the design—never mind the deal—stick to Robbie, it would be a political disaster which is, of course, what happened. He was absolutely right."

Even the usually low-key Senator was getting upset just in telling his side of the story.

Brent let him go on.

"Robbie asked Terry 'What next?' and Terry said he didn't know. It was all very complicated and it was three boxes of papers but he told Robbie that he thought that, somewhere, somehow, in all that paper there just had to be a flaw that Robbie could use to make some changes in the development. Somebody had to have made a mistake, somewhere, sometime, during about 75 years. He said to Robbie that he didn't think the project could be stopped, but that maybe it would be enough if Robbie could force some changes in density and design to make it politically acceptable.

"Robbie thought that was fine and Terry continued to spend weekends on those boxes much to the annoyance of his wife and children. They were kept at his house and worked on in what his wife laughingly referred to as his spare time. It took him about three months of incredibly complicated analysis of each individual parcel, going back over 70 years to finally discover that there was a single small water-lot in the middle—sort of a keyhole at the end of Gilford Street—that Ottawa had given the city in 1918 so the city would always have water access at its street endings. The catch was that if the water-lot—it was tiny—66 feet by 132—about a fifth of an acre was to be used for any non-public purpose, it had to be returned to the federal government. For Terry, the game then became one of quietly and patiently playing footsie with the city's lawyers to get the water-lot signed back to the federal government through a quitclaim, then for Robbie to refuse to turn it over to Harbourview Developments until he had extracted some concessions."

"And what happened so that things fell off the rails?" interjected Brent.

"Well, the spider in the soup became Graham Small, you know, the genius behind West Coast Advertising. He and Robbie's Executive Assistant Gillie Robson were good friends. Gillie used him as a source of political information about Vancouver, and Graham used Gillie as a source about what was going on in Ottawa. In Graham's business it's useful to appear to know what's going on in politics. There was a long outstanding offer from Graham to Gillie to come back to Vancouver to join him in the ad firm as a VP once Gillie had the political stuff out of his veins. It would pay about three times his EA salary. This was no secret.

"At one lunch, as I understand it," George continued, "Graham told Gillie that he thought the Harbourview Developments project was going to be a disaster for Robbie in the next election. Gillie let it slip that Terry Everest had a solution to the problem but it would take time to jell. On another occasion, Gillie also told Graham, in responding to another entreaty, that he—Gillie—had told Robbie he would be leaving in a few months and Robbie should begin to think about who should replace him as EA. Indiscreetly, Robbie discussed some options with Gillie, but offered that he would not be promoting Terry, 'Too valuable where he is', said Robbie. This, unfortunately, Gillie also passed on to Small.

"Graham, who is a clever guy, apparently began to consider the possibilities of the circumstances. He knew that the All-Seasons guys and the Harbourview Development folks were both concerned about some negative things Robbie had said in public and had concluded that there was—or might be—a glitch somewhere. That is, as I said earlier, an abominable no man. Gillie had also confided to that damned Vancouver Sun columnist Alex Feltham—an old newspaper crony—that the project would never be built as it was, and Alex told everybody in town that by writing it in his column. So...."

"So?" said Brent.

"So Graham then approaches the All-Seasons VP and establishes that they are in fact very worried. Very, very worried. The VP says he thinks that Robbie will find some way to screw them up, but they didn't know how. Graham says he can fix it. His price is the worldwide ad account for five years. He knows that will make him rich. They agree, but it's subject to a timing clause, so Graham has to move quickly.

"Graham says he needs the help of one of the shareholders in Harbourview Developments. Surprised at the request, but agreeable, the shareholder does what's asked. Now—I'm not going to mention any more names—the laws of libel being what they are, and what I am about to tell to being very close to bribery."

"Okay, but I still don't see the connections, here," admitted Brent.

George continued.

"Simple. Graham says to Gillie, 'Look, the business is really growing. I really need you now—not a year from now. I can pay X dollars—lots more than you're currently making and you've already told Robbie you'd be leaving, so it's a little sooner.' Gillie considers, and asks Robbie if this creates a problem. Robbie doesn't object.

"Then comes the critical part. Terry of course finds out later the same day that Gillie is leaving and asks Robbie about the EA promotion. Robbie in that charming way he has—you've seen that charm—says, and again I quote, 'You're too valuable where you are.' This outrages Terry, who really wants it and knows he's earned it. The next day—the very next day— the president of Abbott Broadcasting—quite coincidentally, of course," said the Senator, sarcastically, "calls Terry and takes him to a fine lunch at the Rideau Club the day after. Terry is still fuming. It was a fine lunch. Good wine. Lots of it. Compliments are offered about the job Terry did on that legislation the previous year. As I say, some alcohol was consumed, which led to Terry letting down his hair. Anyway, by 2 p.m. Terry has agreed to consider the offer of a VP, Operations at Abbott which, again coincidentally, the president has the offer all typed up and ready for signing in his jacket breast pocket. With very generous salary numbers, mind you.

"Terry returns to the office and again catches up to Robbie after Question Period, about 3:30, and asks Robbie if he's heard the last word on the EA job. Robbie praises him to the skies, tells him how absolutely central he is to all of Robbie's hopes and prayers, and says no to the promotion."

Brent by this time has finished his lunch. The Senator, because of his monologue, stops speaking for a minute while he, too, cleans up his plate. Brent sips his wine.

George continued. "Terry goes back to his office and writes out a letter of resignation, effective two weeks hence, and has it hand-delivered to Robbie, who was in a Cabinet committee meeting. Robbie gets the letter, thinks it's a bluff, takes Terry to dinner and tries to charm him. Terry is really pissed off but Robbie just doesn't get it. There was some confusion in Robbie's mind after the dinner as to exactly what Terry's intentions were, or so he says and expects the letter of resignation to be just forgotten. But Terry leaves, as scheduled, two weeks later, and goes on holidays with his wife to Europe, where Robbie cannot reach him. He sneaks back into Ottawa after a month, does not answer Robbie's messages, and moves to Toronto."

"It's then announced that Abbott has a new VP?"

"You got it."

The waiter arrived to remove the plates and silverware. Another was right behind him with the coffee.

"OK. This has all been an interesting story, but what does this have to do with Harbourview Developments?" Brent asked.

George smiled and gently waved his hand. "Let me tell this my way."

"Well, what Graham Small knew was that one of the low-key Directors of Harbourview Developments was also a director and major shareholder in Abbott, and was someone that was on very good terms with the president of Abbott. All he had to do was to pass on to the president that Terry was very, very unhappy working for Robbie, and if the Abbott folks wanted him, that week—that very week, like right now—would be a perfect time to make the pitch, especially if it were a generous one. So, Abbott did, it was, and Terry left. It was, of course, common knowledge in the industry that everybody was sort of after Terry because of that legislation the previous year. But Abbott got there on exactly the right day with exactly the right offer, when Terry was feeling badly betrayed and sorry for himself and bought him a great lunch."

Brent thought about all this while he sipped his coffee.

"But how did this lead to the Harbourview Development mess?"

"George smiled again. "Simple. Suddenly Robbie, who's a very busy man, is minus two senior aides. The replacements are decidedly the second team—you know them, we've discussed this. Neither of them knows the Harbourview Developments file. In fact Terry still had the files at home so the new guys don't even know where to find the files. Suddenly, there is nobody on Robbie's staff to play footsie under the table with city hall anymore, and nobody is watching those sons-of-bitches at the NHB. Then one day the quitclaim is sent to Ottawa, and the day after that the waterlot gets included in the package by some NHB gnome, and the horse is out of the barn before Robbie and his half-asleep greenhorn staff even know about it."

"Then how did the media discover that Robbie bungled the opportunity to stop the project?" asked Brent.

"I don't know the answer to that one. But I suspect it was someone inside Harbourview Developments. By this time, even though they won, they had come to hate Robbie. So they leaked the story—without too many details—that Robbie had bungled. There was even a hint, as you know, that Robbie had done it for a sizable political—or maybe 'personal'—contribution. Whatever it was, it sunk him."

"And how did you learn all this complicated story?"

"That's an interesting question with a complex answer. First, a lawyer in my firm did some of the legal work for Harbourview. Second, I had a long lunch with Gillie when he got back here, and he expressed concerns for Robbie's political health if Terry left. Third, a legal colleague of mine in Toronto called me at the time to discuss Terry—he was working on the formal offer of employment and let it slip that there was urgency involved. And, fourth, I know most of the people, and after All-Seasons gave its ad account to West Coast, I just put it all together. Easy. Getting rid of the abominable no-man."

"What does Terry think of all this?" asked Brent.

"I hear he just doesn't care. He's still mad at Robbie. And he lives in a nice big house in Toronto and doesn't have to look at the monstrosity."

"So," said the Senator, finishing his coffee, and rising to leave the table, "that's how we got a huge, dense, ugly, concrete wall at the edge of Stanley Park. You know, we Liberals would have been a lot better off with no development there. Just a nice 14 acre open space with some shrubs and a few trees. A park just outside a park. Maybe Robbie would have got re-elected. It's interesting to think of the things that might have been, and how one person can make such a difference."

Brent said, "Yes. But back to practical matters. What should we be doing to get ready for an election?

(As anyone who has visited Vancouver's Stanley Park knows, there is no huge, highrise and hotel development adjacent to the Park. Instead, there is a 14 acre park.)

Lobbying

The Plan

After the last executive arrived, Bill Long asked everyone to take a seat. There was a shuffling around as most refilled their coffee cups, and a few took a croissant or Danish pastry to their seats around the large oval boardroom table.

The executives waited for Bill to begin his presentation. He had been hired to develop a roadmap for their industry to follow out of their 15-year nightmare of government interference with their industry. They had told him they were fed up and were prepared to accept any advice, make any effort and spend any amount of money to achieve some meaningful change in their circumstance.

They had, they related, made other attempts to try to address the challenge, going so far as to try to hire away from government the very senior official that was at the heart of their problem, but no strategy so far had produced so much as the slightest hope of relief. They had finally come to Bill, who had the reputation for being the best government-relations strategist and political adviser in Canada. He had told them it would take six months to develop a strategy, and he told them the cost. These senior executives, used to making decisions in the several hundred million dollar range, initially objected to an initial fee-plus-expenses contract in the mid-six-figure range, but Bill had countered, "If you accept my advice, this will be a very, very small percentage of the reward, but also a small percentage of the cost of doing what must be done. Either you're serious about this, or you're not. If you just want to keep whining about things, don't bother me. If you want to get serious, then face the reality that change comes at a substantial price and with great effort."

They dithered but finally had to agree. They were desperate. Today they would find out if it were worth it.

"Gentlemen," Bill began, "I want to thank you all for being here. I know you're each very busy, but it's my firm belief that the success of what I'm about to propose is entirely dependent on timing and a delay of a month or two right now might well make this project much more difficult."

The 12 men present were the chief executive officers or chief operating officers of the six multinational pharmaceutical manufacturing companies in Canada, as well as senior officers from six companies that didn't have manufacturing operations in Canada, but a major distribution presence. Two were from the United States, two from Britain, and one each from France and Switzerland.

"I know that some of you have travelled a long way. I hope you find today's presentation worthwhile."

Bill didn't believe in elaborate presentations. He thought that more often than not they detracted from the message. Instead, his would be an oral presentation with a large pad of paper on an easel that he would use if he needed to make the points he wanted to emphasize.

He began with a historical overview designed to bring the foreigners into the same frame of reference as the Canadians.

"I suppose I should begin with the Harley Report. Dr. Harry Harley was a Member of Parliament who chaired a Parliamentary Committee on the pricing of prescription drugs in Canada 20 years ago, in 1963. The conclusion of his Committee's Report in 1965 after months of hearings and much research was that most of the prescription drugs your companies sold were priced higher here than in any other country in the world. Any other country in the world." He emphasized the last sentence as he repeated it.

There was a murmur of disagreement and one company president who Bill remembered as Al, said, "There were a lot of half-and quarter-truths in that Report." Heads nodded, more murmurs.

"I don't dispute that," responded Bill. "I only repeat what the news media said what the Report said because that's the perception by many people, in the government and out who accepted the veracity of the Harley Committee report and that perception is the reality you're facing, and must address.

"Look, I could go back to the early 1920s, and talk about the roots of attempts by our government to address Canadian drug manufacturing policy, prices and patents. The issue you're trying to address today, in 1983, didn't begin 15 or 20 years ago. It began a long time before that. But until Harley, for many years, government action was essentially timid. It was the current government that responded to Harley, that has seen it's legislation result in dramatic decreases in drug prices and, of course, in the profits of your companies. We've also seen a significant increase in generic drug manufacturing in Canada and for that the government's very proud of itself. Case closed. You've to get the battles of the past 18 years behind you, and move on. There are changes coming here that will result in new opportunities for your industry. But forget past calumnies and let's look ahead. We—you—have to look at the opportunities."

Al nodded. "Okay, so we look ahead. I promise to be quiet while you spell it out."

Bill looked around the table. The response was a general agreement. Four of his audience had taken the opportunity to light cigarettes. Bill hated cigarette smoke, but said nothing.

"Let's go on."

"Now, as you know, the Harley Committee recommendations led to the Minister of Consumer and Corporate Affairs, Ron Basford, introducing Bill C-102 in 1969, which amended the Patent Act to allow for other drug companies to copy your patented drugs by obtaining a so-called Compulsory License and paying you a modest licensing fee. A very modest licensing fee. Over the past 13 years a significant Canadian-based generic drug manufacturing industry has sprung up to manufacture not just drugs for which they obtained compulsory licenses for the manufacture of drugs to which you hold a patent, but they also have manufactured drugs that were no longer subject to the patent monopoly and have begun selling those, too, at much lower prices than you charge. So I can see why you are angry."

"Angry is not the appropriate word," interjected another company president. Bill couldn't recall his name for a few seconds, then it came to him. The guy's name was Harley. Bill smiled to himself.

Harley went on. "I operate a division, the Canadian division, within a worldwide corporate structure. Through no fault of mine, and solely because of this goddamn legislation, my division shows almost the lowest profits in the world. It pisses me off!"

"Well," Bill responded, "if you take my advice, do as I tell you, stick with it in the face of new challenges as they spring up, and realize it will be a permanent war of growing complexity, then we can get back almost to the good old days. But likely not all the way to the good old days. Will that satisfy you?

"How long is this going to take, and how much money?" This from Al.

"I think we can do it within three years, but five at the outside. The cost will be about, I think, a hundred million dollars, but that's a very rough number."

The look of astonishment on the faces of everyone was immediate. A president—Andre, Bill remembered—stood up, saying, "You're mad. I'm not going to listen to such nonsense."

"Sit down, Andre," said Al, "We've paid a lot of money for this lecture, so lets stay until the end." Andre sat.

Bill began again.

"I think rather than take you through this one piece at a time, I'd better give you the big picture then we can discuss the details. OK?"

It was okay.

"Let me list off the opportunities facing us. First, Brian Mulroney replaced Joe Clark as leader of the Tories last month. This is good. Mulroney is a stronger believer in markets than is Clark, and he's greedier." This comment produced a perplexed look on Al's face.

"What I mean, Al, is that Mulroney really wants to get things done. He'll take gambles others wouldn't, in the name of greater success. Clark is far more cautious, irrespective of his putting the leadership of his Party in play, gambling he'd get re-elected leader." There was no response from Al, and the others remained quiet, listening.

"Second, I believe that Mulroney will win the general election next summer, and he could well win big. Very big."

"I question that," objected Andre. "Trudeau has made startling comebacks before. And what if the Liberals choose another leader?"

"Let me digress to answer that, because my strategy depends absolutely on Mulroney becoming PM. The Liberal Party has become a tired and divided Party. Divided on many levels, over many issues—the deficit, the extreme nationalism of the Foreign Investment Review Act, the effects of the National Energy Policy, the disagreements over the repatriation of the Constitution and adoption of the Charter, and so on. There's a revival in separatist sentiment coming in Quebec over the constitution that can, and I believe will, be harvested by the Tories. Mulroney understands Quebec, particularly rural, backwoods Quebec, better than just about anyone I know. He's done well as a lower class boy from Baie Comeau, but he remembers how people in non-metropolitan Quebec think and he relates, he communicates with them. You watch. And I think Ontario is tired of Trudeau and of Liberal nostrums. And I don't care who will be the Liberal leader, he's just not going to have the time needed to heal all that Party's and the county's ills before he's got to go…call an election. I've had a close look at the possible replacements for Trudeau. None have what it would take. Some of your money has been spent on very sophisticated and expensive polling."

Andre put up his hand, and Bill indicated he should speak.

"Turner?"

Bill began a grin that developed into a short laugh.

"Likely the worst choice, for four reasons. First, politics and the country have changed and the government has changed, in huge ways, since he left politics eight years ago.

"Second, he hasn't kept up, he's still a product of the mid-'60s, if not the '50s. And he doesn't realize he hasn't kept up. His closest advisers have also mostly been out of circulation. I just don't think that, at 55, he can adapt.

"Second, he's made many enemies within the Liberal Party establishment, the folks around Trudeau and Chretien, over the last few years, as a result of his sniping at them and their policies. Only a little has appeared publicly, but his private comments have been scathing. And they've not remained private because of their very juiciness. So there are lots of people—long-time Party fundraisers and organizers, who will just quietly walk, they won't help in a campaign if he's leader.

"Third, he's seen by too many in the Party as too right-wing. So what exactly the Party will stand for, what a government led by Turner will do, in policy terms, will be a mystery to a great many Liberals. Confused people are poor campaigners.

"Fourth, it was the political theory of Keith Davie that the Liberal Party—a great centrist Party—only lost elections when it was outflanked on its left by the Conservatives. And that's what Mulroney will do—appear to take his Party to the left.

"But, Turner, or no Turner, the Liberals are toast. The next question is, 'What can we do to take advantage of it?' The answer lies in Quebec, of all places."

"Quebec?" It was, again, Andre.

"Quebec. As I said, some of the outrageous money you've spent hiring me went into highly detailed opinion polling and other in-depth psychological research. Those of you," he pointed to four people around the table," who have been represented by ineffective and unhelpful Liberal MPs, yea these many years will, I can tell you, no longer have that problem, or burden, come next summer."

Andre, disbelief in his voice, questioned this statement." How can you say that? The Tories haven't even managed to think about scrounging up candidates in Montreal yet."

"Because", Bill retorted bluntly, "candidates in Quebec are not usually very important. For the past 15, 16 years, Trudeau has been important. But things change. Trudeau, who's now going to depart the scene, has left an 'après moi, le deluge' legacy. He is unpopular. His Party is the one that dishonoured Quebec by shoving a constitutional amendment down its throat. Mulroney will articulate and harness that discontent and take a substantial number of seats—maybe half, maybe a few more—and the political landscape is going to change in Quebec, maybe forever."

Al waved his arm, and Bill nodded towards him.

"Look, I'm not a francophone, but I get along in the language. I've lived in Quebec for, lessee, most of the last 20 years and I just don't see that happening. You're going to have to persuade me."

"Okay, here goes. If you've lived in Quebec for 20 years, you know it's a very fluid and dynamic society. You arrived not long after Duplessis died, when the Provincial Liberals were articulating a 'maitre chez nous'—'masters in our own house,' for our offshore friends—strategy for Quebec. You saw the nationalizing of the power generation industry to create Quebec Hydro, you saw bombs blowing up post-boxes, you saw the FLQ crisis and the election of the separatists, then their defeat. You've lived through Montreal going from the pre-eminent commercial centre in Canada—the pre-eminent commercial centre—to an economic backwater, second to Toronto and quickly slipping because of all this turmoil and change. And you watched Pierre Trudeau bring French power to Ottawa and national affairs. All that change is upsetting all the traditional allegiances, loyalties and perceptions. Opinion in Quebec is, right now, very fluid and I'm betting big that Mulroney is the guy who benefits from it."

"How do we fit in, then?" Al asked.

"You fit in by, first, taking a leading role in finding three or four Tory candidates to run on the West Island of Montreal where you guys have your plants and offices. You make sure these guys understand your businesses and how the guys in Toronto are taking jobs away from you. You create a fundamental resentment."

Al interrupted. "What the hell are you talking about?"

Impatiently, now, Bill said, "Look the Patent Bill—C-102—has resulted in a brand new generic drug manufacturing industry in Canada, and it's almost all located in Ontario. So, the way you tell these guys—the candidates—the story is that Ottawa under the Liberals stole jobs from Quebec, from their constituencies, and one of their jobs when they're elected is to get those jobs back. It's a simple, easy to understand argument dealing with a very complex issue. Politicians like simple."

Bill looked for questions. There were none. Al nodded. Andre smiled.

"So, we find three, maybe four pliable potential candidates, we make sure they get nominated."

" Yes, Andre?"

"How do we do that?"

"A detail, Don't worry. I'll get it done.

"Then we make sure they have enough money and organization to get elected. Then after the election we ask for our legitimate grievances to be addressed. They'll have gone to Ottawa, anyway, well briefed. At this point it's just a matter of managing them."

"To do what?" asked Al.

"First, to get the government to do some studies on how C-102 has worked. With the right terms of reference the independent study will show it's been bad for Quebec. Mulroney will have got elected standing up for Quebec and its hopes. And our four guys just keep pushing."

"Yeah," interjected Rene, who to this point had said nothing, "but those sons of bitches, those public servants in the Department of Consumer and Corporate Affairs will drag their feet until Mulroney has been pensioned off."

Bill looked up at the ceiling for perhaps 30 seconds.

"I wasn't going to go into this right now, because it is a little off-topic, and a little longer term project, but I intend that we get rid of the Consumer Affairs Ministry. I have…other clients…similarly afflicted and the best thing is to…ah…get rid of the Department. Scatter the various divisions about the government, undermine their programs—some of which will survive—and get the individual program budgets cut. The whole focus of consumerism in the government will be destroyed. There will no longer be a Minister of Consumer Affairs to harass business."

"You think you can do that?" said Andre, in disbelief.

"Yes, I got rid of another department once. I can do this, just time and money.

"Now, I'm not saying this will be easy, which brings me to one of the things I have to ask of our American friends, here. I understand the drug industry in the U.S. is among the largest political contributors. Are you guys prepared, do you think, to get your hands dirty?"

He didn't wait for an answer.

"What Mulroney will want to do, first thing he becomes Prime Minister, will be to try to…um…normalize…uh…relations with the US. Because of Trudeau, Reagan and his people have almost entirely frozen Canada out of things important to this country. Mulroney has been getting an earful from the business community and, of course, until recently he was the hired gun in Canada for Hanna Mining. He personally knows the score."

"So, what're you askin'?" said Marvin, a vice president of one of the largest US drug companies.

"Simple. You guys have got to get Reagan to say to Mulroney, 'Before we do anything to help you, you Canadians have got to show some good faith by changing your laws so you respect our patents in Canada, our intellectual property laws. Once you do that, then lets talk.'"

"Mulroney might pee his pants, but your problem is on the way to being solved, at least temporarily."

Al waved his arm again, and Bill knew what the question was.

"Why temporarily? Because Mulroney won't be there forever, the Liberals will come back some day, the Provinces are going to get more involved in all this because they are the Medicare administrators and, if you haven't put in place a better mousetrap, you'll be, within a few years, back to where you are now. So the plan, THE PLAN—capital letters—that I'm giving you has a long term insurance policy in it to protect you. And that's where the many millions of dollars I spoke about comes in."

The mention of money in large amounts got everyone's attention.

"You see, while the plan to get Reagan to talk to Mulroney will work, and getting some mouthpiece MPs elected is important, Mulroney is like every other politician, frightened of public opinion, insecure. Now, as Harley—not you—said, 'Canadians pay the highest drug prices in the world.' If you guys get your way and drug prices go back up, way up, Mr.

Mulroney won't be happy because voters won't be happy, and your generic drug manufacturing opposition will make sure that voters won't be happy. So we need agreement on some ideas to, shall we say, restructure things?"

"What's your…plan?" asked Andre.

"First, you guys do little drug research in Canada. That's one reason why you have no friends, supporters or allies in dealing with your Ottawa problem. You have to change that. Big-time."

Two of his audience began to protest. He waved them to be quiet.

"It's true, don't try to bullshit me. I've seen the numbers. Well, you've all got to decide to do more research here. I'd like to see if, over few years, we can seduce all the medical researchers in the universities to support you. They're influential. You've got to start talking about doing research, boasting about it, raise the profile of what you're doing. Maybe change the name of your organization to something that includes Research. That gives a payoff for higher prices that Mulroney can boast about.

"And, I hate to tell you this, but there's no alternative, you're going to have to agree, as part of the package, to a scheme of drug price controls."

The room erupted, as everyone began to speak and some to yell, all at once. "What'n hell do you mean?" said one. Al could be heard distinctly saying, "You're off your rocker. I've never heard such nonsense." And Andre, saying nothing, looked around at the uproar calmly, took out his cigarettes, lit one, and tossed the package on the table and leaned back in his chair.

Bill stood silent for about two minutes, pokerfaced, answering no one during the tumult. He motioned for everyone to sit down, which one by one they did. Several had used the impromptu break to refill their coffee cups.

"That was a test to see if you were listening."

Some of his audience responded with a guffaw or a smile.

"It was also a statement of factual necessity. You can't allow it to be said that Mulroney has sold out to the drug lobby. This has to be packaged in terms of the broadest public interest. That is, it's in Canada's interests, and our researchers at the universities, that more research take place here. It's in Canada's interests that the integrity of the patent system be restored. 'We're not a nation that pirates other countries' intellectual property.' And so on. But Mr. Mulroney has also to be able to say, 'My government will still be protecting Canadians from excessively high drug prices.'

"Thus, we have to design a pricing scheme that gives Mulroney some camouflage.

"Keep in mind, too, the shape of the future. With Hospital Insurance in the '50s, and Medicare in the '70s, came governments paying more of the total drug bill. And with that came provincial drug insurance plans and they're trying to keep costs down by mandating the use of generic rather than brand-name drugs. That's only going to be a greater trend, with greater pressures on you from the provinces and hospitals. Hospitals will increasingly band together to buy in large quantities. Provinces may eventually do the same. Divide and conquer. You guys are going to have to start to lobby, to participate in the political process at the provincial level, as well, but that's a lecture for another day.

"So, gentlemen, that's THE PLAN. First, we take over part of the Quebec Conservative Party—enough to get our people inside the Government caucus to voice our interests. Second, we then use our power in the U.S. Congress and in the President's office to lever Mulroney into putting patent reform at the top of his list of things to do. Third and while that's going on, each of you has to get whatever authorizations you need to participate in this, then to begin rethinking your whole research effort in Canada. Fourth—and most importantly—we have to reach out to potential allies in the universities, and get them lobbying, and arguing in the media, for more drug research in Canada. Fifth, we have to develop a model for a price control board that will not depress prices more than a little, and make sure that people who...um...understand the industry are appointed to it.

Sixth, we begin to pressure the new government for the dissolution of the Consumer Affairs Ministry.

"Finally, and maybe I should have put this first, you want to have a re-look at your national organization and how you do business. For instance, your industry's behavior was considered totally outrageous during C-102. Your industry cannot have a president that yells at a Minister so loudly that he can be heard in the halls of the West Block through two sound-insulated doors. The Minister decided it was time to start regulating all lobbyists and he hired a young Montreal lawyer named Joe Oliver to write a report and draft legislation in 1969. It didn't go anywhere at the time, but you can no longer behave that way. You need to re-examine your industry association's mandate and its people. Probably a good idea not to have as a president someone out of the industry. You want someone with great communications skills, and political smarts, maybe someone with something of a national reputation. Maybe a former consumer spokesperson of some sort, like Beryl Plumptre. Maybe a politician of some sort, defeated or retired. I'd like to start looking for someone. That okay?"

Al was the first to speak.

"Bill, I know little about public affairs and government and politics. I'm a scientist and a businessman. I can't really judge if you're reaching well beyond your grasp here. I look forward to reading your formal report next week and looking at your proposed budget. You have here a plan of breathtaking ambition and scale and I can't judge if it isn't just fantasy. But I'll say this to you and to my colleagues here, we are desperate men. We have here an industry that's in deep trouble and I guess if we don't do something big here, each of us will be doing something else, for someone else, somewhere else, before long.

"We asked for a strategy. It's going to take a while and a lot of money to do this. I gather that ordinarily you work by the hour or by the month on some kind of retainer. Would you be willing in this case to work on a success basis? That is, very modest billings against defined achievement targets, with a very large fee if we are successful?"

Bill had hoped this question would be asked.

"In principle, yes. But understand that I earn a good living serving the needs of a number of clients. To make this one go, I'm going to have to reduce my other commitments. I'm 45 and I'd like to retire a wealthy man sometime before I wear out my welcome here in Ottawa.

"So, if we're talking a success fee of," and here he almost lost his nerve…" $20 million, yes, I'd be most interested, because I can in fact guarantee success."

His audience did not react.

"Sounds okay to me," said Al, "but obviously we," he motioned to those around him, "have to chat."

"Let's shake on it. You guys will get your binders by Monday. But keep in mind we have to get going." Bill worked his way around the table, thanked each of them for coming to Ottawa and saw them to the elevator.

Bill walked back to his office, shut his door, and put his feet on his desk. He looked sideways, out the window and over to the Parliament buildings.

He thought. "A great plan. Retired at 50, with $20 million in the bank. Time to get to work."

How Ottawa Buys Airplanes

Every so often in some sort of osmotic pressure way, Ottawa decides that the Air Force, as it used to be called, needs some new planes.

At the end of the Second World War, Canada had the third-largest aircraft manufacturing industry in the world, and some of the finest aeronautical engineers. As the companies began to look at the postwar market, one thing was obvious—Canada needed a really good airplane to link up Canada's vast and scattered frontier. The de Havilland company then developed the world famous Beaver in 1947, which lead to larger and increasingly sophisticated aircraft—the Otter, the Twin Otter and so on to today's short-takeoff-and-landing technology.

Canadair, based in Montreal, decided to compete for the commercial airliner market and developed the four-engined North Star in the late 1940s by significantly modifying the well proven Douglas DC4.

Others wanted to explore the developing jet engine technology and began working on civilian jet aircraft. The world's first jet passenger aircraft was built by the A.V. Roe Company—AVRO—in 1949. It was a great plane, and had it been allowed to be developed would've been in commercial production in 1952, six years ahead of the Boeing 707. It didn't have the design problems of the British-built Comet, built contemporaneously. But Ottawa wanted AVRO to focus on developing, and then manufacturing the first—and as it turned out, only—Canadian designed and built fighter aircraft, the CF100, needed for the Korean War, and let the Jetliner go.

AVRO soon began to hear tunes of glory in the idea of developing an advanced fighter jet, and began—at Government urging and expense—to design and build what would be generally considered the most advanced fighter aircraft in the world, the AVRO Arrow. One of the the best teams of airplane designers in the world was gathered together, and six aircraft were built, one flying very impressively by May, 1958. Unfortunately, political and financial concerns caused the Diefenbaker Government to order work stopped on the plane the following February and incredibly to order that all models be cut up into small pieces. The 14,000 people working for AVRO were instantly unemployed and, in a single stroke, Canada's capacity to design and build modern-world class jet aircraft was destroyed.

After that, Canada's air forces were dependent on the products of other countries.

What Canada was flying by 1960 were Sabres and CF 100s, good planes but no longer modern. Canada needed a new plane, and replaced the twin engine CF100 with 200 Lockheed-designed single-engine CF104s, built under license by Canadair of Montreal. They went into service in 1961.

Then, as a supplementary aircraft—CF104s kept falling out of the air—Canada arranged to buy some Northrop-designed CF5 aircraft, also built by Canadair in Montreal, beginning delivery in 1968.

But the international development of advanced aircraft was moving apace and by 1974 the Royal Canadian Air Force—by now called the "Air Command" of the Canadian Forces—which drove every pilot crazy—had begun to lobby for a modern replacement for the 20-year-old CF104, and the too-small CF5.

One day in 1974 my partner William came back from a lunch with an air force General to break the news to us of what was to happen next. I was one of five partners in a consulting company that kept track of what was going on in official Ottawa so we could advise our 25 or so business clients of possible and impending problems that the Government might be causing them. We didn't lobby. We just talked to a lot of bureaucrats—and listened very carefully. We did no work related to government procurement, and none for the aircraft manufacturing business. But William had great contacts in the military and they were often a good source of information about industrial strategy. Hence, the lunch.

He related that the government had decided to give in to air force lobbying and begin the process to indentify, negotiate, and buy a new generation of fighter planes. He then swore us to secrecy, and told us how it was going to go. We listened, fascinated.

First, the air force was going to "long-list" five or six aircraft just to make the competition look fair and open, put them through their paces, then short-list two, which would be considered acceptable, with the final decision to be made on the basis of which manufacturer had the best "industrial offset package". Or so the Government planned. The air force had other ideas about plane purchasing decisions than "industrial offset packages," however.

This latter requires some explaining. As noted, Canada had seen its own capacity to design and build aircraft and related components, avionics and so on, atrophy. Most of our most capable engineers, veterans of the Arrow disaster, had decamped to the U.S. to help develop the man-in-space program and the race for the moon. And while Canada had assembly lines, if Canada were to buy foreign aircraft without conditions relating to "Canadian content," even assembly would not be done in Canada.

So the government set standards, not only for "Canadian–content" for planes built for Canadian use, but for planes built for other countries—countries that naturally enough had similar policies. It was in fact, a mug's game.

And so the air force long listed the Grumman F14 Tomcat, the McDonnell Douglas F15 Eagle, the Panavia Tornado, France's Dassault Mirage, General Dynamics' F16 Fighting Falcon, and the F/A18 Hornet, also by McDonnell Douglas.

We partners watched the unfolding panorama over the next few years.

It took about a year to blow-off the two European fighters and the F15—too-big and too-heavy— and the F14, largely because it was a plane designed for the U.S. Navy.

This left the General Dynamics' F16 and the McDonnell-Douglas F18. The industrial offset battles began.

Now, within the government, there were bureaucratic factions favouring each manufacturer, and contacts—not to say intimacies—had been built up over years and decades. So each manufacturer put their best initial packages forward. In confidence, of course.

But the details of each company's proposal were soon leaked to the other company by their bureaucratic partisans. It wasn't long before Ottawa resembled nothing as much as an Arab bazaar. That is, the bidding kept going up. And all the analysis that was being done was not limited to the Defence Department. No. There was a Department of Regional Economic Expansion, dedicated to trying to improve economic activity in the poorer regions of the country. There was the Manpower Department, arguing for more training programs in the industrial offset packages. There was of course, the Department of Industry, wanting a better deal on technology transfers to improve Canadian productivity, innovation and manufacturing capacity. Peripherally, there was the Ministry of Energy and Mines, which also had economists it wanted to keep busy, the Labour Ministry, likewise, and the Finance Department, with no particular axe to grind but wanting to keep its nose in everywhere, nonetheless.

So, in any Cabinet meeting, there were at least six Ministers with a strong Departmental position to articulate, as well as the so called "Regional Ministers', arguing the cases for their respective Provinces. And nobody agreed with anybody.

The Prime Minister had wanted to have a decision in hand by the end of 1977. But there was nothing like a consensus among the legions of departmental economists drawn into the fray. So the struggle of cost-benefit analysts carried on through one long and acrimonious Cabinet meeting after another. Months passed, well into 1978. By this time the provinces had been drawn in, and their fierce lobbying added to the bitterness and intransigence of the struggle, and to the confusion. And the offset package promises kept growing and became more complex, became surreal, with the two proponents making commitments that increasingly lacked credibility. Ministers with provincial positions to argue broadened rather than narrowed the debates.

By the end of 1978, the Trudeau government was losing interest as it became more focused on the gloomy prospects of the next election. Instead of a new fighter aircraft program and the jobs it represented getting votes at least somewhere, it by now looked like a vote-loser everywhere.

The fighter replacement program wasn't an election issue, and the Joe Clark Conservatives took office in June with a promise to make short work of the choice of a new fighter plane. They soon found themselves up to their eyeballs in the swamp of confusion and disharmony created by the Liberals, the provinces, the economists, and the media, by this time realizing they were in a major donnybrook. Only the air force was showing patience as it watched, with some bemusement, all the fuss.

After nine months in office, the Clark government was replaced by the revived Trudeau Liberals. Refreshed from a short break from the travails of government, Pierre Trudeau returned to 24 Sussex Drive with a lengthy to-do list and one of the top items was getting a decision on the new fighter jet. The special Cabinet meeting to discuss the matter was an ill-disciplined shouting match. Trudeau ended it early, because the meeting lacked focus, not to say civility.

Determined to get a decision, he scheduled another meeting for the following week, this time with the attendance of the General who headed up the air force and General Dextraze, who headed the Defence Department.

Trudeau summarized the situation from unbiased and complete notes prepared for him by the Privy Council office. Then the debate began, as ill-behaved as earlier ones. Trudeau cut it short by asking Dextraze to try to summarize the matter from his perspective. He did so, but clearly there was still no Cabinet consensus.

There was a pause in the discussion. One of the Ministers, deep in the whole debate, spoke out.

"Hey, I've been in dozens of these discussions for, what? five years. It seems longer. The talk is all about industrial benefits, offsets, the politics of seeming to favour this region or province over some other. I'm just sick of it.

"But at no time have I ever heard any discussion about which was the better airplane. General Dextraze, which is the better aircraft? I want a simple, straight answer."

Deztraze deferred to the air force General who had so far been silent. His heart had nearly leaped out of his uniform, however, when he heard the Minister ask the question.

"Minister, the air force has no position on that. Both planes have been extensively tested, both are fine, modern aircraft that will do the job. The air force will be delighted with either plane."

The Minister was not going to be denied a substantive answer, as the air force General well knew.

"Okay, General, the air force is not taking a position. What, then, is your personal view? You're a pilot. You've flown these planes. Which—in your personal view—is the better aircraft?

The General drew breath slowly. He knew he had everyone's attention. He had been waiting for five years for this question. He had carefully practiced his answer, because he knew—the air force knew—that at some point this question would be asked. This exact question. He looked around the Cabinet table and looked the questioning Minister in the eye. The formerly raucous room was quiet.

"As I say, they are both good planes. The air force would be happy with either. But you ask me my personal view, my personal view. Well, I've personally flown all the high performance aircraft in the world, post Korea. I assure you these are good planes. But you ask my personal view as a pilot," he repeated.

He paused.

"Well it's this. If I were flying a $25-million aircraft over the North Pole and I lost an engine, I'd like to be flying a plane with two engines. The F18 has two engines. The F16 has one."

He sat back to watch the Cabinet reaction. There was a stunned silence. The clarity of the answer—and the clarity of the choice—was dumbfounding. The minister who had asked the question leaped.

"That makes the decision simple, and very simple to explain. The industrial offset packages are comparable if incomprehensible, I think we all agree, but every voter can understand that the lives of our pilots are valuable, the planes are expensive, and the best decision all around is to buy the two-engine plane. Who can question it?"

Around the table, heads began to nod. Trudeau immediately picked up on the quiet but clearly emerging consensus.

"Colleagues, we have a decision. Thank you all, General Dextraze, and you, General. You were very helpful in clarifying things."

One minister, gathering his papers, turned to a colleague and said, "We had made this very difficult for ourselves. The answer was, in fact, quite simple."

His colleague replied, "Voters like simple."

And so it turned out exactly as William's friend the General had foretold five years earlier. Every one of the long-listed planes had two engines except the F16. In the short-listing, the airforce got rid of all the other two-engine planes except the American F18. And the airforce knew that, at some point, someone would ask, "what did the pilots want?" They wanted an American plane with two engines.

And that is how very expensive and complex aircraft purchasing decisions are made in Ottawa.

Ministers

Reputations

The phone rang. The private-number phone. It was just before seven in the morning, and he stared at it. The reason he came into his office early most mornings was the phone didn't ring, and there were no staff members around to bother him with petty matters. He could read some of the mass of paper he had to master each day for Cabinet meetings and appearances in the House, or to be factually unassailable in any jousting he might do with the media.

Picking up the phone, he said, "John Allen".

He recognized the voice. The message was short, to the point. Allen felt a huge hole in the pit of his stomach. He had a feeling, suddenly, that his face had frozen. He blinked.

He responded as though nothing were amiss, "Thank you. Yes, please keep me informed. I appreciate it."

He hung up.

His face slowly unfroze. The hollowness in his innards persisted. He felt a choking sensation, and said to himself, "Oh, God, I should cry, but I can't allow myself."

He remained motionless, his elbows on the desk, the pile of paper forgotten, his memories swamping him. He remembered their last conversation, last night, after dinner. He helped her with the dishes. They had had their discussion, their "mature discussion," as she put it, during and after dinner. She had been calm, maybe too calm, he suddenly thought. She kissed him on the cheek when he left about 11 o'clock. There was no hint of this.

She'd killed herself that morning; she'd jumped off the 14th storey balcony of her condominium. It must have been after he'd left for The Hill. That would have been about six. Why didn't he hear any police or ambulance sirens? There must have been some. Why did she do it? Why? There was never any hint of such a thing happening.

The voice on the telephone had been a reporter from the Globe whom he knew as well as any wary politician ever know reporters, but one for whom he had a high regard, whom he regularly but carefully helped with stories being worked on. Never leaks, of course, never anything secret, because he was a little old-fashioned that way. He thought the oath of office meant something. No, it was just that, from time to time, the fellow from the Globe needed a hand in connecting the dots. Understanding Ottawa is often about connecting dots if you're on the outside but sometimes even when you're on the inside, or think you're on the inside.

The Globe guy was a veteran. He had a reputation for discretion, for accepting confidences, and respecting them. He wasn't one of those latter-day journalism school graduates who worshipped Woodward and Bernstein, and who thought a corrupt Richard Nixon lurked behind every possible political story. He wasn't included in Pierre Trudeau's description of the members of the media as "crumbs."

And his Globe "friend" was, as far as he knew, the only one that had maybe—he wasn't sure—connected the dots and guessed that he and Marian were lovers. At least, that is what Allan concluded from the phone call. He and Marian had been very discreet. Very, very discreet. It only worked because the two of them had condominiums on the same floor of the same building. It wasn't a busy building or, at least the 14th floor, which had only six units, wasn't busy. He doubted in the past two years even two people had seen him come into or leave her apartment. And there were times, too, when business found each of them in the same hotel in the same city outside Ottawa. They had openly had dinner together occasionally in as public a place as Allen could find so that anyone seeing them would naturally assume it was business. He wasn't one of those to go skulking off with his mistress to Chez Pierre out on Montréal Road, a little restaurant with, apparently, no electric light like one of his colleagues and his spectacularly beautiful Special Assistant. He lunched with many journalists, even ones he loathed.

He wondered for a minute how the Globe guy guessed, or maybe knew. Or maybe he just called because he knew that John and Marian were neighbours, on the off-chance he had heard something. But Allen had wondered before today if he knew. Something he said once. But how? Had Marian said something to him, however subtle? They were both journalists, and they drank together, and shared confidences. But from the beginning he had made Marian swear that she wouldn't even hint of the relationship with anyone. It could destroy his reputation if it were to become known.

He grinned to himself for a brief moment. Mike Pearson, in his memoirs about his Prime Ministry in the '60s, was explaining to the reader his thinking on some matter, and how important secrecy was. Then he wrote something like "...if it should become known (and in Ottawa everything becomes known)...." That insight was one of Allen's favourite aphorisms about Ottawa. There are no secrets. Almost. It's a town where everybody itches to tell somebody almost anything. That's the secret of successful lobbyists' and journalists' gathering of information to persuade their clients and their editors that they're in the know. That is, they've learned how to scratch the itch.

There was no point thinking about that now. He thought of Marian. The made-for-television truly marvelously attractive face, not of a 20-year-old, but of a late-30s, one-time beauty pageant contestant, who was probably too smart to win. He thought of her body. "Spectacular," he had told her one night as they undressed. He thought of her warmth, and her perfume, and the taste and feel of her mouth. He immersed himself in the thought of these things for a few minutes, and tears formed in his eyes as he clenched them shut, and then shook his head. He wiped his eyes with a handkerchief.

"Why?" he said out loud, in a low, agonizing voice.

He knew it wasn't her good looks or great shape that drew him to break his marriage vows, though. It was her mind. He started to grin to himself as he thought about how stupid such a declaration would sound, if made publicly. "I was in love with her mind."

The fact was, the media cross-examined him nearly daily on the complexities and details of his sprawling portfolio, and he knew the media liked him and respected him, because he always both knew his brief, as lawyers say, and he knew how to give journalists precisely the accurate quote they needed for their story and provide it in the terse language the headline-writers loved or with a different slant for radio or television.

He was proud of that talent, honed fine over a dozen years in Parliament, and more years before that in local politics and in the courtroom. He had a reputation, and he knew it.

No, the appeal of Marian was that she had a mind as quick and slippery and shiny as mercury, and sharp, very sharp. It was a complex mind, subtle and reflective and multi-dimensional, and with it came the most seductive sense of humour. He had never met anyone like her.

When she was interviewing him while playing her role as a television interviewer he was always on guard, especially after their affair began because he had an increased appreciation of that marvelous mind.

"What a waste," he thought. "What a godamn, godamn waste."

She had that instinct that some reporters have of understanding from the barest outline of a story the shape and colour and meaning of the whole big picture even before—sometimes—all the members of the Cabinet understood.

Mind you, he had often thought some of his colleagues were not appointed because of their brains.

And so when she interviewed him he knew that she was going to work him hard and he had to be careful. He had become so careful, an empathetic colleague had once said, and was speaking so slowly in answering her questions, that it sounded as if Allen had developed a southern drawl.

He shook his head again, and again he grinned a little, thinking that they had been on TV at least a dozen times together, and every time she worked him hard and every time he walked away unblooded. He wondered what effect it would have had on their relationship if he had allowed his professional skills to slip even a little.

His mind wandered again to her face and then to the previous night's conversation. The hollowness in his gut returned.

He had told her months ago that what had started, for both of them, as a friendship, had just gone too far. It was becoming serious for him. He said he was falling in love with her. Had fallen in love with her. She had laughed. Not at him, he thought, but at the very concept. She was not, he reflected, very sentimental. He knew she'd taken many lovers over the years. She had been posted overseas and he knew the stories of her picking up with a local guy for a while, then lightly saying goodbye when she moved on.

She dismissed the stories and the relationships they represented. "It's a little like the 'country wives' the Scottish fur traders had in the frontier days of the Hudson's Bay Company," she once said. "They took up with a native woman for a year or two then went to the next trading post to take up with another native woman, all the time writing affectionate notes back to the wife and kids in Edinburgh."

If she had any deep romantic feelings for him, they were unexpressed. "Was that the problem?" he asked himself.

Thus, last night they had shared a bottle of better-than-he-usually-bought Bordeaux. Between sips, she stirred, shook and sliced various things for dinner and would then sit down with him. But not next to him. The coffee table was between them, and they kept up a running conversation about happenings in Ottawa. He always tried to just talk about what he knew had already been in the media. She always tried to talk about the stories being worked on by the press gallery but hadn't yet broken. He wondered if she was attempting to have him confirm suspicions, or attempting to keep him slightly off balance. Or maybe—sometimes—to warn him of upcoming trouble. She gave no clues.

He had to say this: he was frequently astonished by how well informed she was on so many matters that he considered highly confidential. Sometimes it worried him. But sometimes it helped him, too. He gained a perspective of how a story might play that allowed him to make comments in Cabinet that his colleagues later thought were amazingly prescient and that demonstrated superior political judgment. If only they knew.

After his first glass of wine he said to her that, if anything, his feelings were becoming stronger and that thinking about her was taking up entirely too much time. He said this lightly. Or he tried to. He hoped she understood what he was trying to say before he said it and would forgive him, but he was afraid of her reaction. A woman scorned and all that.

She told him, in that direct, reportorial manner she had perfected, to stop beating around the bush.

So he said it. He said he had to make a choice. He told her he loved her. But it was to the point that he just could not continue with the secrecy. It wasn't only unfair to his stay-at-home wife, Linda, but it was unfair to them all.

Marian listened, and interjected that she wasn't unhappy if he wanted to carry on as they were. She wasn't going to press expectations of marriage on him, nor did she want to make the relationship public. She observed that she was doing a pretty good job of covering up by dating others from time to time.

Allen had thought about that for a minute, as if reconsidering what he was trying to say. Then he told her flatly that it had to end. There were two reasons, he had said. First—and he admitted this sounded odd—he was having pangs of guilt. Second, it was sure, eventually, to become public no matter what their efforts at secrecy.

He didn't need to explain that this would destroy his marriage and his shaky financial situation, since he had little other than a half-paid-for house and a modest Parliamentary pension. It might well cost him his seat at the Cabinet table. It would certainly cost him his chance at promotion.

Fundamentally, it would ruin his reputation. All his reputations—for prudence, truth, loyalty, sound judgment—all of them.

They both knew there was a third reason that went unsaid. A fatal third. The Prime Ministership.

Mulroney had been Prime Minister for six years. He had run the Progressive Conservative government high up on the shoals of unpopularity in the aftermath of the Meech Lake deal a few months earlier.

His ego wouldn't let him drop a topic about which the public was beyond weary. The government's and maybe the country's salvation might well lay in his early resignation and a new face with new policies and priorities and a new agenda for the '90's that might keep the Party together. The creation of the separatist Bloc Quebecois was a worrying development, as was the emerging Reform movement out west.

John Allen had a good shot at the succession, he thought. Others that he respected agreed and had volunteered help and to raise funds. So far he'd said and done nothing but they both knew that, if it became public that he had being carrying on an affair, it would destroy his chances with, at least, the right-wing, family-first traditionalists in his Party with whom he was on good terms but who were leaking away to the new Reform Party.

So, for the future of the Party, for the country, for the leadership, the hard-headed decision had to be made. She had to go. They both understood this without their speaking of it. While he hoped she knew that it broke his heart, he couldn't read her reaction.

She stared at him, then quietly said, "You've given this long thought."

He admitted this was true.

She had nodded. "I think dinner is ready."

Over dinner they talked about nothing but what was going on in the House. It was like a long- married couple talking about the family business.

After dinner, they returned to the soft seats. While she poured coffee, he did the brandies, putting two glasses of cognac in the microwave oven for 10 seconds. Both of them liked good cognac warmed. He had put hers on the coffee table and walked over to the windows and looked out on the lights of Ottawa. Not far away there were the well-lit green roofs of the buildings in the Parliamentary Precinct. He loved those buildings. Linda hated them.

They drank their cognac slowly and talked little. He finished a second cup of coffee, then rose and said he had to get back to his apartment, that he had papers, cursed papers, to read. Nothing more had been said about his earlier decision.

She walked him to the door, kissed his cheek, and said, "Goodbye, my love."

He startled himself with that memory, tears welling in his eyes. When he'd confessed his love for her months ago, she'd treated him, he thought, like just one more "country wife". Could there have been more to her feelings? Why hadn't she said anything before? Had he misjudged, made an enormous mistake?

He sat at the desk, then looked at his watch. He had been in reverie for about 15 minutes. He shook his head, again, and pressed the intercom button.

"Yes, Minister?"

"Martha, I'd like coffee, please. A Thermos of coffee."

His lawyer's mind began to work. What were the implications of her death for him?

Then the sudden crashing thought. "Is this going to get out?"

He thought about that for a few minutes. His Globe friend seemed to know, maybe. Who else might? He cast about for any other vague comments anyone might have made that would indicate knowledge or suspicion. He couldn't think of any. But then, the seeming suicide of a beautiful, talented, Ottawa press gallery newswoman with an international reputation wasn't an every-day story that would just drift away. She was a prominent member of a reportorial family that was forever curious. There would be questions. The police would have questions, too. He was a neighbour. They would certainly interview him. What could he say? While the truth might leak out—just the truth that they had had dinner in her apartment— the admission that they had had dinner "several times" might start tongues wagging. A lie would be dangerous and, if detected, politically fatal.

What about physical evidence? Was there a note? Could the police get finger-prints off his brandy glass? He dismissed this thought immediately.

Marian was fastidious—the glasses would have gone into the dishwasher, and the dishwasher started before she went to bed. If she went to bed. The wine bottle? Maybe. Both of them had handled it, though.

But any policeman would see that someone had been there for dinner. There would have been pairs of tell-tale items like brandy snifters and wine glasses in the dishwasher, to begin with.

Well, he thought, a dinner or a glass of wine between neighbours didn't an affair make.

But what about his reportorial "friend" from the Globe? That might be problematical. Most of the journalists he knew would sell their grandmothers into prostitution for the sake of a big story. This was maybe that kind of story: "MINISTER'S MISTRESS COMMITS SUICIDE." He could see the page one headlines in his mind's eye.

He thought for a minute, and rubbed his eyes with his thumbs. He had to deal with the Globe guy, his one source of information and his one risk of exposure.

Picking up his private line phone, he dialed the reporter's number.

"Hello", the Globe guy answered.

"Harry, it's John Allen."

"Yes".

"Are you in a place you can talk? I wonder if you could give me a more complete picture of what you called me about earlier."

"No. I'm filing. I'll have to call you back."

Allen thought for a few seconds. "I'm going to have to start my day here momentarily. Could you make lunch?

A pause.

"Yes. Would Hy's on Queen Street be all right? 12 o'clock?"

Allen was looking at his crowded schedule for the day. "I have a Cabinet Committee until 12. How about 12:15? I can make that."

"See you there. 12:15."

John Allen stood up. He stretched his six-foot frame, did a few stretching exercises, and went to his private bathroom.

He then walked over to the window, and looked out over the Ottawa River and the unremarkable neighbourhoods of Hull and beyond to the still-green hills of the Gatineau for fully five minutes. It was a lovely view. He shook his head. "How could she?"

He went back to his desk, the coffee arrived, he poured a cup, then sipped it.

He sighed. There was nothing he could do except sit and wait. He had to see how the suicide would play in the media. He thought about suitable responses should he be asked for a comment. Volunteer nothing. Reply truthfully. Try to bring the question back to what a great person she was. A careful lawyer's approach.

"Yes, of course I knew her. Everybody in Ottawa knew her. I guess everybody in Canada knew her."

"She was a great person. It's a great loss, a sad day for Canada."

These all sounded fine. And they were sufficiently bland as to not be used as quotes that would draw attention.

He thought of other possible questions and answers.

"No, I know nothing about what might have caused her to jump. Her death is a great loss to journalism. And to the country."

"Yes, we did in fact have condominiums in the same building. She would often mention it on TV that two Ministers lived in her building. And four other Parliamentarians. Ministers have to live somewhere. But I rarely saw her."

He hoped these would suffice. He doubted there was anything that would lead any reporter to any pointed follow-up question.

A perfunctory knock at his office door was followed by the entrance of the corpulent body of Hugo, his chief of staff.

"Minister, we have to discuss some scheduling things, and that Cabdoc, before the Deputy arrives."

"Yes, Hugo," he sighed, "but I have a heavy day, so let's keep it simple." His mind slipped into business mode.

Hugo abbreviated his agenda, and raised only two of the serious political issues that required attention. They quickly went through them. Allen's mind wandered twice into the land of doubt.

Can this thing be kept quiet? he thought to himself. If not, can the damage be contained? No answers came.

Hugo rose to usher in the Deputy for the next meeting, and then sat down to take notes.

Allen's meeting with the Deputy Minister was perfunctory. No surprises. No insights. He wondered if the Deputy had any flaws. The perfect-Mandarin face was always in place. The mind always carefully focused. Allen wondered, as the Deputy droned on, if he had a mistress. He guessed anything was possible.

The meeting ended just before 10. Another trip to the bathroom, then he picked up his Cabinet four-ring binder that contained his Cabinet documents in a large, black leather zipped case and said, cheerily, to nobody in particular, "Off to Cabinet," as he left the office.

The Cabinet committee meeting dragged its way through four items, while Allen was uncharacteristically quiet. He couldn't get engaged in any of the issues. None concerned his Ministry, so no comment was really called for. He doodled, as he often did, and he thought of Marian, which he had been doing more and more, recently, but the context was different. "Why had she done it?" he asked himself again.

Then his mind wandered to his lunch with Harry. A tentative plan began to form. He would have to be very careful, and play it by instinct. But he knew that whatever he did he would be taking enormous chances. Could he just sit tight and hope? He thought not. Better try to tie up this one loose end. Tie it up firmly.

The committee clerk spoke up to say it was 10 to 12, and would Ministers like lunch ordered? This brought the discussion of the last item to an end satisfactory to everybody. As one, the Ministers and their officials rose from their chairs and headed towards the doors.

Outside, he handed his Cabinet documents binder to a Special Assistant who had arrived with a message that he should call Martha if he wasn't going back to the office.

He took the elevator to where there was a phone near the Centre Block private entrance that he could use to call his secretary.

And what did she want?

"Have you heard that Marian MacDonald killed herself by jumping off her balcony early this morning?" Cautiously, for he sometimes thought

Martha was a mind reader, he said it had been mentioned by someone in Cabinet.

"Fine. Just so you know."

He wondered for a moment what Martha might know. He quickly rejected any need for worry irrespective of what she knew or thought she knew. She was a totally loyal Sphinx.

"I'm off to lunch at Hy's with Harry Martin. I'll be back to the office for my House Book about 1:45," he reported. It was always important that a Minister keep his office aware of his whereabouts, lest the unexpected happen.

"Be careful," she replied, before hanging up. He was not sure just what she meant. Did she—could she—know more than he thought she knew? Or was she cautioning him about talking to a reporter?

The walk down the steps in front of the House, short-cutting across the grass of the Parliamentary Precinct, down O'Connor to Queen Street to Hy's took less than five minutes. He found Harry in a booth. He looked around for people he knew and calculated the likelihood of being overheard as being negligible.

"Sad news," he said, sitting down.

The reporter nodded. "Terrible."

"Are there any further details you can give me? Was there a note?"

"No note. The cops confirmed that. An examination of the apartment convinced them there'd been someone for dinner, but the dishwasher had run a full cycle, the bed was unmessed, and there was a near empty bottle of scotch on the coffee table, and one glass. No idea how much it had in it when she started, of course, until an autopsy.

"A cop told me off the record that they concluded she was alone when she jumped. But there is a medical examination to come, looking mostly for toxicological results and alcohol readings. And, I suspect, any evidence of sex, but nobody said anything."

Allen said nothing. Maybe Harry had a hidden recorder running. Best to say as little as possible.

Harry went on.

"It's been general knowledge around the Gallery for months that she'd been fighting depression. Been taking something for it. The gossip around the Gallery this morning is that's what it was. Case closed. But you knew her well, didn't you? Did you see any of that?"

They both knew what Harry was asking. Was there a surreptitious tape recorder?

"Well, I was on her show several times. We were neighbours in the same building. I had lunch or dinner with her numerous times. She was a fiercely competitive reporter, as you know, and maybe she thought a few drinks might get me to lower my guard. But I noticed nothing different." And he hadn't. It was the truth.

He was momentarily sad. He knew nothing about the depression or the pills, yet everybody else did, apparently. Was he that emotionally blind or selfish or stupid that he'd not noticed? Or maybe there was nothing to notice, maybe she had told her colleagues and not him.

"There's also a story around the Gallery that she had a sugar-daddy, or something. Know anything about that?" rejoined Harry.

"No," said Allen. "But she was very attractive and it wouldn't surprise me if somebody with some money to spare decided to spend it on her. There are worse things to do with money." He said this last with a small smile.

The waiter came by to take drink orders and leave menus. That gave Allen a few seconds to think.

"What might the Gallery do with that suspicion?" asked Allen.

"Well, as near as I can tell, there's no evidence, and if anyone has suspicions that they want to take public they haven't raised their voices yet."

Allen thought. Then the two glasses of wine arrived. Neither had looked at the menu. Each ordered from memory. Allen allowed himself, sometimes, one glass of wine before Question Period. There was a long silence as each of them had a sip.

Allen grew tired of the vacuum.

"Well, the problem with anybody in the media starting something like that is the effect it has on people's reputations. The poor lover—if there is one—is likely catatonic with his grief and sense of loss. The arrangement—if there was one—was probably secret for a reason. And the poor bastard would likely do anything he could to keep it private, for any number of imaginable reasons. And a journalist who tried to make something out of this might get a short term fix of a front page story, but today's front page is tomorrow's fish-wrap. His reputation might be damaged for trying to make something out of that poor girl's death, and likely nothing could ever be proved anyway." It had been a long summary of how he felt, and of the facts as he saw them. A lawyer's summary.

"Yes," said Harry, slowly, "It could damage a lot of people's reputations. And I agree with you about what would happen to any reporter that tried to make anything of it without a lot of evidence. A lot of evidence. Whispers wouldn't satisfy a managing editor, anyway."

Allen felt his stomach muscles relax. He hadn't realized they were tense.

"Yes," Harry continued, "it's a matter of fact that everybody's reputation, including Marian's, would suffer. It wouldn't do any good to start trying to even investigate such a story without some evidence of foul play."

Allen relaxed a little more, and sipped his wine again.

He thought again about a hidden tape recorder, and decided he was becoming paranoid. Time to leap.

"Harry, to completely change the subject, I'd like to have one of those conversations with you that never took place. Are you game? I've been wanting to talk to you about something for a while."

"Always."

Allen decided he could not accept the terse response.

"No, Harry, I want to have a conversation that you must promise will never be written down, will never be passed on, will never be discussed by anyone but you and me. I have to have your solemn promise."

The reporter looked at the politician. Reporters survive on cutting the corners of confidentiality a little close, sometimes. This time, clearly, the rules were different. So, no story here, but curiosity led him to make the commitment.

"I promise. Cross my heart and hope to die."

"Harry, there are a number of things coming together in my life that are leading in a particular direction. I've been thinking of not running again in '92 or '93—whenever. I've now decided I will. Second, I've been having a look at how my Ministerial staff operates. You may know that my press secretary is leaving. I'm looking for a replacement. Of necessity, someone from the Gallery, if at all possible. Someone with a reputation for integrity, someone who respects confidences, someone that I can let down my hair with and who will give me frank, unvarnished advice. I'd be grateful for any suggestions. The reason I need someone with experience on The Hill is because my Chief of Staff has hinted he'll be leaving in the next six months or so. If the new press secretary works out, I would want to see if a promotion would be in order. I think too many Ministers have too many Chiefs of Staff that are not sensitive to media matters."

What Allen was talking about, Harry knew, was at least a 50-percent increase from a reporter's salary for whoever took the job, more perks, and an opportunity to leave the Gallery, which is interesting work for only so long. A senior job in the office of a senior Minister can, after a while, lead in many interesting, profitable, and challenging directions.

Harry looked at him. Allen was letting Harry scratch the secrecy itch. He wasn't surprised, but certainly curious. He'd heard rumours, but said nothing. Allen continued, taking a greater chance. Ministers lost their portfolios for what he was about to say.

"I think the Boss will step down soon. Meech has harmed him. He's lost his confidence—although that might only last weeks. He has an enormous capacity for self-delusion—larger even than Diefenbaker, maybe. Internally, there are problems with Cabinet and with the performance of individual Ministers. You know that. Reputations of governments and of Prime Ministers, once shattered, are difficult to rebuild. None of this is any secret. The government's polling numbers are very bad and were it not for the huge amount of third-party money spent to promote free trade in the last election, we might well have lost even then. Against Turner." He said this last with sarcasm.

"Our government, our Party, needs to be led by a new man, someone with a reputation for action, a reputation for honesty, a reputation for integrity. And a man—or woman—of course, of vision. Some of my colleagues are short in one area or another. Reputation will be the making of the next leader, and will elect the next leader Prime Minister. You may not agree, but that's my view."

Harry waited silently for the next sentence, but he nodded.

"I'm putting together, although none of the people I have in mind know it, a team to take to the Langevin Block, to the PMO. I want the best people. And I trust you absolutely to never say a thing about this conversation, or ever write about it. I have told you this because of your reputation for respecting confidences."

Allan stopped and looked at Harry.

Harry looked back at Allen. He said nothing, waiting. Just then the food was served, and Allen made it clear with a wave of his hand that he had nothing more to say.

Harry chose his words carefully. He spoke slowly.

"I agree with you. And to complete your thought, I think you might even have what it takes to be a good Prime Minister. I'll say nothing to anyone. As to suggestions about a press secretary, I'll give it some thought, although I might be interested myself."

Allen finished chewing a forkful of medium-well-done filet, and looked at Harry.

"I hoped you would."

Quietly he added, "You know, you have the kind of reputation in journalism, and in other ways, that someone like me would need to help me get where I want to go. Give me a call after you have thought about it. There's a big ring here worth trying to reach for."

"It's funny, you know. Everybody thinks that Ottawa is all about policy and ambition, and who's in and who's out, who is going up, and who down. It's not. Ottawa is, as you know, all about reputation."

Harry was slow to reply.

"Yes, reputation. I had a friend in the Gallery who used to say, misquoting somebody I'm sure, 'Get a reputation for rising early, and you can sleep 'til noon'."

Why Jim Thompson Never Became Prime Minister

Benjamin Franklin is credited with the aphorism, "the only way three people can keep a secret is if two of them are dead". This relating of events is the reverse of that. Seven people participated in an important meeting many years ago and we all swore to silence, for reasons that will become obvious. All the others are now dead and I feel released from that promise. I think that the story provides the answer to a critical political question that many people have asked over a lot of years: why didn't Jim Thompson seek the leadership of his Party—giving him the Prime Ministership—when it was more or less offered to him on a platter?

His decision to refuse has been one of the abiding mysteries of Canadian politics because surely the history of our country would have been very different had he chosen to return to public life and led our country at a key time in our public affairs.

It's been many years since these events took place. The reader may ask how so much later I can write this little memoir and purportedly quote the participants accurately. The answer is straightforward. Although, other than the chairman, none of us—by agreement—made notes of the meeting described herein at the time, I took the trouble immediately after the meeting, while comments and impressions were still clear in my mind, to write out everything I could recall. What you read below is a version of those notes, expanded to explain to the reader who the participants were and why, in my view, they said what they did.

One good thing about outliving everybody else is that no one is around to contradict one's own version of history. However, it's a historical fact that Jim Thompson was a near certainty to become leader of his Party and Prime Minister, and he chose not to. There has to be a credible explanation for such an ambitious and successful man to do what he did. This memoir is put forward as that explanation.

The meeting was held in Ottawa in a boardroom on the 12th floor of 90 Sparks Street, the silver Royal Bank building at the south-east corner of Metcalfe, immediately behind the Langevin Block, the office building on Wellington Street that serves as the Prime Minister's departmental office. As each of us arrived and looked out the boardroom's wall-to-wall windows over the top of the Langevin Block to the view of the Parliament Buildings, I would guess most of us were moved by deep private memories. All of us had a long and intimate commitment to our Party. Most of us had worked and had offices at one time or another in the Centre Block. Thus, the view of the buildings, the Peace Tower, and the big red maple-leaf flag fluttering against a flawless blue sky that bright sunny day must have affected each of us at some emotional level.

Coffee was on a sideboard and I was the third person to arrive, at 9:20 for a 9:30 meeting. As I filled my cup we made small talk about the weather and general matters. In retrospect it was clear that no one wanted to talk politics until everyone had arrived. The meeting, called the previous afternoon, could begin no earlier than 9:30 because two attendees were coming in on overnight. This was a measure of the haste and urgency to organize the meeting.

The group was a cross-section of the most senior people in the Party. The two who were there when I arrived were Martin Harrison from Vancouver and Dulcie Murray from Toronto. Martin had been an executive assistant to Jim Thompson 20 years earlier, during Thompson's early Ministerial days. He was still straight and tall in his late 40s, reminding those who knew him of his time playing championship basketball.

Martin had subsequently become a very successful lawyer. Unlike some of the rest of us, he had not been a young political activist at university and upon his leaving The Hill he largely withdrew from political activity. However, any time Jim called, Martin was there to help. Hence he would chair the meeting, having convened it at Jim's request.

I remember thinking that Dulcie Murray was a most interesting woman, She was tall, about 45 then, with red hair and striking looks. She was bright and politically astute. And she had guts. Her talents had carried her to a top executive position in a multinational company, but she never gave up her love for politics and could be depended upon at any time to respond to a call for help by the Party. In a day when there were no controls on political donations, her annual personal contributions were often in five figures. She sometimes gave more than some of the Banks. Looking at her I remembered that there had been a rumour, years before, that she and Jim had been lovers a long time ago. I reflected momentarily that this meeting had been convened at Jim's expressed wish, and the attendees were people he named as those whose views he most respected. I was feeling a little embarrassed by the thought of being included on that kind of list.

The fourth person to arrive was Senator Don Sawyer from Toronto, bringing a jolly, rolly-polly presence to the meeting. He also brought decades of experience in electoral politics and a good sense of what Party people—not only the caucus on Parliament Hill, but the activists—would be thinking. Everyone attending would have agreed that Sawyer was the ranking expert on the Ontario political situation and, despite his jovial demeanor, he was quite capable of cutting anyone's throat in the Party's interests. I expected that he was invited for all those reasons, but thought that he and Jim were not personally close, despite his having once been Jim's Parliamentary Secretary. It was likely, too, that Jim preferred him inside the tent at the beginning of a Party contest, rather than outside. Sawyer, in any event, would want to go with the winner, which Jim was.

Immediately behind him the last three arrived. Harry Dhaliwal was from Calgary. A Sikh, but not a religious one, he had also worked in a

Minister's office after his MBA. He then parachuted himself into the bureaucracy, where he had quickly proven invaluable in energy policy matters. After a decade there, it was a short leap to a vice presidency of an oil company. He was a business star, with his name in the news all the time. He was also very knowledgeable about Alberta politics.

Mark MacDonald was a Halifax lawyer and, despite his rumpled appearance very skilled. He had chaired a Royal Commission and served as an adviser in some sort of United Nations inquiry. In the Party, he was a backroom guy, mostly involved in raising money. He didn't come to Ottawa any more often than absolutely necessary and his attendance was something of a surprise to me. I knew of three or four other Maritimers who were closer to Jim, but Mark had that Maritime reputation for being canny. Maybe that was it.

Pierre Dupont was a very rich Montrealer. Slim, small, with silver-grey hair and a $2,000 suit, I recall thinking that he was the epitome of Old Montreal Money. But he didn't just sit back and count it. He was a director of half a dozen blue-chip companies, as well as at least two charitable and one cultural foundation that I knew of. His long and generous service to Canada and to the Party was, we all knew, something of which he was proud. He was unselfish in the selfish business of backroom politics.

I was, at the time, president of a large trade association based in Ottawa, working as a lobbyist after also doing a spell in a Minister's office and some years in the senior bureaucracy. I was there, probably, both because I knew Jim well, and because I had the broadest view of government, the Party, the country, and the business community.

We were, then, the seven people that Jim Thompson wanted to hear from concerning the most important decision of his life. I don't know how the others felt, but I was intimidated.

Martin called the meeting to order and after we all filled our coffee cups he began.

"I've spoken to each of you separately on the phone and thank you all for downing tools on short noticed and coming to Ottawa. Except you"—he teased, addressing me—"you're already here." I grinned. We were old friends.

"In short, the PM indicated three days ago that he will step down as soon as the Party chooses a new leader. Jim called me that afternoon saying a number of people had called him more or less immediately, urging him to go after the job.

"His response—which you have all seen in the media, was that he thought that when he left Cabinet, and Ottawa, he'd not be back. However, he told the media he wanted a week to think about it and committed himself to not saying anything to anybody over the next week while he considered the matter.

"Now, you all know Jim. He wants the facts. He wants clear, direct, blunt advice. And he's not about to dawdle over a decision. He's unlike many in politics, but that's the way it is.

"It's his view that he need not consult far and wide—until he has in fact made a decision, anyway." This was a little joke reflecting the expectation that, if Jim did decide to go for it, he would then want to phone everyone he knew and ask their advice, making a large number of Party people happy that they had been "consulted."

"He believes that the people in this room have all the knowledge and experience and judgment to provide the advice he needs to make the right decision. I'd be lying if I thought he didn't want to go. But again, as you know, he is a cold-blooded decision-maker and looks at this no differently than a $10 billion corporate takeover.

"When I called you yesterday, I asked each of you if you were prepared to participate in a 'meeting that never happened'. Each of you said yes. I now want you all to reiterate your commitment to each other to never speaking to anyone about this meeting, irrespective of what comes out of it. Never. We will only produce the best advice for Jim if we can each speak very frankly. Do I have agreement?"

Everyone present nodded and mumbled assent. Martin, after saying he would take notes for his report to Jim, asked everyone else not to, and began his agenda. What is the state of the Party? What are the prospects for winning the next election? When should that election be? What is the state of the cabinet? Of the backbench? Of Party finances? And what immediate changes of policy and governmental direction are necessary, if any? Finally, what would Jim's prospects be of winning the leadership and the next election?

These were discussed in detail over the next couple of hours. There was not a lot of dissent among the seven of us. Everything looked reasonably positive.

About 11:15, Martin began to pull it all together.

"Let me then summarize: We are agreed that the Party is not in great organizational shape but that a leadership campaign and a year's solid rebuilding effort should put it in condition to win the election, given some new, well qualified candidates putting a new face on things, and a solid performance by a new PM if coupled with some new approaches to abiding problems.

"Does that meet with everyone's agreement with respect to the Party?"

Someone said that it was a good summary.

"OK. The government and the cabinet," Martin went on. "I think it fair to say that we know who will contest the leadership, and let's leave them aside for now. If Jim runs, we will have an opportunity to address that issue. I think we are agreed that the government hasn't been performing as well as we'd all have liked, that there is evidence of some tired people that have been kept in harness too long. The Solicitor General is one. The Minister of Transport has been spending about 80 per cent of his time on one file while the rest of the Ministry has been falling apart around him. If this is not addressed, it'll cause us real problems in the West, in particular. We have a serious case of foot in the cow-pie disease by the Agriculture Minister. Same problem. The Minister of Indian Affairs is in trouble, but what Minister of Indian Affairs is not? The Immigration Minister has to go.

"In summary, nothing that can't be managed. Our advice, I gather, will be that should he win the leadership he'll have to immediately change at least five Ministers, and give the new ones both the time and the support they need to effect some significant changes in policy and direction.

"Is that a fair summary?"

Dulcie said that we should really add the Trade Minister to the list of under-performers. We all understood what she was saying and there was a murmur of agreement. He was simply accident prone, politically speaking.

"Fine, so far. Does anybody expect any problem raising adequate funds quickly for a leadership run?"

Senator Sawyer led in the laughter. However, it was a question that had to be asked.

"Finally, does anyone doubt that if Jim seeks the leadership that he'll win?"

There was no response. It was understood the job was his for the asking.

"Does anybody have serious doubts about his ability to do the job?"

"None whatever," said Mark MacDonald.

"I guess that's it unless somebody has something to add?" Martin phrased it as a question because he had, I think, noticed that Dulcie was restive, seeming almost to be fighting with herself about whether she should say something.

"Dulcie?" She had said little during the previous two hours, I now realized.

"We have not discussed the wisdom of his seeking the leadership. I think that is, ultimately, the key question that simply, above all else, must be addressed," she said, slowly and precisely.

There was silence from the others as we waited for her to go on.

Dulcie looked around the table for about 10 seconds. If any of us had ever not realized how strikingly beautiful she looked, those thoughts disappeared during those 10 seconds. The expression on her face was a mixture of doubt and anguish. Usually a very difficult person to read, she couldn't be read in those 10 seconds, either. But she was clearly troubled. She said, "We have, I think, a huge problem that we just must discuss. It can't be avoided. It's Toni."

He was referring to Jim's wife.

"What's the problem?" asked Mark, likely the only person in the room who did not understand the issue. Mark was from Halifax and while he was a very good Party man and lawyer, he also was far outside the Toronto-Ottawa-Montreal gossip circuit.

Dulcie didn't understand this, I guess, and snapped, "Well, she's crazy. Mentally unbalanced."

There, she had said it. Then her voice and manner relaxed, and she spoke carefully and analytically, making her case almost in corporate boardroom terms.

"Ever since Olive Diefenbaker, the wives of Party Leaders and Prime Ministers are public property. I think we can all remember the last time we had someone at 24 Sussex Drive who was…well…not part of the team. The Trudeau government in the mid-'70s was in complete disarray for about two years while Trudeau and his wife sorted out their differences. We just can't avoid discussing the issue of having a…Toni… in there."

Mark, ever the quiet lawyer, persisted. "I still have no idea what you're talking about."

Martin, interestingly, spoke first. He had been Jim's EA. He would be considered, I think, the hardest of hard-core loyalists in Jim's world.

"Well, I wouldn't say she's crazy, but she certainly causes friction over unimportant matters wherever she goes."

I smiled to myself at that considerable understatement.

"Before my day, she put up a constant fuss about the size of the Coca-Cola bottles on government executive aircraft. Coke was phasing out six-ounce bottles in favour of tens. She insisted on six ounce bottles, which were nearly impossible to find. She made my predecessor's life intolerable over the issue, every time she flew on a government plane to some event. As you know, Jim liked to have her along in those days. I just simply ignored her and eventually the problem went away. But she made all sorts of irrational interferences with what we were trying to do in Jim's office." He ended with a shrug.

"Surely," Mark said, "this's not grounds for calling someone crazy."

"Well," interjected the Senator, "I was his Parliamentary Secretary when he was Minister of Finance. The president of his wife bank wrote him to say that they had closed her account and told her not to return to the bank, ever. He detailed several of the many disruptions she had caused. The president of the goddamn bank thought he had to write, for God's sake. The letter asked Jim to talk to her."

Then Pierre Dupont, usually very quiet spoke up.

"My daughter worked in an exclusive lingerie boutique in the Yorkville area of Toronto. One night my daughter called. She pays no attention whatever to politics and asked if I knew a woman named Toni Thompson. I said I did. She told me that she had come in the store that morning. One of the clerks who knew her from an earlier confrontation just disappeared into the back area to join the owner. That left my daughter and a woman who speaks perfectly good English, but with a noticeably heavy Polish accent, to serve her.

"As it was related to me, Toni asked the Polish-accented clerk to see a certain brand and line of lingerie. The clerk told her that over the past six months the manufacturer had discontinued the line. Toni apparently and quite loudly disputed this information. The clerk, trying to be polite, repeated the information, elaborating a little. Even more loudly and abusively, Toni told her she was wrong. The distracted clerk tried to calm her down whereupon Toni yelled, 'Does anybody speak English here?'

"At this point the owner appeared and managed to get Toni calmed down. Since then, and before then, I have heard other, similar stories, and worse."

I thought I had to speak up. "Yeah, there are a lot of stories. Some are not pretty. A few years ago I witnessed a confrontation she had, this time with Jim. He was out on one of his trips doing political stuff and checked into the local Westin Hotel. He had a modest suite because the Party was picking up the cost. There were about six of us sitting around just before dinner, having a drink in his room.

"There was a knock at the door, and in came Toni, explaining that she decided not to sit at home in Ottawa by herself that weekend and had flown out to join him.

"Completely surprised, Jim asked her to sit down and said he would make her a drink. She immediately complained that, in the small suite, there was no place suitable to sit, and she made some other snotty remark, asking Jim's ministerial assistant why were they in this crummy hotel rather than the Fairmont, which she preferred and which had larger suites.

"Jim interrupted her, saying the choice of hotels was his, not the assistant's, and he was at fault. She seized on this and standing there in the middle of the room started yelling that, yes, it was his fault, that everything was his fault, that he was a fuck up and that he fucked up everything. Yes, she used that language in front of staff and local political activists—and went on and on at the top of her voice, screaming. Jim managed to get her calmed down eventually by promising to move to the other hotel. Everyone was so embarrassed at having witnessed the scene that we all made our excuses and left the two of them. We went to dinner by ourselves. The local Party folks who had not heard about her were quite baffled."

Mark, by this time a little baffled himself said, "Ah, yes, but if that's the best you can do...."

He was cut off by Harry.

"No," there was sadness in his voice, and he shook his head. "I witnessed a confrontation between them when he was still in the Cabinet. There was some kind of reception one night and he wanted to go home early. She had maybe one drink too many and wanted to go to an after-party at the Press Club. He had some heavy duty legislation in the House the next day and said he had to work on his speech. He asked an assistant—not someone from his own staff, incidentally—who happened to be there, to go along and keep watch. About an hour later, the assistant called Jim at home to tell him that he was concerned that 'she was getting out of control,' and Jim ought to come down, which he did.

"When he arrived, she was standing about halfway down the bar, surrounded by a half dozen guys, mostly reporters. Everybody was well on the way. He said, from the end of the bar, very quietly, 'OK, Toni, it's time to go.'

"She looked at him for about 15 seconds, then turned to the bartender and said, 'Give the man'—and motioned towards Jim—'a sarsaparilla.'

She was sarcastic. You will remember that Jim had gone on the wagon that year to lose some weight.

"He said about the same thing again, asking her to come along.

"She then turned away from him towards a couple of the press guys and said, 'Do you know how long his… thing…is?' "She emphasized the word 'thing', so everybody knew what she was talking about. 'It's about this long.'

"She said this holding her thumb and forefinger about an inch apart. 'Some man,' she said, again very sarcastically.

"At that point, Jim pushed into the group, grabbed her by one wrist and just physically yanked her out of there, with her yelling and screaming. I can't recall ever witnessing anything like it. She wasn't seen in public for several days and when she was, it was said that she had what looked suspiciously like a black eye."

"I suppose to her list of faults it should be added that she is a sort of thief. At least, the media would report it that way," said Senator Sawyer. This got a reaction of surprise from everyone except Dulcie.

"It might not be that clear, but it is well known both here and in Toronto that she will go into an exclusive clothing store and look at a lot of things, try on a few, then say that she was not sure and she'd like to take them home to see if they went with something else or make some other excuse. Few low level clerks would have the temerity to demand she pay for them before they left the store. A lot of it she just never brings back. Or she would pay for it, wear it once or twice to events, and then return it for a refund. But she also has the bad habit of picking up accessories, like a scarf, putting it on and walking out. Again, given who she is, or was, this is written off as an eccentricity, but some stores now won't let her in the door."

"I have trouble believing this." said Mark. "I've never heard of such a thing. I've never read about it in the papers. Surely something like this would get reported?"

"Maybe now, but not then," Harry continued. "All the gloves are off, now. But at the time the media gossiped about this sort of thing but didn't report it. That's not the case now. And what a Minister's wife might say is much less reportable than what a Prime Ministers' wife says—and does. We found that out in the mid-70s."

"Well," interjected Dulcie, "I guess that's my point. A Party leader, a Prime Minister, has to have wife who's...presentable, I suppose. And behaves herself, at least in public. Toni is—and always has been—a spoiled rich girl with no respect for anybody or any thing. I guess it's a changed world out there and I can't conceive that Jim—and I love him as much as any of you do—could run a government while keeping such a willful wife under wraps. I just can't think it can be done. Now, I've said my piece." There was relief in her voice.

I recall chuckling at this point because, when Dulcie said, "and I love Jim as much as any of you do," the Senator, who was sitting right beside me, commented sotto voce, "More." I wondered again if the relationship between Jim and Dulcie was more than just rumour.

There was then an uncomfortable silence. Martin asked if there was more to add. Pierre spoke, likely for all of us, "There are, I agree, many other stories. They're all distasteful and shouldn't be repeated." I always thought of Pierre as a gentleman a little more refined than the rest of us. It was the perfect response. This issue had been fairly raised and was well understood. Further elaboration would serve no purpose.

"What's the answer?" offered Mark. "Surely this is something that can be controlled. She can be kept away from the media. She can be isolated, surely. There has to be a solution. The stakes are too high here to not find some answer." His voice had risen, and his hands were gesticulating. I'd never seen him more animated. He was the quintessential lawyer seeking the great compromise. There was none.

Martin, who had briefly been a newsman before law school, and who understood the breed very well, answered in a low voice. "Yes, in theory she could be isolated. But then the act of isolating her becomes news in itself. Then the old stories—and let me tell you, you didn't hear the worst today—will start to leak out. She has hurt a lot of people over the years. Jim has his share of political enemies. No, I'm afraid it couldn't be contained. When Jim was here, on The Hill, gossip about her...eccentricities ... were common. But with him being away from The Hill, and her not being newsworthy as 'the wife of,' for the past few years, her ongoing behavior has not been of media interest. But a leadership campaign will start to bring it all out. If he became PM her ego is such, I am sorry to say, that she would be uncontrollable." He had spoken slowly and deliberately, again, I think, summarizing the sense of the meeting.

"Does Jim understand how bad she is?" said Mark, sympathetically. "If so, why no divorce? Nobody can live with a person as…," he searched for words, …"unstable as that. Life must be hell."

It was Senator Sawyer who replied. "Well, she's still, as you say, unstable. As First Lady, you're right, Martin, she would be worse. Jim is more aware than any of us of her problem. She did not seem to be that way when they were first married, but he's a devout Catholic, and while I think—I guess I know—that he considered divorce some years ago when…." He stopped talking for a few seconds while he reordered his thoughts, and I recognized for the first time that maybe he had a closer relationship with Jim than I had thought. I then remembered that one of the Senator's legal specialties was matrimonial law.

Harry and Martin both looked towards Dulcie. There was nothing to read in her expression.

"Anyway, he rejected the idea and he knows that doing anything to sever the marriage would devastate the kids. They know she's a nut and they have made peace with that. And then it would all come out. He'd be as ruined in business as he'd be in politics."

It was, again, Mark who asked, "You think he'd be ruined?"

The question wasn't answered.

"Well," continued Mark, "can she be treated? There have been huge advances in mental health treatment over the years."

Martin and the Senator both started to speak, but then Martin motioned for the Senator to go ahead. While he spoke, Martin nodded agreement.

"The theory is all right, but she fails to grasp that she's doing anything wrong, or unacceptable. Attempts have been made to get her to counseling, to no avail. And, if she's not prepared to face reality, no one can make her."

All this was digested for about a half minute. The Senator rose, saying he was going to the men's room. That gave others a break—one to get coffee, two others to talk quietly to one another, and one followed the Senator. Dulcie sat upright, staring straight ahead, saying nothing since first raising the issue. I was down the table from her, but I think she had tears in her eyes.

Senator Sawyer returned to the room, poured a cup of coffee, slowly added milk, then sat down.

"Yes." he said, "I guess he'd be ruined. Like you Mark—hell—like all of you, I just can't see a solution. We just can't have a crazy woman married to an effective Party Leader and Prime Minister. Maybe she's not crazy, but I can't think of another suitable word. She'd be impossibly disruptive. In any event, I think it's over. If anybody thinks differently, speak up, but I think Martin is in the best place to fly down to Toronto and break the news to Jim. Martin?"

Martin nodded.

Senator Sawyer went on. "It was agreed at the beginning of this meeting that none of us would ever speak of it again. I think, more than ever, that remains necessary. For Jim's sake, let's keep this all to ourselves."

I recall thinking that, in a mere half hour, this had descended from one of the most optimistic rooms in Ottawa to one of the most depressed. The joy of the call to the Party colours to which everyone in the room was prepared to respond, dropping work, loading cases on law partners, spending one's own money and irretrievable time, happily immersed in politics, in a common cause, had in a very few minutes disappeared. More than that, everyone knew without expressing it, the Party and the country would now have to choose a leader from lesser lights. The opportunity for excellence—and that was what Jim represented—was lost. It was an awful realization.

Everyone gathered their papers and cases and quietly went out the door. Even in the elevator, there was silence. This from as gregarious and loquacious a group as you would ever meet. In the Royal Bank lobby, Dulcie paused and, I thought, looked a little lost, a little uncertain. Unusual for a woman of such verve and self-confidence.

I asked her if she might be free for lunch, that it was a few minutes early but we could get a good booth at the Canadian Grill in the Chateau Laurier, and a drink, before the lobbyist crowd arrived. She nodded assent.

We went out on to Sparks Street and cut down to Elgin, walking quickly in the cool fall air across Confederation Square, saying nothing until we were seated in our booth. A waiter very quickly took our drink orders.

"Did I do the right thing?" she asked. Her eyes showed her uncertainty. "For God's sake tell me I did the right thing." Her eyes glistened.

"You did," I assured her. "Somebody had to say it and, to my astonishment, while it was plain as day, it was just not something that had occurred to me, nor to the others. I know all the stories. I know the problem. We all do. But we all just got focused on one aspect of dealing with the issue of whether he should run or not. Thank God you spoke up. You likely saved Jim and the Party and the country years of unhappiness. Thank you, on behalf of all of us."

I raised my glass in a silent toast. She responded by raising hers.

Her eyes looked less troubled.

As far as I know, none of us ever spoke to one another about the meeting again. Two days later, Jim announced he was not going to run, "for personal reasons," that serviceable excuse that says both everything and nothing. There was media speculation about the decision, but nobody guessed—or at least published—the real reason. The new Prime Minister subsequently appointed Jim to a number of commissions and Boards over the next few years, and asked him to do some work that was important to the country internationally, things he could do without involving Toni. The work brought him pleasure and honour.

Toni died a decade after that fateful meeting, and Jim eight years later.

Dulcie returned to her work, and continued her commitment to the Party, with no gossip about any man in her life. She never married.

I remember thinking that day, as I walked back to my office, that Jim would have made a truly great Prime Minister were it not for something most people would think an irrelevancy: his choice of wives.

Some Odd People Get into Politics

He was a son of a bitch when he was drunk. Even after only a few drinks, he was indiscriminately argumentative—with his wife, his friends, his business associates, his employees, even the golf pro that tried so hard to improve his game. Sober, he was charming and funny, warm and generous, so they put up with it.

But you'd never have thought he had any future in politics.

Barry was a contemporary of my Old Man, born in the late 'teens, young adults during the bad days of the 'thirties, and off to war where he learned to be a man, to command, and to manage men. After the war, he came back to the small lumber town on British Columbia's frontier and, after a false start or two, discovered he had a talent for business. Like many men who came back from the war with the life-broadening experience that front-line combat gives and with luck, he was able to turn his ability, his ambition and his attitude into business success, rising above his parents and his contemporaries in the '50s to become modestly wealthy in the '60s, and with some prominence in the community.

While he was a son of a bitch when he was drinking, as I say, Barry was otherwise charming and a good judge of people. So his employees put up with his drinking because he hired good people who forgave him his faults, and his good judgment showed in the tolerance of his friends, in the people he did business with and in choosing a wife. Everybody in the little town knew Marie and agreed that, whatever luck and judgment he had, Barry had outdone himself in landing Marie. But, as I say, he was known to be a son of a bitch when he was drinking.

Then one day he stopped drinking. He became a consumer of vast quantities of coffee, until he realized that interfered with his sleeping, then he moved on to decaf, soft drinks and tea. The change in his personality, reputation and business success was profoundly for the better. His businesses became more successful; his friendships thrived and, as his reputation grew, so did the honours he earned from his charity and political work. He was an odd person to get into politics, lacking polish and formal schooling as he did, but he ran for Parliament and served two terms, was a modestly successful Cabinet Minister, then left of his own choice. "Too much travel, too much wasted time," he said by way of explanation. "And too much time away from Marie."

People eventually forgot what a son of a bitch he had been when he drank. He lived a happy life. That was clear. Then, in her 60s, Marie died. A cancer that got away from the doctors, he said, bitterly and briefly. He wasn't one to be too forthcoming about personal things. It was a large funeral, and everybody who was anybody in town attended, along with a lot of nobodies that liked Barry and Marie. It was very sad because Marie was too young and no one was sure what would happen to Barry without her. Some said that the kids—he had fathered four—would see he's looked after.

About six weeks after the funeral, my Old Man called to invite him to lunch. Barry sounded happy to accept and when they met, the Old Man noted how drawn he seemed but how well he was masking his grief.

The waiter seated them and asked for a drink order. "A beer, any brand," said the Old Man. The waiter turned to Barry, who seemed lost in thought. "A draft beer. A pint of Canadian," he said quietly. The Old Man could not contain his surprise. He remembered when Barry drank, and what a son of a bitch he was.

"I thought you didn't drink," said the Old Man, who couldn't restrain himself.

Barry looked past the Old Man into a distance far away. Fifteen long seconds dragged out. He looked sad, years beyond his age, for those seconds.

"I don't. But I think today I owe myself one."

Not content to leave well enough alone something that was obviously intensely personal, the Old Man said, "Why did you quit?"

Barry started to tell the story. The Old man told it to me the way he remembered hearing it, years later, when Barry was gone. He said he never told anybody else.

"Barry", the Old Man said, "got that distant look in his eyes again, and that sad look on his face."

"You know I used to be a son of a bitch when I drank, I guess."

The Old Man nodded.

"I was hard on everybody. It didn't make any sense. But everybody around me suffered. The guys I worked with and who worked for me, my friends, mostly Marie and the kids. I'd come home and if the kids were still up, I would rant and yell and scare hell out of them. If they weren't still awake, it meant I had likely drank even more, and I used to beat up Marie something awful. I guess the kids knew."

"I didn't know that. That side of you," said the Old Man.

"Well, Marie went to extremes to cover up. She had bad bruises, and one time we had to go to Vancouver for medical treatment. No secrets in the Regional Hospital here. It went on for years. I don't know how she took it, or why.

"One night I came home drunker than usual and just went to bed and fell fast asleep, clothes on. When I woke up, the room was still dark. I didn't know where I was—you know that feeling sometimes when you first wake up? I was cold and uncomfortable, and I tried to roll over from my back to my side and I couldn't move.

"Then I realized my wrists and ankles were tied to the four-poster bed, holding me there and I realized I was naked, and lying on a cold plastic sheet. My tongue was dry and my mouth felt dirty and I couldn't move and I was still maybe a little drunk and I was confused. I realized I'd woken up because I had to pee. I yelled, 'Marie!' as loud as I could.

"She came through the door within a few seconds, turning the light on."

"'You're awake. Good. Now we can talk.'"

"Talk?" I said, "What in Christ is going on? Why am I tied down? Where are my clothes? What's happening?"

I was yelling. I was angry. Real angry.

"'Yes, talk. You see, I'm just not going to take it any more. Your drunkenness, your beating me, your terrorizing the children. I just CANNOT take it any more.'" She was very calm.

"Then I'll stop," I said. Loudly. Impatiently. But still very angry.

"'No you won't. You won't until you know how it feels. You won't until you understand I'm serious. You've said before you'd stop, but you didn't. So now we have to do it my way.'"

"Your way? You can't believe that this is the way to deal with this?"

I tried to struggle against the ropes, but they were tight and tied well. I yelled, loudest I could, "GET ME THE HELL OUT OF HERE!"

"She watched, with a determined...troubled... look on her face. It was a look I had never seen in nine years of marriage. She left the room and came back a minute later carrying a small kid's-sized baseball bat that we'd bought for Junior."

"'Now', she said, 'you son of a bitch, you're going to learn about how it hurts. You're going to learn how the hurt is so much worse when it's done by somebody you love. You're going to suffer humiliation. You're going to be here for a couple days while you think about things. This will hurt, but it will hurt me as much to have to do it.'"

"Again I struggled. The ropes wouldn't give. "LET ME OUT!" I screamed, not giving a damn who heard.

"'Yell all you like,' said Marie. 'The kids are at my sisters for a few days, everybody thinks you and I have gone to Vancouver, and the near neighbours are away. Yell all you like. Nobody will hear. You see, I've been planning this party for a while and we're all by ourselves. I knew when I heard the neighbours were going to be away to get prepared and I knew I could depend on you to come home drunk.'"

"Suddenly, she brought the bat down like she was trying for a home run or chopping a stubborn piece of wood. She hit me across the chest. I was more surprised than hurt, though, with that first one. She didn't even pause. She then brought the bat down with all her strength—I swear—across my gut. This time I yelled. Jesus it hurt. You know, after Italy I was in Normandy and I was hit and spent some time in the hospital. That hurt was nothing like this little baseball bat. She hit me a couple times more—just as hard, across my thighs, then a couple more across my knees and legs. God, it hurt. Then she stopped. She was out of breath. And there were tears running down her cheeks."

"'That'll do for now,' she said, walked out of the room, turning the light off and closing the door. I lay there, still screaming in agony. I can't describe how I felt. Hurt, Jesus, yes. But outraged! How could anybody do this to me? To me? This was my wife. I loved my wife. How could she do this? Then I started to cry. I hadn't cried since Holland—the second time I was wounded. It only lasted a while. The house was quiet, and I guess I still had some booze in me and I fell asleep."

At this point in the narrative, the waiter brought the beer. Barry sipped his slowly, savouring it.

"I awoke again I don't know how much later. I was really uncomfortable on that cold, sticky plastic sheet. I was stiff and, my God, I was sore. But then I realized that what had woken me was that now I really had to take a pee. I yelled, 'Marie!'

"She came in the room, silently. Softly, she said, 'What?'

"I gotta pee somethin' awful."

"'So, pee.'"

"No, you can't mean that?' I couldn't believe it. Even in the war, scared as I was, cold as I was, pinned down under fire as I might be, I never peed myself. 'I can't.'

"'You can and you will. You're going to be where you are for a couple of days.'"

"No."

"'Yes. Get used to it.'

"Then I realised that she had the bat with her. And she repeated the routine, but backwards. First two real hard ones on the shins, then the thighs, then the stomach, then the chest. You ever been hit really hard on the shins? My God." He shook his head remembering. He shuddered.

"Then she left again, again with tears in her own eyes. After a while, I called again. I was in agony with having to pee. She didn't answer. I laid there then I just couldn't hold on any longer. I started to pee myself and I cried. I couldn't help myself.

"I won't go into a lot more detail. You get the picture. I was there two nights and most of three days. She would come in with towels and soak up the urine, and clean up the other, then throw everything in the washing machine. She brought me bread and hot soup, and fed me like I was a hospital patient. And she would beat me—three, four times a day. Beat me bad.

"Between cleanings and feedings and beatings we would talk. She told me how much I had hurt her. And she cried in the telling. And I cried. By the end the telling was hurting me more than the beating and I gotta tell you, I was black and blue nearly everywhere from ankle to neckline.

"We talked about my drinking and why I drank—insecurity, I think, and the war.

We talked about the kids, and friends, and the businesses. And we talked about divorce. Why she hadn't asked for one, or even run away, even when she knew I was out drinking and when I'd come home I'd beat her. I loved her. And she loved me. A woman with less love would have cut and run. She thought I was worth salvaging.

"I had a lot of time to think, mostly in the dark. My anger and resentment and hurt slowly changed to complete mortification. How could I have been such a shit to everybody? At some point I realized I had to change my ways.

"On the third afternoon, she came into the room, without the bat for the first time, I guess. She asked me if I wanted loose. Jesus."

"'OK, you son of a bitch'—she was back to her language of the first day, not recognizing what had happened since. She had a butcher knife with her. I really didn't know what she was going to do with that knife. But her voice was harsh and bitter.

"'I'm going to cut you lose, and maybe you'll kill me right here and now. Or maybe you'll just leave and never come back. But if you stay, we both better understand two things. If you ever drink again, you'll beat me up again. And if you ever beat me up again, you better kill me, because after the beating you'll go to sleep, and I'll kill you. Do you understand what I am saying? Do you really understand?'

"She watched my eyes. She was looking into them for truth.

"I began to cry. I told her I would never take another drink; I would never harm her again. I told her I loved her, to please let me go.

"There was real doubt in her eyes, I can tell you. I think she thought that as soon as I was loose, I'd kill her. She knew I killed people in the war, close up, messy-like. I'd done it before. But she cut the ropes. I pulled myself together. I was so goddamned stiff and sore I could hardly move. I didn't say anything, went to the bathroom and drew a hot bath and lay there for an hour. Then I got dressed and went for an hour's walk. She had left the house during my bath, but when I got back she was there, cooking dinner, a fine dinner.

"We never spoke about the incident again and I never had another drink. But she's gone now and I think I can trust myself just this once."

He lifted his glass, in an imaginary toast.

The faraway look returned to his eyes. Lunch arrived and they ate in silence. He finished the beer. They were good friends and didn't have to talk to understand one another.

The Old Man said that, as far as he knew, Barry never took another drink. "But," said the Old Man, "he was an odd man to get into politics. The only politician I think I ever knew who didn't drink."

Thinking in Egypt

As Frank walked up O'Connor Street toward The Hill, his mind again focused on the future. Frank—The Honourable Frank Wright, P.C., M.P., a Member of Canada's Parliament for these past 18 years, and a Privy Councilor—denoting, in his case membership in the Cabinet, for 12—was a troubled man. He had been an active politician for most of his life. Active at university and in the backrooms, organizing and raising money, a municipal councilor, and then mayor. Finally, a run for a seat in Parliament at 50 in a constituency the big city political wizards said he couldn't win, in a part of the country they also said it was useless to try to organize. But Frank was ambitious, and he had organized, planned and worked—worked hard— for ten years against the day when he thought that in fact he could win.

All the stars lined up for that election 18 years ago. His Party, then in Opposition, was unexpectedly up in the polls just as the Prime Minister thought he had a better chance of winning an election then than later and was wrong. The longtime incumbent in the riding had unexpectedly stepped down having allowed his organization to deteriorate. Caught with a second-rate candidate and a rusty organization, the Prime Minister's Party lost to the popular mayor.

Frank thought about that first campaign as he walked up O'Connor Street into the glare of the newly risen spring sun. Most ministers had their chauffeur pick them up at their residences in the morning, driving them to The Hill or to their departmental offices, during which they read papers from their briefcases. On those few days when it was fit to walk in Ottawa—a city of tropical summers and arctic winters—Frank preferred to walk. By now the winter snow was gone, but the morning was chilly and the puddles of water on the street were frozen. It gave him unhurried time to think. He was of the view that in the harried and pressured life of a Cabinet minister there was too little time to think. Thus, he relished the walk on those days that were suitable.

When he had first arrived in Ottawa, he concluded that if he were there even for only four years real estate was a good investment, so he had bought a condominium in a new high-rise along the Rideau Canal. When, after becoming a Minister two years later, it became clear that he needed to move Donna and their two teenage boys to Ottawa they bought a house in the pleasant and affordable Alta Vista area and rented out the condo. The boys were now gone, so they rented the house out and moved back to the condo. No snow to shovel, and within walking distance to The Hill. Usually his route took him down—or up, really—O'Connor Street.

His thinking these days was increasingly retrospective, he realized. He wondered if his subconscious was trying to tell him something.

He remembered being disappointed initially at not being included in that first Cabinet, 18 years ago. Two years later, when the late-night call came quite unexpectedly from the Prime Minister, he was grateful that he had experienced two years on the backbench to understand the ways of parliamentary life that would have otherwise eluded him had he joined the Cabinet right away.

He had learned the sense of powerlessness of the backbenchers of every party, in Opposition or not. When he became a Minister, he always remembered and he cultivated the company and advice of the ordinary parliamentarians. He benefited, too, from the realization that most of the members of the other parties were decent people whose motivations for getting into public life were much like his own. Long days of public hearings as the parliamentary committees he served on, crisscrossing the country, followed by long evenings of drinking and sharing experiences, perspectives and ideologies had given him a broader view of the country and of the other Parties than he had when he arrived.

When he became a Minister, he therefore viewed Opposition members' suggestions and proposed amendments to legislation with a more open mind than did most of his Cabinet colleagues. And he chaffed with the backbenchers under the niggardly budgetary rules of Parliament of the day. The pay was not great and he had himself taken a cut in net income of more than 40 percent when he was elected, what with new and greater personal expenses of maintaining two residences, foreign to Joe Lunchbucket. It was difficult to keep an extra residence in Ottawa, and to cover travel, entertainment and other expenses in the constituency that had to be borne and that were not adequately covered by his then parliamentary salary and tax-free allowance. But Donna worked, and that helped.

He could never adequately explain to the ignorant that the so-called "percs" of subsidized meals in the Parliamentary Restaurant and "free" airline trips back and forth to his riding were something he would have gladly traded for full compensation upon submission of receipts, as in the private sector. Or, preferably, the pleasure of going home for dinner every night, after a half-hour commute, rather than fourteen hours every second weekend in an airplane.

It bothered him, sometimes even yet, that some journalists earning twice the salary of a backbencher for a small fraction of the work, the hours, the pressure and the responsibility would occasionally write cheap-shot articles about parliamentary salaries and benefits. He remembered an era now long past when there were no provisions—or limited opportunities—for spouses or children of MPs to travel to Ottawa. Any time he, as a Minister, had a government aircraft traveling anywhere, he would have a member of his staff notify backbenchers from his destination area of every Party of any spare seats, so spouses, children or staff could hitch a ride.

This attitude made him not only a better Minister but gave him insights into Opposition party and backbench thinking that was very useful in Cabinet, since he learned a great deal on those intimate flights on the executive jet.

Frequently, it was he that the then-PM would turn to for comment during Cabinet debate when the Opposition's opinion was relevant.

He crossed Somerset Street after waiting for the light, his mind recalling some of his early days on The Hill when, he realized later, he knew so little he was potentially almost dangerous.

That is, as one long-experienced politician frequently put it, "everyone in public life in only ever one sentence from political oblivion." He walked the next block thinking of the politicians he had seen destroyed over his life, slowly or quickly, by failing to obey that maxim.

As he crossed Cooper Street against the light because there was no traffic his mind turned to more immediate concerns. There were rumours. There were always rumours, of course, and one learned to live with them. To ignore them was dangerous. And so he had made a practice of listening to the "tom-toms." The current rumours were of Cabinet reassignments—or a "shuffle" in popular parlance. Frank wondered what his subconscious was trying to tell him as he considered the possible veracity of those rumours.

It gave him feelings of guilt occasionally, that he spent more time than he often thought useful sifting through the detritus of idle speculation that consumes so much of Parliamentary reporting. However, on two occasions the effort had allowed him to salvage his political career.

The first time, he was an inexperienced Minister. His department had been nursing for many years a legislative initiative that his Deputy Minister persuaded him to take to Cabinet only weeks after he joined the Cabinet. Somehow—because it was in retrospect plainly a flawed and politically ill-advised piece of legislation and probably economically bad as well—Cabinet approved its introduction in Parliament. For some weeks there was general silence about the Bill as it sat on the Order Paper awaiting second reading. Then an enormous controversy erupted, emanating from the Big Business community in Toronto.

Frank was taken aback by its ferocity. In his 28 months in Parliament he had seen nothing similar. Indeed, he could recall nothing quite like it going back a decade. He defended the Bill publicly as he had to, but privately he paused. He was by nature a careful and methodical guy. He was troubled by both the bitterness of the criticisms of his Bill and the defensiveness of his Deputy, who had assured him of the innocuous nature of the proposed policy.

Thus, when the House Leader wanted to call the Bill for second reading debate, Frank demurred, arguing he could not be in Ottawa that week—for it would be a lengthy debate and he had prior travel commitments. Then he quickly arranged some departmental inspection tours.

In Toronto, he had quiet chats with several senior party members—the kinds of people whose names show up on no party executive lists or in the media. He had lunch with the editor-in-chief of the most thoughtful newspaper. Without coming out and asking their views about the Bill, he learned enough. He did the same kind of thing in Montreal and two other cities. He had drinks with two of the best-connected columnists in the country, people who played a major role in setting the agenda for serious policy debate in Canada. He made sure to listen carefully, and to think afterwards about what had been said or left unsaid. He called an old friend who was a top-rated university economist and spent a quiet Saturday afternoon getting his take on the substance of the Bill. And he contacted an expert in public administration, also an academic, for his views which were freely given and damning.

He returned to Ottawa after a week of this sort of research and contemplation and reflected on his new perspective different from what he received from his Deputy. He approached four of his colleagues and without telling them of the results of his tour told them of his concerns. Three of them told him the reaction was just all Opposition politics and to ignore it, but the fourth said that the Bill was in real trouble, and that Frank best be very cautious.

Frank had more respect for this last Minister than he had for almost all of his other 24 colleagues together. He asked for advice on how to deal with it. His colleague told him to just wait a few weeks, but keep the Bill from a parliamentary debate that would commit the Government to pushing it through. He did this. Then he learned that the senior fundraisers for the party had met with the PM and reported a severe falling-off in business donations. It was, said one of them, almost like a conspiracy by the business community to pressure the government by denying the Party much of the money it needed to accumulate to fight the next election.

With this information in hand, Frank had plotted his next move carefully. He knew that the PM had no respect for the business community, and would only bend reluctantly. By the time that happened precious fundraising time would have been lost and, in acting late, the PM might be forced to over-react by firing Frank, who wasn't naïve about the irreplaeablity of Ministers.

Thus, Frank gave a carefully phrased, not-for-attribution story to a trusted columnist, telling her that the department in analyzing the public response to the proposed legislation was arguing internally that the Bill ought to be allowed to die on the Order Paper. That is, not be proceeded with until it could be seriously re-thought.

The column ran. The departmental spokespersons, of course, denied the story. The PMO charged that there had been a leak which of course gave credence to the story. The reaction from the business community was ecstatic, even to a denied leak. The party fundraisers called to say they hoped the rumour was true.

The next week, Frank proposed to Cabinet—without going into any sordid details—that the Bill be allowed to die. The Cabinet, with what Frank thought was indecent haste, agreed. His colleagues of course thought he was acting on departmental advice, while his Deputy thought that the Bill had been dropped because of direction from Cabinet or the Prime Minister. He realized then that many of his colleagues were, as Walter Lippman had observed many years earlier, "insecure and intimidated men". It was an insight that would serve him well.

Walking out of the Cabinet room afterwards, his most esteemed colleague said, "You have the makings of a political genius. You handled that very well. It has no ones fingerprints on it. Very good."

Thus, over the next 16 years, and four more portfolios, interspersed with four years in Opposition, he had developed the reputation of being the Prime Minister's firefighter. Some Minister has made a mess? Frank was sent in to tidy it up in a way that neither embarrassed his predecessor nor appeared to signal some massive change in policy. A new initiative that required a deft political touch? Frank was fingered to implement it. He had been told, early on, that politics was like swimming among sharks, which you could do with impunity as long as you didn't bleed. But if the sharks smelled blood, they would tear you apart. He thought that working hard at not bleeding was worthwhile.

Thus, through it all, nobody had ever laid a political hand on him. He was squeaky clean ethically, respected sufficiently by Opposition members that they often gave him an easier time than he deserved, and not sufficiently colourful to attract too much—or the wrong kind of— press attention. Perhaps even more important, he didn't have the "royal jelly" that would have caused him a problem when the Party chose a new Leader. He thrived, in part, because no one saw him as a threat.

But now Frank was 68. He'd been around for a long time. He had never—amongst his five portfolios—had a senior Cabinet job. He'd never had Finance, or Foreign Affairs, or Transport. He regretted this. His opportunity to do something big, he told his wife two or three times, was not to be his destiny.

More to the point, an election was just around the corner. There was a clamoring for a changing of the guard, for more young people, for more women, in Cabinet, and for new ideas, for different ways. A demand for renewal. His riding was perceived by many—although not by him—as "safe". There were pressures—polite pressures, to be sure—for him to step aside. There were rumours that the Party organizers were out trying to recruit a "star" candidate, then to force him out. He had never tried to direct the Party apparatus in his province so most of the Party apparatchiks were not his people. He had always known this was a risk, but he calculated that he was strong enough in seniority and in Cabinet to withstand these sorts of pressures.

But maybe for not much longer.

He stopped for the light at Laurier Street. Five blocks to go, to think about these issues.

An election could be expected as early as 10 months, he thought. These days preparation—election readiness—started earlier and earlier. Or it could be as late as 18 months. The Cabinet had not had a formal session to consider it, but his own view was that the new PM wanted to make some changes in both personnel and direction sooner rather than later. So, what happens next? Should he dig in and fight to stay, or try to bargain a nice sinecure with the PM, such as a Senate or diplomatic appointment, just go gracefully into the night, or try to find something in the private sector before he was pushed out?

As he crossed Slater Street, he decided that he should start to make careful arrangements to ease himself out. Maybe. Or maybe not.

His ruminations were interrupted by his Chief of Staff, Francois Dufour, who had walked down from the Centre Block to meet him. He often did this when he wanted 10 more minutes with Frank than the schedule allowed for some discussion of political or departmental matters.

"What's up?"

"Nothing critical. I just enjoy your company."

Frank knew this wasn't the reason, but let it pass. Then it came.

"Minister, what have you heard about possible election dates?"

"Nothing. You know both that there's been no discussion of it in Cabinet, and that I am not one of the PM's intimates who would be brought into the first round of discussions of the possibilities if he wanted to consider it. Why do you ask?"

"I had breakfast with Wilson an hour ago. He called yesterday saying he'd wanted to schedule a chat with me for some time—an assertion I believe to be untrue—and he said he had a breakfast cancelled and asked if I were available. Well, when the National Director calls, one goes if one is either ambitious or even curious. I am mostly the latter."

"You do yourself an injustice." Frank wanted to hear more.

"Well, it was most confusing. He says that work on an early election is now getting underway. While he didn't ask me to not tell you this, likely because he thought I wouldn't agree, and I suspect another reason, he told me that they might want to second me to the PMO for a period to work on election planning. I told him I couldn't leave you in the lurch."

Francois had given him three important pieces of information.

"Francois, if you want to go, I think you should go. But give me a month or six weeks to iron out the wrinkles of the transition. I think Billy is about able to fill your shoes—not as well, of course, but adequately. Wilson should understand."

"Billy has had a really great teacher," responded Francois, referring of course to himself, and he smiled, a little slyly.

"Now." said Frank, "you said that you thought Wilson had another reason for not asking that you not tell me about the approach. What was that?"

"I think it's a signal that you start to prepare yourself for leaving the Cabinet. I hate to put it that way, but that's what I thought. I'm sorry."

He was sorry too, thought Frank. They had worked together for five years, and he thought Francois was first-rate.

"I think its time to start thinking about that sort of thing, too," responded Frank. "I had recently come to the same conclusion." He did not say it was a conclusion reached only one block back.

"What are you going to do?"

He took a deep breath while he made an instant decision.

"I'm going to take the Easter Break, and go to Egypt to think. A week of scuba diving in the Red Sea. Don't look at me like that. Egypt's a great place to think. Nobody speaks English, or knows who I am. Canada doesn't exist. So I'm pretty well alone with my own thoughts, uninterrupted. And in the silence of the clear waters of the Red Sea, I know I will see the future. I want to get Billy in today and the three of us have a look at my schedule and see how I can squeeze two weeks away from here as soon as the House rises for Easter."

Francois could hardly not show his astonishment. He had known Frank for something like eight years. Worked for him for over five. Thought he knew him well, but this? Most Ministers would have responded by thinking how they could scheme to resist the pressure to step down. Frank, he thought, was almost welcoming it.

"The Red Sea?"

"Yes, best diving in the world. Been there twice before. Want to go again. It's a very good place to think, and I want to be where I can think without interruption."

They arrived at the members' entrance to the Centre Block and took the elevator to the fourth floor. It was still early in the day, and the sound of their heels on the grey marble floors echoed against the stone walls. They said little more. When they arrived at the north hallway office, it was 8:15.

Francois said, "You have a half hour before we meet to discuss the day. You want to include Billy?" Frank nodded. The transition was underway.

Three weeks later, an Air Canada flight took Frank to Frankfurt, and an EgyptAir Boeing 767 flew him to Hurgada, a tourist destination on the Red Sea about 400 kilometers south of Cairo. A minibus took him and a group of 14 others south another 150 kilometres to Quseer.

Pre-Christian Romans would see the dock area as unchanged in two thousand years, he thought to himself, except for the rubber tires on the donkey carts, and the ubiquitous cell phones.

He gathered his clothes-bag and dive gear from the van and, under the hot April sun, walked down the ancient stone wharf to his boat. His was the fifth. There were two beyond his. They were all about the same. Approximately 36 meters long, each accommodated about two dozen divers in roomy, air-conditioned cabins.

The boats were run by Egyptians, but owned by Germans, he thought. It seemed that, generally, if you wanted to dive the southern Red Sea, you flew via Frankfurt and did business with the Germans. If you wanted the north—Sharm el Shekh—you went via London and did business with the Brits. He hated London and did not much like the Brits. So here he was. The diving was better, anyway.

An hour later, the boat left, under a cloudless and very bright blue sky. It was hot and he knew he would have to keep out of the sun. The other divers were 14 Germans, a Swiss, two French, four Swedes, and two Italians. With me, he calculated, that made 22. Eight, including the Swiss, were female, none distinctively beautiful. Most spoke enough

English that he could get by. None knew very much about Canada, and none were very curious about him. He liked it that way.

He was buddied up by the dive masters with the Swiss woman. After a single dive he realized that she was a skilled diver and was happy with that arrangement. Being partnered with an inexperienced diver could have made things difficult, if not dangerous, and certainly unenjoyable. She was a private person, and didn't ask anything more personal of him than how long he had been diving. His response, "Thirty years, about 500 dives," satisfied her. She didn't want to dive with a guppy, either.

Thus, Frank spent six days, notionally with 21 other divers, but intellectually and emotionally by himself. He got some sun, enjoyed the Egyptian food, did three or four dives a day, had two good Egyptian beers each evening after the last dive, and spent a lot of time thinking, usually on the shaded top-deck of the boat.

He thought about his years in government, about what was happening currently, and he reflected on past and current lost opportunities. Not just his, but the larger picture. He wondered about the direction the PM was going to be taking. The government, he realized, was a little adrift and thought of many things it should be doing. He sighed. Not his problem.

At the end of it, he'd made up his mind. He'd go to the PM, acknowledge that he had been around a long time, and offer to step aside and help his successor in the constituency get elected. The Party had been good to him. He had the opportunity to get out while the getting was good, on his own terms. He would take it.

He took the bus to Cairo from Hurgada, enjoying the experience of mixing with the hoi polloi and then wandered around that city for three days, accompanied by his wife. The week he had been diving, she'd been in Paris. She'd been overjoyed by his suggestion for a surprise holiday, and asked him if there was some reason. He told her.

Of course, he had had to use his Ministerial passport, so the Egyptians tried to interest him in some of their official hospitality. He allowed himself to attend one diplomatic gathering with the Canadian Ambassador, but begged off on all the other invitations. He tried to make it clear to the Ambassador that he and Donna would appreciate some peace and privacy. Nonetheless, he knew that Egyptian security was never very far away and while he considered Cairo safe, for her sake he appreciated it.

They sneaked back into Ottawa without fanfare on a Sunday and on Monday he called Therese, the PM's private secretary and asked for an appointment. He was to see the PM over lunch on Wednesday.

By Wednesday he was acutely aware of the growing speculation about Cabinet changes, and thanked his luck that he had got back to take the initiative rather than receiving a phone call telling him he was out.

Going into the PM's office in the Langevin Block for lunch, Frank looked out the windows across to the Centre Block. "All this coming to an end," he thought. "Better to do it now, this way, than later, bitterly, even regretfully and hurt. Take the high road."

The PM greeted him.

"I hear you've been away. Great tan."

It wasn't with great warmth, Frank thought, noting that the PM had not asked him where he'd been, but then this PM was not a very warm guy. Few Prime Ministers are, he knew, when they're off stage.

"I'd heard you like lobster salad," said the PM. "So I thought we should have that. I like it too. And some good Mosel. Another of your favourites, I'm told.

You and I haven't had lunch together in, what, six, seven months?"

Frank nodded. "Eight, actually." This meal and the PM's manner made him think of the Last Supper, somehow, or the last meal given a prisoner before the hanging.

"Thank you for releasing Francois to Wilson," began the PM."Having someone in on the planning of the election early gives me much more confidence than I would otherwise have in the outcome. So, thank you, again. I appreciate it personally."

"Francois's a good guy. Very capable. Honest, frank, politically sensitive. He has a great career ahead of him. He has saved my sorry ass more than a couple times. I'm glad he has this opportunity."

The lobster salad and the wine were served. Frank again looked out the window. Wistfully.

"But," said Frank, "it was in connection with the coming election that I wanted to see you." He saw no reason not to go right to the heart of the matter.

"I've taken a short vacation to consider my future, do a lot of thinking and I wanted to tell you of my conclusions." He put a forkful of lobster salad in his mouth. The PM took a sip of wine and said nothing.

"I've been around for some time. I assume you're looking to make some changes, to bring in new talent, give hope to younger guys. Thus, while I do not really want to give up public life, I suppose I should face these facts and tell you frankly that I'm quite prepared to step aside as soon as you decide on the changes you need to make." He took another forkful of salad, and indicated it was the PM's turn to say something.

"You say you're not ready to leave public life. What did you have in mind?"

"Well, I'm just back from a week of scuba diving. I went to Egypt to do some thinking. I know that I'm healthy. I don't feel 'old.' I've lots of energy. I enjoy what I do, and think I have some talent for it. At the same time, we can't all stay here forever. So, if there is some other task you'd like me to do, I will happily undertake it. But I'm not going to cling to a Cabinet post like a limpet.

"But please understand I'm not talking about any quid pro quo, here. The Party, you, and your predecessors have been good to me. I want to leave—or continue to serve outside the Cabinet—in whatever capacity I can. But as I read it, my time in Cabinet is over."

"What other things did you have in mind?"

"Oh, nothing in particular. An ambassadorship, or the UN, or whatever. There has been discussion of a Royal Commission on our energy future. As I say, wherever you think I can be of help. Or maybe I just go and hang up my track shoes." He ended with a shrug, having said it all, he recognized, with a tone of resignation in his voice.

"Why do you think I want you to go?" the PM asked.

Frank thought for a minute. It was a question that surprised him.

"Well, as I say, I've been around a while. You're facing an election shortly. You'll want to put a new face on things. That's reality. I'm an old face."

"But not a tired face, you say."

"No, not a tired face. In fact the dive holiday gave me time to recharge some batteries and to start to think about some things. Do you know how bad, how really bad, how negative and destructive our overly-complicated income tax system is? Not intentionally, but collateral damage to tax collection. I gave some thought to that. The rule the government has that no other department can research and propose tax policy changes other than Finance is just awful, and is a huge hindrance to governmental policy-making, for instance. We should do something about that. We have to have a close look at our institutional arrangements for coordinating federal programs with provincial, and look at developing what I call 'needless overlap of programs strategy' to economize. There's too much waste when we do something and the provinces do pretty much the same thing." He paused. The PM looked at him expectantly, as if he wanted Frank to go on. So he did.

"We have a shelter problem in this country—not just a problem of the relative few that are homeless, but a huge shortfall in rental housing production. We have a housing distribution problem—too many old couples rattling around in large houses, while too many growing families need that housing, and could make better use of it. Existing policies discourage making that housing available to those that need it. And about 40 per cent of Canadians are tenants, many badly housed, and our tax laws penalize them while favouring home owners, who are already better off, financially. Tax policy discriminates against those who would invest in new rental housing, so little gets built. The problem is, again, our tax laws and the concern the Finance Department has for revenues to the exclusion of a broader public interest." Again, he paused, and again the PM signaled for him to carry on.

"I don't know how we can keep accepting hundreds of thousands of immigrants each year without proper policies in place for them. For instance, to properly house them, educate them, integrate them. On immigration, we are just not thinking our way through the implications of the wide-open family reunification policy. It is potentially a fiscal and demographic time bomb. And so on." Without further encouragement, he continued.

"On foreign policy, I think we have to really re-commit to the UN as the cornerstone of our foreign policy. You know there was a time for many years when Canada as a matter of principle was the first country to pay its dues every year. That's no longer the case, reflecting how our commitment to that world organization has slipped. I could go on, I guess, but...."

He paused, realizing he'd already gone on a little long, and displayed an uncharacteristic passion. But, he thought, "What the hell?"

"So, no, not tired." There was eagerness and impatience in his voice.

The PM looked at him querulously, but said nothing.

Frank refilled his wine glass and drank half of it. Ah, a good, chilled Mosel.

There was a long pause. Frank had made his point, had finished his meal as he had talked, and now he just wanted some coffee and to get away.

The Prime Minister continued his silence, ate the last of his salad, and sipped the last of his wine. He sat back in his chair, appearing pensive. Frank glanced out the window, again, to the view of the Centre Block. He'd really hate to leave. He knew it, but he had done what he knew was right.

Finally, the Prime Minister spoke.

"Frank, the rumours are true. I am shuffling my Cabinet the day after tomorrow. I've not spoken to anyone yet, and hope to do it all, very quickly, tomorrow. You can do me one last service, if you will?"

Frank got the message. One last service. He nodded.

"You've been around a long time. You're careful with your judgments. I want some advice."

Frank nodded.

"What do you think of the current Finance Minister?"

This was not what Frank was expecting. George—the current Finance Minister—he considered a friend. He had gone out of his way to support Frank a couple of times when that support was crucial to Frank's success in Cabinet. Frank sort of felt that he owed George one.

"You put me in an awkward position, Prime Minister. George is a friend. I'm loath to be critical."

"That's why I asked. It's easy to get tough judgments from a man's enemy."

The PM was waiting for an answer.

Frank sighed.

"Well, he's a fine man. A real human being. A mench, I guess. But the portfolio is too big for him. He busies himself with a thousand loose ends and does not, I think, see the Finance portfolio for the lynch-pin of the government's whole being that it is, or should be. So, he's a little more than adequate. But he's a lot better than two of the people some folks in the press have suggested as his replacement, if that helps."

He hoped he'd not been too critical of George.

The PM looked at him, somewhat strangely, Frank thought.

"You have it all exactly right, and exactly wrong."

Frank was confused, and said so.

The Prime Minister paused in his reply.

"Frank, I agree you've been around a long time. Over these last few months, since I took this job, I've had to look at all my former Cabinet colleagues with a very critical eye. Some people that I like very much I have to retire tomorrow. I hate the prospect. But the future of this government depends on tomorrow's Cabinet changes, how well we do over the next few months, and if we're successful in reinvigorating this government. It needs reinvigorating. I've concluded that small changes on the periphery won't do. Some senior people have to go. And we need some new ideas and approaches."

"In part we have this opportunity because the other guys fumbled in bringing in new guys, adapting to change, developing new ideas. They had momentum and I think they've lost it. I think we're getting our momentum back. But it requires that I grasp opportunity with both fists and gamble.

Frank waited for the axe.

"Frank, I plan to rebuild my Cabinet around you and your experience. Yes, I'm bringing in some new blood, five new, young but promising faces. I hope they'll do well. But I want you to be the new Finance Minister. I agree with you about Finance. I want proposals for modernizing our tax laws, for encouraging more research and development and for more education investment. Housing, too, if you like. Move aggressively just as soon as you can extract policy and new ideas from those guys in the department. Or go outside. Recruit from the universities or Bay Street, or wherever. The point is, I want to take this government forward, and quickly. I do have to balance a Cabinet containing a few young hotshots with bright smiles with some experienced talent. Your long service and experience—and most importantly your sure touch with things—gives you the confidence you'll need to be bold, and me the knowledge that the spark-plug of the government is in good hands. Frank, as much as I know that I have to take a chance on some new people, I need guys with the surefootedness of long experience to make sure we don't bugger up.

"Have you got it in you? Will you do it?"

Frank was dumbfounded. He'd thought this all through so carefully. Mentally, he had all but retired to the cottage. He had his feet up on the table, the television tuned to an old movie and a cold beer in his hand. Suddenly, he had to focus on a very different future. His mind began to think rapidly about the implications of the PM's message. Then he stopped it before it got out of control. Finally. A chance, after so long, to do something...important!

"Yes, Prime Minister, I have, and I will. You've caught me by complete surprise." Frank's voice was humble. He felt a little moisture in his eyes.

The PM was smiling. He realized the coup he had pulled. He waited for Frank, who thought for a minute.

"When do we start, Prime Minister? Can I have Francois back? I'll need him. And I'll want a new Deputy Minister.

Defeat

Sometimes Things Just Turn Out Badly

In politics, electoral defeats, even expected defeats, are always difficult. Some politicians are clearly bitter from the realization that they don't have the numbers as the first few votes are counted. Others smell it coming during the election and become bitter even before the balloting. A few welcome it, given that they didn't have the courage to quit, but are resentful anyway because of the voters' rejection. Most never really get over it. Oh, they hide it well enough for a while but underneath after a few years and sometimes a few drinks, in some circumstances, the hurt and bitterness and resentment will come through.

Pete was determined he wasn't going to be one of those bitter guys. He vowed this to himself halfway through the campaign when he realized he was done for. No, sir. He was going to run a good campaign, for the sake of the troops if for no other reason and it would be a clean campaign. He wasn't going to mud-sling—although some of the troops thought he should be hitting harder. No, he wasn't going out with anybody saying good riddance to a bad loser.

He had a reputation outside politics and a life before politics. He had made a fine living as a journalist and as a writer of novels. Politics—one term in Ottawa—had been a mid-life lark. "Maybe I really did it only to get more grist for another novel," he sometimes thought. He had made a career of having a journalist's detached perspective and he wasn't going to lose it in a losing election campaign.

So when the seat-won numbers came in nationally on election night—the national party numbers from back east his troops were shocked. A loss of 36 seats to the B.C. border. There'd be a weak minority government at best or a possible loss nationally, depending on holding a few seats in BC. But he knew that the feeling he had that the voters were just not listening to him were accurate and it wasn't personal. Voters weren't listening to the Prime Minister most particularly. "Maybe," he thought in mid campaign, "the folks are not listening to me because they're not listening to the PM." By the end of the campaign, that explanation seemed compelling.

In fact, more than a few voters had said they were sad that they couldn't vote for him because they were so goddamned mad at that SOB Trudeau.

What could he say? He half-agreed with them, Trudeau was an SOB, and he didn't take these voters' comments personally.

On election night, the Liberals had held on to a bare plurality—109 seats to 107. It would have been a tie except that Norm Cafik held on to his seat by an unimaginably thin four votes.

But it was a defeat for Trudeau in every possible way except the one that really mattered. "The SOB could still hang on, with luck," Pete thought later.

Pete gave the requisite "victory speech" to the troops, an appropriate "good loser" quote to the media, and made his way to NDP headquarters to concede defeat to Harvey Watson. If there was anything that was hard to take that night, it was the jeers and catcalls from Watson's beered-up supporters as he pushed through the half-drunk, overjoyed crowd. They lacked any sense of class, he thought. He carefully measured and catalogued the mood, the atmosphere, his feelings and his emotions, self consciously filing them away for the day when he might have to describe the scene or something like it in a novel. He took in the noise, the odours, the electricity that is always in the air around a winner, even a Harvey Watson.

Oh, yes, there was another thing that was hard, he suddenly thought. Karen. His wife of 30 years hadn't been able to handle Ottawa, or the drinking that resulted from the pressures of being an MP or the frequent separations caused by his travel to cover his sprawling riding, or being separated from their friends—Ottawa was a cold city in more ways than one—and she had called it quits. It hurt that she's not here tonight. He had not thought of Karen much during the campaign. She'd hated campaigning in '68. Now there are no more campaigns. Maybe she'll be back, he thought now.

He congratulated Watson who was a nice guy, but no gret talent, not someone you'd vote for after admiring his life of accomplishment. In fact, his fundamental personal decency was his best feature. But now he was an MP. He'd be getting deep into complex problems, working longer hours than he ever had before and dealing with demanding and unreasonable constituents. Pete felt sorry for him. Pete knew he was a lot smarter than Harvey and he knew how hard it'd been for him.

He had a chance to think about what he'd say on the walk over to NDP headquarters and he said it well. Graciously. Sincerely. The boisterous crowd sensed both his grace and his sincerity, and quieted down to give him a fair hearing. They gave him a more than cursory hand of applause when he finished and stepped from the stage. Pete felt good about it all. And he filed it away in his memory.

He said to Watson privately, after he'd conceded, "Let's get together in the morning. I'd like to have a smooth transition. I want to get away for a while."

The relief on Watson's face was visible. Maybe his Party or his new constituents didn't know how over his head he'd be, but it was obvious that Watson knew. "Good for him," thought Pete.

"11:30 at The Café alright?"

Pete nodded.

He slept well. "Maybe the best sleep in four years," he thought as he shaved the next morning. He had to call Ottawa, and talk to Margarite. She was a prize, as secretaries went. She'd been active in politics at university before coming to Ottawa from New Brunswick 10 years earlier.

Unmarried, she loved her job and loved politics. She loved "The Hill". She was dedicated to Pete and more competent than all but perhaps a dozen other MPs' secretaries.

She'd arrived in Ottawa while the Liberals were still in Opposition in 1962 desperately interested in politics but with only the prospects of hope. Margarite had some savings—enough for a small apartment in an older building best described as seedy—and found some part-time work, and volunteered in the office of a Liberal Opposition MP for six months until the Diefenbaker government was defeated in the '63 election. By then, given that she "knew everybody on The Hill", and now had some experience, she landed a job in a Minister's office as a junior.

Margarite had thrived. But when her Minister was defeated in 1968—how that happened she could never figure out, because the incoming Trudeau tide washed more than a few underachievers up onto the beach—she found herself working for a backbencher.

She drew Pete and soon settled in. She came to love him in that way some secretaries do, not romantically but admiringly. She quickly mastered the vagaries and personalities of his far-flung rural constituency, and the peculiar politics and personalities of B.C. It was so far from New Brunswick and from Quebec, which she also knew so intimately. Everybody who knew the staff on The Hill was aware that she did a great job for Pete, and a couple of Ministers' offices tried to hire her away. They offered better money, but she stayed.

"It really made no sense, and now she was out of a job because he was out of a job," thought Pete, not wanting to face that reality. With the secretaries of more than 30 defeated Liberals looking for jobs on The Hill, it was not going to be easy for Margarite, despite her great reputation.

He had to talk to her. He practised what he'd say while he shaved.

He called her at a quarter after eight, 11:15 in Ottawa. She would be in the office by then, likely horribly hung-over from the previous evening. He suspected from his observations as a journalist that politicians and their outriders drank more in the agony of defeat than in the pleasure of victory. She answered the phone right away, and professionally. "Pete

Fleming's Office." Upbeat. Positive. Professional. When she heard his voice, her own dropped—or rather it sagged.

"You saw the results from here?" he offered.

"Yes, I'm sorry. Sometimes things just turn out badly." She had lost her boss in the previous election and had wondered earlier that morning if she were a jinx.

"Nothing to be sorry about. I just wasn't cut out for politics and it's an easy way out."

She knew this was true. His heart wasn't really in it, not like serious, career politicians, the guys for whom the political game came before money or family.

He paused, trying to think what he should say next.

"How're things in Ottawa?"

"Well, about as you'd expect."

She sighed.

"There is a raft of close races, military votes not yet in, recounts, and God knows what. It's very tense and very uncertain. It's expected that the bozos who ran that awful campaign will be resigning within days if not hours but, other than that, until everyone gets a better fix on the final seat numbers and Cabinet meets and assesses the damage and maybe the future, nobody knows. Of course, Trudeau may decide he can't stay on in any event, with such a result. I don't know if you've looked at the regional numbers, but Liberals carried only 53 seats of the 190 in English Canada. It's now a very much Quebec-dominated Party, with no seats at all in at least two, maybe three provinces. Some in the media are seeing it as a near total repudiation of Trudeau by English Canada. Even he should be able to see that. Other than that, everything is speculation. Lots of people around here lookin' for jobs, though."

"Including you?"

"Including me. So far, anyway"

"Well, don't worry. I'm off to see Watson at 11:30. I'm not planning to go back to Ottawa—not for a while, at least—I can't see the purpose and I really can't afford it. I'd like to pass on all the constituency files to Watson. Can you clean out the personal stuff? I think he knows just how difficult the job is, and he'll be very happy to keep you on, if you want that. Do you?"

This wasn't what she expected. In those days, defeated MPs had no big severance arrangement like later, no pension after one term, they didn't even have their plane fare back to Ottawa paid for if they lost, and didn't get their moving expenses back to the constituency paid for, either. It was grim. The day an MP was defeated, he was off the payroll, cold turkey.

"Well, sure, I'll clean things up, and stay long enough to show him around, but I don't think I could work for," she paused, seeking the right words, "one of them."

He knew what she meant. It was a partisan business. He couldn't fault her.

She changed the topic.

"What are you going to do with the apartment and the furniture? Will Karen come back and pack up if you don't?"

"I've not yet talked to her, so damned if I have any idea. As you know, I expected to be defeated, but I've not given any of this any thought. I'm stuck with the lease anyway for seven more months. I have to start to make some money before long so I can keep up those lease payments. Look, I'll call you again later, when I know more."

His meeting with Watson went well. Watson was delighted with the offer of an office, of constituency files, and of an at least interim competent secretary to help him get settled.

They discussed other things, and Pete tried to give him a little advice about an MP's life in Ottawa.

Then Pete went back to the office to call some of his defeated colleagues. One of them who had bought a house in Ottawa and expected to stay there at least until spring offered after not much hinting by Pete to store Pete's furniture—"a few things," as Pete described it—until spring.

He tried to call Karen. No answer. He checked. She'd not tried to reach him. That depressed him.

He then called Margarite again. She was still in the office at 6:30 in Ottawa, and admitted she'd got to the "D" files in the hours since their last conversation.

"Look", said Pete, "I've managed to get Larry to let me store the apartment's contents at his place until spring. I just can't afford to store them commercially and I can't afford to move them back here until Karen and I get things sorted out legally, I don't even know what's mine, what's hers, and what belongs to the Sally Ann."

Margarite knew of the financial crunch, because she had had to do the typing. She knew that when Karen left, even without being asked Pete had started sending her half his parliamentary salary. That kind of thing was why Margarite liked him so much. His sense of fairness. And it was why Pete was so broke, as well.

"So—and I know you hate the thought of moving—but could you find it your heart to straighten things up, separate out the personal, and hire a moving company to move the stuff?" asked Pete.

This was, he knew, a sensitive point. When she had moved to Ottawa as an impecunious just-graduated student, Margarite had rented the cheapest place she could find. It was a lot shoddier a decade later, but she was still there despite her vastly improved financial circumstances. She hated moving. She hated even the thoughts of moving. So there she stayed.

There was a long pause, then a resigned, "OK."

Margarite thought about what she had undertaken for the rest of the evening. By the end of the day at 8:30, she was at F.

The next day Margarite called three moving companies. She described the size and contents of the apartment, and its location. One said it did not want the job. The other two weaseled on price quotes, but it was clear it was going to be expensive. She called a truck-rental company and got what she thought was a reasonable deal.

Pete called first thing the next morning. "How soon do you think you can get them to clean out the apartment? I've talked to Watson again. It occurred to me he would need a place to stay and so I've sublet it to him until June, sight unseen." Triumph was obvious in his voice.

"I can get it cleared out over the weekend. Will that do?"

"Great. Thanks a lot," he said, perfunctorily. He moved on.

235

"Look, I've about got things under control here. I need a break before going back to earning a living. I'm taking off by car for a couple weeks down the Pacific Coast. Going to do a little fishing. We'll see how far I get before half the money runs out and then I'll turn around and come home. I'll call in from time to time."

She finished the office files to the letter 'Q' by Thursday night. In the meantime she had lined up the truck for Friday morning. She had called all the friends she—and Pete—had on The Hill. She explained the situation. She didn't want anybody in on this who didn't understand the difficulties beforehand. But most had been over to Pete's at one time or another and had seen the apartment.

You see, this was not just a small one-bedroom, new-efficiency-apartment-with-an-elevator-and-a-view favoured by most MPs—because most left their spouses back in the constituency—that contained a minimal amount of furniture. Not Pete—or, rather, not Pete and Karen.

Karen had decided that if Pete was going to be spending most of his time in Ottawa, so would she. The home in B.C. had been leased out, and most of the accumulated detritus of many years of marriage had been moved to Ottawa in 1968. But that wasn't the last of it. Karen decided that she wanted to live in a roomy apartment in a building with "character". That meant renting—in this case—a large three-bedroom unit on the fourth floor in a building built before elevators were installed in apartment buildings.

Four flights of steep, narrow stairs! That was why the moving companies were so difficult. They knew the building. What should be an easy half-day job in a modern building was a backbreaking day long-job, for three or four times the crew. And moving employees really didn't like that kind of work. One flight of stairs—fine. Two, maybe. Three, not very happy. Four, not at any reasonable price.

But Margarite had IOUs out all over The Hill. And Pete had friends. And everybody understood being in a financial jam. And so 25 of them volunteered, if volunteered is the right word.

"Maybe shamed would be better," thought Margarite.

Her very large crowd of helpers managed to get the apartment cleared out and loaded into two trucks—she needed a second one, finally—by the early evening on Friday. Saturday morning they drove over to Larry's house.

Larry inspected the two trucks unsympathetically. "Look," he said, "Pete told me he had a 'few things'—and I quote—to store. Look at my house. It's smaller than that damn apartment. So, no."

Margarite got on the phone to try to catch Pete, but he had left Friday morning. No one seemed to know of his plans, other than he was "headed south, along the Coast." She thought about the alternatives. This was, of course, decades before the invention of mobile phones and email. Putting the furniture in storage was a costly last resort, something she didn't want to do on her own.

Saturday afternoon Margarite went to the Automobile Association to get maps and tour books for the states of Washington and Oregon, and phone numbers for some motels and tourist bureaus along the Coast. Then she went to the office. She started calling motels and fishing lodges, north to south. At every one she left a message, and asked for the name and the phone number of the next motel to the south.

As she went, she asked about likely fishing holes. Hopefully, he would stop somewhere and get her message. All Saturday afternoon, Sunday and Monday—she worked her way as far south as Astoria, Oregon. Then he called—he was still north of Gray's Harbour in Washington.

She explained the situation. The news confounded him. Although the sub-lease of the apartment to Harry Watson eased his finances a little, a big storage bill would take a large cut of it. Finally, he said he'd have to think about it. "Just leave it with me for a day or two." The furniture sat in the parked vans. Margarite called the truck rental company, explained the situation, cried a little, and they gave her a big discount.

She went back to cleaning out the files. He called on Wednesday afternoon, another note of self-congratulatory triumph in his voice.

"I've solved the problem!" he proclaimed. She imagined the smile on his face.

"How?" she responded, warily.

"I had rented the apartment to Watson, as you know. Now I have convinced him to take it furnished, and for more money!

"All you have to do is get the furniture moved back in! Problem solved!"

There was silence from her end of the line.

"Hello? Hello?"

"I'm here." She gathered herself together and quietly said she'd separate out the personal stuff from the furniture and get the furniture back into the apartment. She recruited the same bunch of 'volunteers' for the job. You would think they'd have mutinied, but they all thought the whole episode was so funny they couldn't resist helping. They spread the work over a couple of days, and Margarite spoiled them all with as much beer and pizza as they could consume, which she added to the truck-rental bill, and which Pete paid with alacrity. He had been offered some freelance work that paid well.

Pete returned to Ottawa for a few days in late January for the opening of Parliament. There was a wind-chill of 50 degrees below. He'd signed a book deal about his time in Ottawa, and earned an advance. He threw a party for the gang, a party that grew in legend. They all forgave him.

Margarite came out of her time with Pete very well, eventually landing a much better job in the office of a senior Minister as his Private Secretary. But she postponed moving from her cheap, grubby little apartment for a further decade.

Pete thought, when he eventually heard the whole story from Margarite's perspective, that he was a very lucky guy. Few people have those kinds of friendships. He decided to somehow work the story into the book.

He smiled as he thought about what wonderful things he had learned from an electoral defeat. And of what wonderful friends he had. And he bought Margarite a heavy new winter coat. Nineteen seventy-three was a very cold winter in the second-coldest capital city in the world.

Jake's Appointment

Jake slept late, Ottawa time. Even though he usually awoke at seven, which made it 10 in Ottawa with the time change. Getting up at 8:30, as he did this morning, was like 5:30, stomach time. He'd forgotten, in his year away from Ottawa, how enervating adjusting to the time change really was, commuting back and forth.

He showered, shaved and dressed carefully. He wanted to look his best for his appointment.

He then pulled open the curtains covering the wall-to wall windows of his hotel room, and stared out over the skyline. He noted, in fact he counted, 13 Canadian flags. He saw it was a bright summer day. It was August, and that meant hot and muggy. Ottawa summers were as hot and uncomfortable as Ottawa winters were cold and uncomfortable. One did not come to Ottawa to enjoy the climate, he reflected.

Taking the elevator down to the lobby, he inspected himself, shoes to hairline, in the mirror. Well dressed. Well preserved, he concluded. Lots of mileage there, yet. A breakfast of toast and eggs while he read the Globe took an hour. He didn't go back to his room, but went out onto Albert Street then turned onto O'Connor to head up the gentle grade to Parliament Hill.

As he walked across the street, he suddenly became aware of how hot it was, even though it was just midmorning. The day was bright, but it was the humidity that made him aware of the heat.

He carried on up O'Connor Street and, as he crossed Wellington, a prominent journalist he had known well crossed the other way. As they passed, Jake looked at him and nodded. The journalist paid no attention, either not recognizing him, or feigning non-recognition. Briefly, Jake wondered about it but then shrugged. A politician out of office, one written off by the national media and from outside the cozy confines of Ottawa ceased to exist for reporters.

He reached the other side of the street and began the climb up the steps to the road in front of the West Block of the Parliament Buildings. He took the steps two at a time. He was, he liked to think, 65 years old but not ready to hang up his jogging shoes just yet. At the top, instead of going straight ahead into the West Block, he turned right and followed the sidewalk to the corner. As he then turned left to cross the road, he stopped to look up at the Centre Block for a minute.

Most people called that particular building the "House of Commons" but it was, of course, more than that. It also contained the Chamber where the Senate met, and where most Senators had their offices. Today Jake had a particular interest in the Senate.

The Centre Block was a beautiful building, he thought. He paused for nearly a minute before he went on, enjoying the shade provided by the West Block, and looking at the Centre Block almost as if he had never seen the building before, rather than as someone who had lived in that building, almost, for a dozen years. He looked at the large Canadian flag on the pole atop the Peace Tower, and recalled that cold blustery day after a long, bitterly partisan, miserable debate as the new flag was run up for the first time. That had been in February 1965. That a country could go for 98 years without its own distinctive flag, he had said repeatedly at the time, was nothing short of scandal.

He began to walk again, beside the West Block then up another set of stairs—one at a time now toward the western entrance door to the House of Commons. This door was guarded, restricted for use only by MPs and their staffs, but he went in anyway. It was all so familiar and he thought that, while the reporters might have forgotten him, the House of Commons guards surely will not have. He was correct, and Jules, whom he had spoken to often while waiting to be picked up by his chauffeur when he was a Minister, was there.

Jules smiled widely, "Welcome back, M'sieu le Ministre," saying his welcome in his fine French.

"Good to be back, Jules. Lovely day, but quiet here, I guess," he responded in French, his own heavily accented.

"Oui, M'sieu. Holidays. Only those with guilty consciences are here today."

"Leaves me out," responded Jake, now shifting to English as he passed on to Jules' left, going around to the right of the flight of stairs that led straight ahead and up to the Commons chamber, moving towards the elevator. He pushed the call button and when the elevator arrived it was empty and didn't stop on its trip to the third floor. He contemplated the hundreds—no, thousands—of times he had ridden this particular elevator, with its interior brass trim polished to a brilliant shine, to his fourth- or fifth-floor office.

"Let's see," he thought, "12 years as an MP, with the House sitting, say, 150 days a year, and using this elevator at least twice a day, minimum, that's at least 3,000 times. Really, it's a lot more than 3,000 times. No wonder I feel at home here."

Emerging into the main hall that ran the width of the building, he swung automatically to the left, then left again, to enter a small hallway, open on the right side, that then curved around to the right. He could have looked down three floors to where Jules stood beside his desk. He didn't look down. Instead, his eyes fixed on the heavily carved frame of the door to the anteroom of the Prime Minister's "Hill Office."

He went through it—it was already open— and saw Jeanne, the PM's long-time private secretary. He planned to greet her with what enthusiasm he could muster, knowing well of her legendary unresponsiveness to those who came to see her boss. Long service, and being privy to almost everything that took place in the PM's office—after the fact, usually, of course—meant she had long ago concluded that everyone who came through the door wanted a favour and she resented it.

But before Jake could say, "Hello, Jeanne, I'm here for an appointment with the Prime Minister," she said, "He'll see you in a few minutes. He's on the phone."

Unsaid was that Jake was five minutes early and even if the PM wasn't on the phone, he wouldn't see Jake until the appointed time. He knew he was to have exactly half an hour with the PM and began once again to put his thoughts in order. This was not difficult. Jake had an orderly if unspontaneous mind and he had thought long and hard about what he was going to ask for.

Presumably responding to some unseen signal, at precisely 10:00 a.m. Jeanne said, "He will see you now."

Jake rose and, when he was halfway across the office the door to the private office opened and Keith emerged. Nobody in Ottawa ever asked, "Keith who?" He was a Senator and the PM's most senior political adviser, and Jake was more than a little surprised to see him. It was mid-August, and Keith was famous for fleeing the capital when the Senate was not in session unless pressing business or some crisis had drawn him back.

"Hello, Jake. Good to see you. How're things on the West Coast?" Keith seemed unsurprised to see him.

"Hello, Keith. Everything's fine. But as much as I love Vancouver, I miss this place." Jake was eternally suspicious of Keith, and trusted him not at all. His very greeting, he thought, oozed insincerity.

"Give me a call sometime. I'd like us to do lunch. I want to ask you about some political things in B.C."

This was a surprise, Jake thought, because Keith never seemed to ask anyone about political things in B.C. Jake was not sure who in hell Keith did talk to in BC, since he never cared about B.C. politically—"there are more seats in metro Toronto than we can ever possibly win in B.C.," he had said frequently. It would be unusual if he spoke to anyone at all.

"I'll do that." But he knew the lunch would never take place.

Keith held the door open for him and, as they passed, Jake wondered what was really meant by the invitation. And if Keith had been seeing the PM, why was the PM on the phone? Were they both on the phone to someone? He didn't have any time to ponder those questions.

The PM rose from behind his big desk and came around it to shake Jake's hand.

Never a warm man, he was as always, business-like. There was no political smile, no effusive greeting. Not from this Prime Minister. They hadn't spoken since the perfunctory phone call the PM had made election night 13 months previously, to offer condolences on the lost election. The PM had been in a particularly effusive mood that night—he had picked up 35 seats, almost wiping out with a well fought campaign the disaster—the near defeat—of the previous contest. Jake had attended two Cabinet meetings after his loss before resigning from Cabinet but the PM had said nothing to him as an individual. He had thanked the three defeated Ministers as a group at the close of Jake's last Cabinet meeting.

"Come in. Good to see you. Thanks for calling."

Jake looked into the PM's blue eyes for some sign that this seemingly unusually warm greeting was serious. He received no sign, one way or the other.

"How're things on the Coast?"

"Good, generally, although there's the NDP provincial government that of course has the province in a mess, and that worries the business community. Mining is a disaster. Your government seems to be doing well, except for inflation, and the federal Tories are fighting among themselves as usual."

Jake immediately realized that he had made four mistakes in his first sentences. The PM had been close to the NDP in earlier years, personally liked the B.C. Premier, Dave Barrett, and gave not a damn for the business community in BC. He cared even less about mining.

"But I'm surprised to find you here during a very hot August when you get so few opportunities to take holidays," he tried to recover.

"Well, a married man with small boys can't travel as in earlier days, of course, but there are other things to do that one never has time for when the House is in session." He got to the point. "What can I do for you?"

Jake, it had to be said, was not one for small talk either. It was one of his oft-pointed out faults. But the PM, he realized again, had even less capacity for it. He remembered, once more, some awkward moments from his time in Cabinet when this prime ministerial failing was obvious. So, down to business.

"Prime Minister," he began formally, "there is a Senate seat vacant in BC. I very much would appreciate you appointing me to fill it. I served in the House faithfully and well, for a dozen years, I have been loyal to you and I was a hard working Minister. There is more I would like to contribute to Canadian public life but by the time of the next general election I'll be, many will think, past my prime."

He had inserted this little joke in the hope of eliciting a smile from the PM. None was forthcoming in the ensuing silence.

Jake continued.

"Thus, I'm very interested in appointment to the Senate. I have a proven track record. A sound reputation. You know I'll work hard."

This latter was an allusion to the PM's well known disdain for a large number of Senators who only showed their faces in Ottawa when the Government Whip in the Senate pleaded with them on the phone or when a recalcitrant Senator wanted to say something in caucus—usually something critical of the Government.

Jake waited for a response.

"Well," the PM, began, carefully, slowly. "You take me by surprise."

Jake, doubted that, but let it pass.

"I'd heard," the PM continued, "that you'd made the transition back to the private sector very well. I hadn't heard of your having any further interest in politics. In fact, I've been to B.C. …lets see…maybe four times the past year outside the campaign, and hadn't seen you at any function. So, as I say, your newfound—or perhaps re-found— interest in the government and in politics surprises me."

"It shouldn't, Prime Minister," responded Jake. "I think you know I left a private sector position in 1962 in which I was being paid nearly $40,000 a year and about to be offered a vice-presidency to become a back-bencher at a fifth that, such was my interest then and it is undiminished today.

"But after my defeat, getting back into the world of making a living in the private sector has required a certain...singleness of purpose. I really haven't had much time for anything other than work...and finding work."

The Prime Minister considered this for perhaps 30 seconds, then went on.

"My understanding—I was not around then, of course—is that you left your well-paid job expecting to join the Cabinet immediately and to take a cut in income of less than half that."

Jake was annoyed. The response was picayune and it was history. Whatever the cut, it was significant and it represented a real sacrifice at the time. Indeed, his wife had repeatedly reminded him of that.

"Not the expectation. I hoped to get elected. I hoped to be asked to join the Cabinet. But seniority seemed to mean more to Mr. Pearson than ability," he went on with some ill-disguised bitterness. It was no secret that the two Ministers that Pearson had brought into government from B.C. in '63 had disliked Jake, and he learned to reciprocate. He'd sat on the backbench for six unhappy years.

The PM decided to let the matter pass.

"Tell me more about why you want the Senate. Surely the challenges of the Red Chamber would be beneath your...talents and—frankly—your interests."

"I'd prefer to go back to the House. That's no secret. Even without a Cabinet seat. But I'd have to wait for probably three more years for a general election. I'd like to get back involved now."

He paused, marshalling some thoughts.

"I want to bring my talents as an economist—one with a pretty good reputation, you have to agree—back to public life. And back to some of the challenges the country is facing."

They both knew what he was talking about. The country's economic growth had stalled but inflation was over 10 per cent a year, the deficit was climbing and the government was being attacked in the media daily for not "doing something". There was much debate about what "doing something" meant. Some thought it meant wage and price controls. Jake was a free-market economist for whom controls were a chimera.

He favoured more fiscal discipline, not a popular view with many of his former colleagues. But the PM had fought and won the previous election campaigning against price controls, and it would be difficult for him to reverse course. But right then, unknown to Jake, the PM was on the verge of doing so.

"In any event," Jake went on, "I think there's an old saying in politics, is there not, that everyone who has served the Party and the country well is entitled to one 'give', that is, an appointment to something. All the others who stuck their necks out in '60, and '61 for Pearson and to rebuild the party in B.C., have got theirs. Larry got the board of Air Canada, Joe got the Bank of Canada, Bill got the Senate, Willy got Lieutenant Governor, and so on. When I was recruited to run, it was a signal in the business community, and in the academic community, too, that B.C. should take a Liberal comeback seriously. I resigned my senior position and worked non-stop for six months before the election, just as I was about to be offered a Vice Presidency and given a big raise."

"I understand the federal campaign committee saw that you were paid for those six months," the PM said. "And Brent never received anything." Five years later, Brent had run the PM's leadership campaign in B.C. and co-chaired the subsequent election campaign.

"Why had that name come up, suddenly?" wondered Jake. It was of no relevance. It was a cruel remark, anyway. The PM was independently wealthy while he, Jake, had grown-up poor. "Had it been expected that Jake and his family should have lived on buttons?" he thought to himself.

The PM went on.

"Correct me if I'm wrong, but I thought you've already had your 'give', your appointment. Is that not true?"

Jake was confused. What was the PM talking about? He had asked for and received nothing. "I don't understand", he said, slowly.

"You know," said the PM, "the election when Brent and Senator Vail were campaign chairs in B.C."

Jake's mind stopped for a second, then it all came back. He had forgotten.

The PM had won the leadership convention and immediately dissolved Parliament, resulting in a general election. He had said he would make no changes in the Cabinet he had inherited from Pearson and would await the outcome of an election to form his own government. It had been an astonishing decision but the leadership race had, in four short months, refocused the country from the decade-long bitter standoff between Pearson and Diefenbaker to a time of change, a new beginning. New people had come forward in the Party and had made it clear they would run in the next election. The kind of people that the PM liked. He wanted to put the past firmly behind him. An election and new faces would do exactly that.

In so doing, however, this new PM had to put himself firmly in the hands of the Party's organizers. He was not the kind of person who harboured a great deal of trust for his fellow man but he knew he had no choice.

He knew very little about the internal workings of the Liberal Party, and nothing at all about how a national election campaign would be put together. But he liked and trusted the fellow he had decided to name national campaign chairman, Jock Andrew, and had seen enough of him over the previous two years to make the gamble. As chair, Jock would choose the chairs in each province and set campaign strategy.

In B.C., two campaign co-chairs had been appointed. One, George Vail, had supported a leadership candidate who had lost badly, but he knew the B.C. Party and its organization better than anyone else. The other had been Brent Farrow, the PM's man in BC.

Things were a mess. No one had expected to face an election for at least another year, and the hard-fought leadership battles were only a few weeks behind them. The healing had not even started and now they were thrust into a campaign. Worse, in some respects, was that polling numbers showed significant increases in seats were possible if the effort were made to seriously contest some historically marginal seats.

Thus, a few days after the election call, Brent had phoned Jake. They met at noon the next day in the third floor bar of the Vancouver Club where George liked to do political business.

There was the usual small talk as they gathered around the end of the big table, and as George took his liquor bottles from his locker and placed them next to where the waiter had put soda, tonic, ice and glasses. Each mixed his own drink in silence.

"I thought we could order a light lunch here, as well?" offered Brent. The other two nodded agreement. He ordered soup and sandwiches for the three of them.

"Jake," said George, "we have an awful problem here." He nodded to Brent, as the other "we". "We were asked to take this on last week, but no one has given a minute's thought to election preparation since '65. We just signed a lease for space this morning. There is no campaign organization. We are almost nowhere in finding good candidates. Money has to be found. We do not even know what we'll do for a policy platform. Yet the polls are very good. There could be the big breakthrough in B.C. that we have worked on for these many years. We now have seven seats, we could have a dozen, maybe more."

Jake heard this with a non-committal look on his face. He considered it nonsense, and had been through these kinds of pep-talks by George and others several times over the past six years. He never disagreed with them, but he simply didn't believe them either. He was struggling to figure out where this conversation was going. But he was not going to argue.

"I don't disagree. How can I help? I can certainly raise money," responded Jake.

George went on. "This redistribution of the constituencies and the redrawing of boundaries has made a mess of things. Done by a bunch of stupid judges, who know nothing about the realities of politics. It's one of the evil side effects of the non-partisan appointment of judges." He shook his head.

"They did dumb things like put Fernie in the same riding with Vernon, two towns with nothing in common, and separated by three other ridings, three mountain ranges and 300 miles. Kamloops riding now contains Quesnel, but not Williams Lake, which is closer and with which it has more in common. Just stupid."

Jake's Appointment

"Anyway, your own riding has been divided in two, with some odds and ends added to the northern part. We assume you're planning to run in the south?"

"Yes, of course."

Brent leaned forward. He glanced around the near-empty room to judge the likelihood of being overheard.

"We'd like you to run in the north. We've someone that we think can carry the south but we have no prospects—none—for a possible winner for the north. Except you."

Brent, for all his reputation as a superb lawyer with a persuasive way, wasn't wasting time by obfuscation.

Jake was astonished. He lived in the south. It contained all his best organizers. That's where his money came from. In the north, which he had usually lost—but barely—it wasn't only a candidate that the party lacked. Little money, poor organization. "Where would one start?" he wondered.

He was staring sure defeat in the face if he ran in the north. "Were they that desperate to get rid of me?" he thought, bitterly.

All his negative emotions fled across his face in the fifteen seconds of silence since Brent stopped speaking.

The waiter arrived with the soup and sandwiches.

"I don't think I can win there," he said, quietly, slowly, without emotion.

"You can," said George, "we've got numbers. It looks good."

Jake glanced at Brent, then at George. These guys would always say they had whatever numbers they needed to persuade somebody to do something. He didn't believe for a minute that they'd done a poll in the riding. They hadn't had time since they were appointed. And they didn't have the money. It was that simple.

Jake thought he had to say something to put an end to this nonsense.

"Well, irrespective of what your numbers say, I've been the MP for most of that area for six years. I know those people. There's little organization and we get no money from that area. It's too late now to start putting something together. Besides, Norm Mercer, my riding president, would have a heart attack."

"We'll get you money," said George, "and we can get you a good campaign manager. Leave Mercer to us; he'll be delighted with the candidate we hope to persuade to run in your riding. We'll do whatever we can to make sure you win. We'll schedule the PM in there during the campaign."

"Sure," Jake thought, "and pigs have wings...."

Then he said, choosing his words carefully, "Well, I wouldn't even begin to think about it unless I were in the Cabinet. A person would need that to not look stupid for trading a safe seat for a near-sure loser."

Brent looked at him in disbelief. "We can't go around appointing people to the Cabinet, or even promising such things." It was a comment made in scorn.

"Well, Brent, George, you asked me to do something I think is political suicide. I'm telling you it can't be done, and I'm the guy in the ring, not you. But it might, it just might, be done by a Minister. I'm not even prepared to consider it from outside the Cabinet."

They had finished their lunches and coffee had been served.

Brent stared at Jake for 10 seconds, then rose, and Gerry followed, both leaving their coffee untouched.

"You'll hear from us," said Brent. Jake lingered at his coffee.

The two organizers paused at the top of the Vancouver Club steps on Hastings Street.

George said, "I gotta go back to the office. I think it's payday." It was a grim joke. Neither of the two lawyers had billed very much since the beginning of the leadership race over four months before, and they were being covered by their partners. It was a joke in each firm that they only showed their faces on payday.

"What do you think?" he asked.

Brent paused a few seconds. "Well, had the PM done the conventional thing, Jake'd be in, even if he had the stupidity to support a loser in the leadership. I'm going to call Jock and see what he can do."

He did. The answer had been hopeful. Jock called him back the next day and said it was a done deal. The PM didn't like it, but the facts of political life had been explained. In the end the PM agreed. Jake was being called within the hour.

Jake's Appointment

The announcement of Jake's appointment to Cabinet was made the next day. The graceful statement by the PM emphasized that Jake was being appointed not only for his personal attributes but to make the point that B.C. would be very important in his future administration. Brent and George, who seldom drank in the morning, took a bottle of rye out of the new campaign office fridge and each mixed themselves a drink. George mixed his with milk, "To feed his ulcer," he said. They toasted their success, because they now had persuaded a first-class candidate to run in the southern part of Jake's old riding.

"I've got 79 things to do today, but I'll get back to Jake's riding and call Mercer in the morning to get things lined up. I don't want him now going off on his own doing a candidate search as soon as Jake makes his announcement concerning changing ridings."

The next morning Brent phoned Norm Mercer about the alternative candidate. When he hung up, he was beet red with rage. He walked across to George's office and slammed the door. He couldn't yell, which he wanted more than anything to do, because the staff—still moving in a week into the campaign—would wonder.

"I just got off the phone to Mercer," he hissed through gritted teeth. "When I asked him about the timing of the nominating meeting, he told me next week. I told him that he should be hearing from Jake, because it was our understanding Jake would be running in the other part of the old riding and I wanted to talk to him about a candidate.

"You know what he said? That he had just hung up from talking to Jake, who had confirmed he would be running in the south."

Brent, in the courtroom the very embodiment of control, was obviously in an outrage.

George responded. "Well, maybe we should have a chat with him. Explain the facts of life. Get him on the speakerphone."

Jake answered.

"Congratulations on the Cabinet appointment, Jake," boomed Brent with feigned enthusiasm. "George is here with me and we want to talk to you about next steps. We want to make an announcement about you running in the other riding and get things underway for a new candidate in the south," pretending he hadn't spoken to Norm Mercer.

"Well," responded Jake's disembodied voice, "I've thought about it as I said I would. I still think the odds of winning are too long. I am staying where I am. I'm running in the south."

Brent and George looked at one another. "Could you repeat that again, Jake? We're not sure we heard you correctly," said Brent.

"What I said was that I would not even think about the other riding unless I was appointed to the Cabinet. Well, over the past 24 hours I've thought about it, as I said I would. I spent all day yesterday making a bunch of calls in the riding. I still think it's not winnable, despite…" he paused, "…despite what you say your polls say." His voice was firm.

George could not restrain himself.

"Look, you ungrateful son-of-a-bitch. We had a deal here. Brent went to the wall for you and cashed in a lot of chips to get your worthless ass sitting at the goddam Cabinet table. Now, you goddamn well hold up your end of the deal." He had said it with emphasis, with iron in it, but his voice had not risen.

There was a momentary silence.

"Look, you might have thought there was a deal," Jake responded quietly. "But there was no deal to run in the north. I made it as clear as I could I would not run there and wouldn't even think about it from outside the Cabinet. Well, I have, as I said, thought about it, made a lot of calls, but nothing has changed. That's the end of it."

George said, "I think the three of us had better meet." They did. Jake had refused to budge. In the election the Liberals won the north riding with a neophyte. In fact they won 16 of 23 seats. It was a landslide. The polls were right.

Jake's mind returned to the present.

"That was a long time ago," he said, lamely.

"Nevertheless", responded the PM, "That was your 'give', I think. You were appointed to the Cabinet. There was a deal, Jake, and you didn't keep up your end."

It was a matter-of-fact statement. Jake thought it sounded more like an accusation. He tried to recover.

"I disagree. Had you done the conventional thing and appointed a Cabinet prior to calling the election, I would have been appointed on my merits. There's no question of that. I wasn't trying to strike a deal; I was honestly and emphatically trying to make the point with George and Brent that I wasn't interested in the other riding. It never occurred to me they could persuade you to appoint me mid-election, and I didn't ask for it, or promise them anything.

"But I did do what I said I would do: I considered the other riding very carefully. I thought it would be the end of my political career. I was wrong, but that's what I genuinely thought. And frankly I also thought that Brent and George were lying to me because I had never particularly got along with them, I suspected that they were trying to get rid of me and make room for others. Well, I hadn't given up my well-paid career in the private sector to get moldy on the backbench for six years and end my career by just going and committing political suicide if I could help it. You may not see it this way, but I had already made enough sacrifices for politics."

There was deep bitterness and anger in Jake's voice.

The PM looked directly at Jake for fully 30 seconds, then spoke carefully.

"Jake, there was a deal the very second you accepted the appointment to Cabinet. You could have turned it down. You didn't keep your word. Now you come in here and make promises about what you want to contribute in the future. I don't need another apologist for the business community in the Senate. What I do need are a few more people interested in strongly supporting the government and the Party. The next couple of years are going to be very difficult. You have no idea how difficult.

"Besides, during your six years in Cabinet, you did the absolute minimum in support of the Party. You rarely made political speeches, or traveled for the Party or helped in by-elections. I consulted Keith about this. You made few contributions in Cabinet of a political nature. Nobody has even seen you in the past year. I checked that with Brent and George just before you came in.

"So," thought Jake.

"Do you know that Brent is likely the guy closest to me in B.C.? Do you know that he asked to go to the Court of Appeal? I said, "No" because he doesn't have a judicial personality, despite being an absolutely top lawyer. I would give him anything else; he doesn't want anything else. And I trust him.

"So, Jake, there was a deal. I came into this business 10 years ago knowing nothing about politics. I've been lucky enough to learn more than a few things, two of which are, first, it's a team and we pull together. Second, if your word isn't any good, there's no place for you.

There was silence as the two men stared at one another.

"Jake," the PM continued quietly, "on the basis of your abilities you could have been—should have been—Finance Minister. Or in Trade or Industry. Big, important, economic portfolios. But I left you to grind away in an unimportant backwater of a Department for six years because that was what you got in the bargain, a bargain you didn't keep. How could I trust you with something bigger? How can I trust you now? You understand why I can't appoint you to the Senate, don't you, Jake?"

In the face of this almost-lecture, the always well controlled Jake felt his face becoming more and more flushed. He squinted, felt water in his eyes, felt his throat constricting with anger. He rose, saying nothing to the PM, not looking at him, turned towards the door and, wordlessly, walked out, slamming the large heavy door behind him.

The PM walked back to his desk and pushed his intercom button. In flawless French he said, "Jeanne, get Brent and Senator Vail on the phone for me, please."

If you would like to purchase more copies of this book, they are available in print or digital format from the FriesenPress online bookstore:

http://www.friesenpress.com/bookstore

CPSIA information can be obtained
at www.ICGtesting.com
Printed in the USA
FSOW02n1831281015
12716FS